ON TIME

PAM JARVIS

BURTON MAYERS

ON TIME

Copyright © 2021 Pam Jarvis

All rights reserved.

Content compiled for publication by Richard Mayers of *Burton Mayers Books*.
Front Cover by Martellia Design

First published by Burton Mayers Books 2021.
All rights reserved.

No part of this publication may be reproduced or transmitted in any form or by any means, electronic or mechanical, including photocopy, recording, or an information storage and retrieval system, without permission in writing from the publisher.
The right of Pam Jarvis to be identified as the author of this work has been asserted by her in accordance with the Copyright, Designs and Patent Act 1988

A CIP catalogue record for this book is available from the British Library

ISBN: **1-8383459-7-6**
ISBN-13: **978-1-8383459-7-6**

Typeset in **Garamond**

This book is a work of fiction. Names, characters, businesses, organizations, places and events are the product of the author's imagination. Any resemblance to actual persons, living or dead, events or locales is entirely coincidental.

www.BurtonMayersBooks.com

DEDICATION

For my ancestors, grandparents, parents and husband who were the bows, and for my children, grandchildren and descendants who are the arrows.

ON CHILDREN:

'Your children are not your children.

They are the sons and daughters of Life's longing for itself.

They come through you but not from you...

You may house their bodies but not their souls,

For their souls dwell in the house of tomorrow, which you cannot visit, not even in your dreams....

You are the bows from which your children as living arrows are sent forth.'

Kahlil Gibran, *The Prophet* 1923

ON TIME

~ CONTENTS ~

	Acknowledgments	v
	Prologue	Pg 1
1	Ancestors	Pg 4
2	Descendants	Pg 13
3	Travellers	Pg 30
4	Family Business	Pg 49
5	Missing	Pg 70
6	Lost and Found	Pg 95
7	On Time	Pg 120
8	Voices	Pg 143
9	Time After Time	Pg 162
10	Fast Forward	Pg 185
	Epilogue	Pg 207
	About the Author	Pg 210

ACKNOWLEDGMENTS

The first and most important people to acknowledge are as always, my partner and my now adult children who have spent the past 30 years supporting me and putting up with me as I research and write. And of course, my grandchildren who are always a joy and an inspiration.

There are so many others to thank who have had a hand in the development of this book, reading, editing and suggesting amendments: Carmel O'Hagan, Berni Dawkins, Jane George and Chris Malone who were with me from the beginning, also Simon George, Gill Ditch, Val Daniel, Nick Thorne, Julie Gallagher, Tom van Breukelen and Sandra Craft. And last but definitely not least, Richard Mayers for all his hard work on this book, editing and formatting.

Thanks too, to the now long dead authors whose quotes I use in the text; Marjorie Williams who wrote 'The Velveteen Rabbit' available at
https://www.gutenberg.org/files/11757/11757-h/11757-h.htm
and Kahlil Gibran who wrote 'The Prophet' available at
https://www.gutenberg.org/files/58585/58585-h/58585-h.htm#link21

I have used Gibran's poem 'On Children' in teaching for nearly 30 years. And it is from these ideas that one of the key themes of this book emerged:

What if your children weren't just your children?

ON TIME

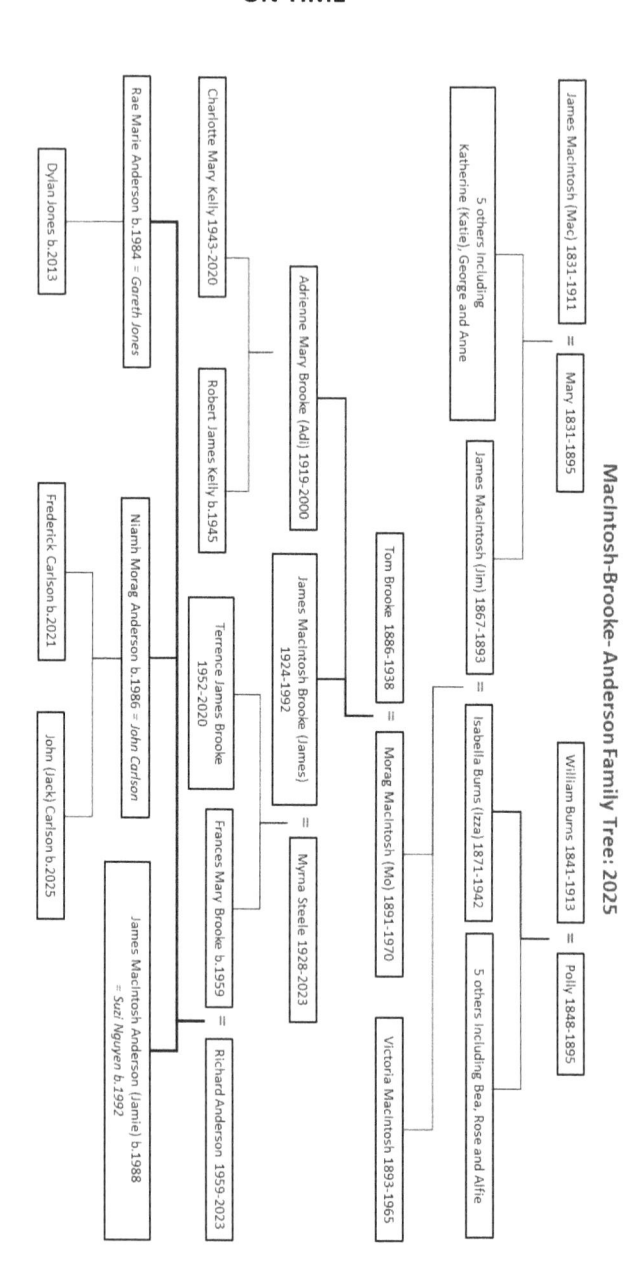

MacIntosh-Brooke-Anderson Family Tree: 2025

- James MacIntosh (Mac) 1831-1911 = Mary 1831-1895
  - 5 others including Katherine (Katie), George and Anne
  - James MacIntosh (Jim) 1867-1893
  - Morag MacIntosh (Mo) 1891-1970 = Tom Brooke 1886-1938
    - Adrienne Mary Brooke (Adi) 1919-2000 = Robert James Kelly b.1945
      - Charlotte Mary Kelly 1943-2020
    - James MacIntosh Brooke (James) 1924-1992 = Myrna Steele 1928-2023
      - Terrence James Brooke 1952-2020
      - Frances Mary Brooke b.1959 = Richard Anderson 1959-2023
        - Rae Marie Anderson b.1984 = Gareth Jones
          - Dylan Jones b.2013
        - Niamh Morag Anderson b.1986 = John Carlson
          - Frederick Carlson b.2021
          - John (Jack) Carlson b.2025
        - James MacIntosh Anderson (Jamie) b.1988 = Suzi Nguyen b.1992

- William Burns 1841-1913 = Polly 1848-1895
  - Isabella Burns (Izza) 1871-1942 = James MacIntosh (Jim) 1867-1893
  - 5 others including Bea, Rose and Alfie
  - Victoria MacIntosh 1893-1965

Annamarie Simons: Family Tree: 2025

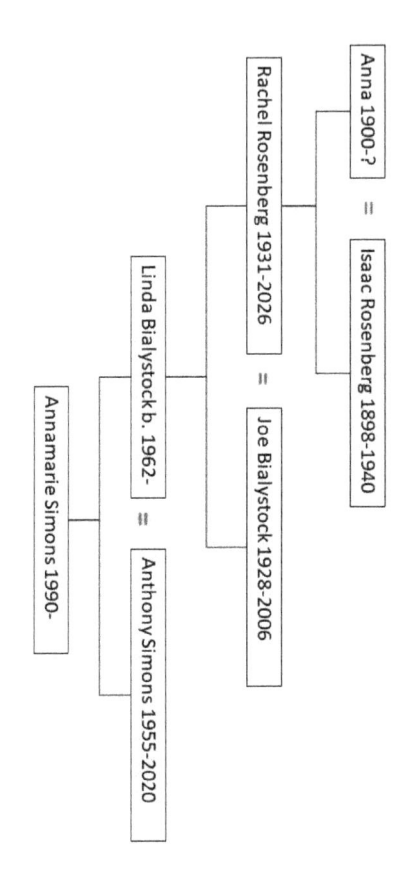

```
Anna 1900-? = Isaac Rosenberg 1898-1940
                │
    Rachel Rosenberg 1931-2026 = Joe Bialystock 1928-2006
                          │
          Linda Bialystock b. 1962- = Anthony Simons 1955-2020
                                │
                    Annamarie Simons 1990-
```

PROLOGUE:
THE EYE OF THE STORM

Rachel: Praha hlavní nádraží [Prague Station], August 1939

Rachel stood in the tumultuous crowd, tears running down her face. Everyone else had their Mama and Papa with them, but Rachel's Mama was gone, and now she was completely alone. She looked around. Everyone else was crying too. Some children were wailing, and most of the Mamas and Papas were shouting, not only at the children, but also at each other. Ladies with clipboards were running around, but they only appeared to be able to speak a few words that the children understood. Mostly they spoke rapidly in a strange language that sounded like a long string of urgent noises. One of them was discreetly wiping her eyes.

No one paid any attention to Rachel. The station smelt of dust, coal, pee and sweat. A feeling was building inside of her like the bubbles in an Oranzada bottle, rising from her tummy to the top of her head. Any minute now she was going to explode, all her fear flowing over like fizzy orange liquid. She remembered feeling like this on the day when the bad men first arrived in Praha. Mama and Bubbe had told Rachel to go and play in her bedroom. They were in the living room talking in low, urgent voices. Mama kept blowing her nose on a handkerchief. Rachel had sneaked out of her room to look through the only window from which she could see the street below, to find out what the strange thump, thump, thump and rumbling noises were.

Rachel remembered peeking through the thick net curtains in Bubbe's little kitchen, a pair of dark brown eyes blinking above the dirty, peeling beige paint on the window-sill. She saw cold sunlight sparking on polished armoured vehicles trundling past, and soldiers marching on the icy cobblestones, their shiny boots moving rapidly up and down in a jerky kicking motion. She couldn't see their faces, only the top of their helmets. They filed swiftly across the small patch of street within the limited view that the window allowed. Everything felt bad and wrong, and it scared her. What if the bad men saw her watching? She'd moved away from the curtain and gone to lie on her bed, so she hadn't got to the point of feeling like she would scream without stopping on that day. But there was nowhere to go and hide now, so her urge to run and scream continued to blossom inside her like a dark flower.

Suddenly, she caught a glimpse of a small boy standing alone at the side of the crowd. She hadn't noticed him before; it was as if he had popped in from nowhere. Rachel scanned the nearby adults to see if his Mama and Papa were nearby, but like hers, they were nowhere to be seen. He looked very strange, nothing like the other children milling around. He had white-blond hair, and he was wearing the oddest clothes, a light blue suit made from a fabric that Rachel couldn't remember seeing before. Most strangely of all, the front of the shirt was printed with a picture of a cartoon train with a smiling face. Intrigued, she took a step closer and noticed a weak silver glow surrounding him. He wasn't crying like the other children, although he did seem somewhat dazed. He turned towards her, bright blue eyes staring directly into hers. Rachel stared back. As their eyes locked, Rachel began to feel the terror that had been pushing at her forehead dispersing, as though it was somehow flowing out of her head and into his.

Out of the corner of her eye, she saw a tall blond man walking swiftly towards her, deftly swerving through the crowd. She turned towards him and then glanced back at the boy, but he was nowhere to be seen. How could he pop in and out like that? Everything was so strange today. She looked back at the man; he was crouching down beside her now.

'Rachel?' he said.

Rachel looked into his eyes and noticed that they were exactly the same shade of blue as the little boy's. Then he began to speak to her in a foreign language. Rachel couldn't understand a word he was saying, but his voice sounded kind, and she began to feel that she wasn't quite so alone.

ANCESTORS

Mac: Sittingbourne, December 1893

Jim's breath grew louder and slower, developing an ominous rattle. Mac knew what that meant; he had been in this situation twelve years previously with his daughter Katie. He didn't need to see the doctor briefly shake his head as he took Jim's pulse to know what was going to happen now. The tragedy that was about to unfold was deeply etched in the doctor's eyes.

Mac felt the weight of a crushing sadness at the inevitability of the situation. A parade of pictures crossed his mind's eye like a magic lantern: little Jimmy toddling across the grass, the sun glinting on his auburn hair, an older Jimmy watching him work and wanting to learn about the tools, always full of 'why don't yous' and 'couldn't you do it likes', some of which were actually reasonable suggestions; an adult Jim clutching the certificate that marked his elevation from apprentice engineer to journeyman, and a teenage Jim and his younger brother running and wrestling on the sand.

'I'm sorry, Mac,' said the doctor. 'I have done all I can. I've given him medicine now to make sure he doesn't suffer.'

Mac nodded. What a waste, he thought. We waited so long for this boy, after three girls we were so surprised. And he was so big and healthy. How can something as apparently trivial as a troublesome set of tonsils lead to this?

'What is Izza going to do?' Mac replied, his thoughts moving to his daughter-in-law a few doors away in his own house, surrounded by his wife and daughters. 'She has those two little lasses, and one only born three weeks ago.'

'It's his tonsils, Mac…. They're poisoning him, and there's nothing I can do about it.'

Mac sighed. The doctor continued. 'Perhaps Izza's family will help out. I know the way that Morag came into the world caused grief to a lot of folks. But of course, you would never give her back now. And after all, you are all Scots a long way south of home, that must count for something?'

Mac shook his head. 'Well, Mo is a bonny wee lassie, and that's for sure. But… we're from the wrong coast and the wrong class doctor. It's not as simple as all that. And she ran away from them to us to have that wee'an. Her father said he would never forgive her.'

The doctor frowned. 'People say a lot of things when they're angry Mac, they don't always mean them.'

'Well… He always seemed like the type that did'.

The doctor thought of Izza's rigid, steely eyed father. Perhaps Mac was right. But now, there was a more urgent job at hand. He took Jim's pulse again. 'I think you need to go and get Izza, Mac. She will want to say goodbye.'

Mac, suddenly blinded by tears, stumbled the few hundred yards to his own house. His mind was full again, strangely not of Jim, but of Katie, lost at only eighteen, twelve years ago now. Such bright young people with so much life, snuffed out like candles. Do they go anywhere, he thought; is there anything left, or is this really the end, the utter waste of promise?

Five minutes later he escorted Izza into her bedroom, where her young husband of less than two years was drawing his last laboured breaths. He regarded her with concern; she was visibly trembling, and clearly not yet recovered from the difficult birth of baby Victoria. She stared through him. He helped her to sit down on the chair. The rasping breath began to slow. Mac sat down on the bed. He listened to the clock tick loudly, counting down the last few minutes of Jim's life.

Fran: Leeds, February 2025

Fran turned off the PC with a sigh; more going round and round in circles on YourAncestry.com with no result. She was getting closer to the conclusion that she was going to have to give up with her quest to uncover the details of the MacIntosh/Burns feud. On the one hand, the reason was obvious. Her great-grandmother Izza was heavily pregnant with Nana Mo when she married her first husband Jim MacIntosh. The birth certificate indicated that the birth was legitimate; however, the marriage was in April 1891 and the birth was in May of the same year. The census in March 1891 also showed Izza still in residence with her parents. I bet that was fun, thought Fran grimly, remembering her Nana Mo's description of her strict Scottish Presbyterian upbringing in her maternal grandfather's house, principally under the gimlet eye of her fearsome Aunt Bea.

Fran was reasonably sure that Mo had told the truth about having no memories of Jim's parents. But nevertheless, she had been born in their house and after Jim's tragic death at just twenty-six, surely his parents and siblings would have been eager to maintain contact with his two little daughters, who had moved to live in their maternal grandparents' house just a few miles away. So why on earth didn't they do so? And why had Mo told her own children and grandchildren that she'd never met her paternal grandparents because that side of the family were living in Scotland? Because that was clearly not true. The census records showed that they were living a few miles away for the entire period of Mo's childhood.

Wistful, Fran flicked through the printouts, tracking the addresses. Did Izza's family prevent her from having any contact at all with her dead husband's family? If so, why on earth would they do that?

She turned to the local newspapers that she had unearthed, tracking Jim's father, also called James but known locally as 'Mac' through the work he had done on the Town Council throughout the 1900s. He seemed like a good man. So why had Mo and her younger sister Victoria apparently never even met him?

The house remained silent around her, apart from the old dog Kylie snoring in her sleep. Fran removed her reading glasses and looked around the room. It used to be her son Jamie's bedroom, but had become her home office over a decade ago, when he had re-located to London to begin his post-doctoral research. The floor to ceiling shelves held an odd mixture of artefacts; principally old toys in boxes that the grandchildren played with when they were in the house, and untidy piles of history books and papers that Fran had been meaning to sort out since her retirement five years ago; the legacy of a thirty-year academic career.

One day, I must get around to some redecorating, thought Fran, even though the walls are not visible behind all this crap. So, then first of all, I need to have a clean out. She felt the familiar inertia permeating her veins like a sedative, a hangover from the lockdowns and bereavements of the last few years. She absent-mindedly patted Kylie's head. Poor Kylie, yet another relic of a previous life.

'Please don't leave me this year, Kylie. Not so soon after all the others.'

Kylie stared back at Fran, wagging her tail. The silence in the house hung heavily.

Who would have thought all those people in one extended family could die within such a short time, Fran pondered. She had lost a brother and cousin to COVID19 in 2020, and then her husband Rich, from a sudden heart attack in late 2023. Then a few weeks afterwards Fran's elderly mother died peacefully in her sleep in the cocoon of her nursing home, having gradually declined into dementia for over a decade.

So now, it was just Fran, soon to be 66, and her remaining cousin, Rob, still hale and hearty at 80 in Salem, Massachusetts, who she had visited last summer for the first time since the effective end to the pandemic. After five long years, Fran had decided to risk it. Neither she nor Rob were getting any younger, and neither of them were quite so sanguine about their chances of living to a ripe old age anymore.

Fran sighed. When it comes down to the real Brooke-MacIntoshes, it is just me and Rob, she thought. Of course, there are the children and grandchildren. But Fran and Rob were the only ones left of the family that Fran had inhabited during her childhood. 'Nearly all gone' she said aloud. She was aware of a cold nose being bumped against her hand 'yes, I know you're still here, Kylie,' she said. A warm, rough tongue licked her sympathetically.

A picture of Fran and Nana Mo tumbled out of the ancestry files. Fran picked it up. They were paddling in the sea, long ago. Fran was aged about two, wearing a sun hat that was far too big for her, and Mo was holding Fran's hand, beaming happily into the camera. It all looked so carefree; but so much was still unknown, and seemingly unknowable. Why didn't you tell me Nana Mo? thought Fran. Were you ashamed of being so nearly illegitimate? Fran's mind moved again to the thought that there must be something more to the story. Why did Mo name her own son after a father and paternal grandfather who, she claimed, she had never known? Was it, as she told Fran so long ago, in compensation for a life never lived, or was she sending some sort of message to her mother's family? Mo had made it very clear to her children and grandchildren that she had experienced many frustrations growing up in her maternal grandfather's house.

Fran returned to her thought of 'just us', remembering

Mo musing in the last years of her life that there was no one who called her 'Mo' anymore, just 'mum' or 'nana'. It was something that had occurred to Fran frequently in the last year, as she moved into the 'mum and granny' zone herself. If only Mo had known that until the end of her own life, there were several remaining MacIntosh relatives of her own generation that she would have been able to visit, had the families not been estranged. Fran flicked through the oldest photographs she possessed, at the back of the MacIntosh-Burns section in her ancestry files. They were of a group of young women in Edwardian dress, all neatly labelled on the back in Mo's handwriting: Mo's mother and her sisters. But there were no pictures of Mo's father, or of anyone in his family at all.

'What a waste,' said Fran aloud.

Her mobile phone rang loudly. 'Niamh' flashed onto the screen:

'Hello'
'What are you doing mum?'
'Family history.'
'Again? Turn off that PC….'
'I just did…'
'And come to the movies and the pizza restaurant with us. The kids want to see the new Disney.'
'Oh-OK.'
'We'll be over in half an hour.'

Fran put down her phone and ran for the shower. It wouldn't do for her daughters and her grandsons to find her still in her pyjamas.

Mo: London, August 1966

'Tell me again why Daddy has such a funny name, Nana.'

Mo looked out of the window at the disappointingly dark, rainy day outside and settled down for story time

ON TIME

with her youngest grandchild. She looked into her granddaughter's intense blue eyes, and the thought 'old soul' popped into her mind. She quickly banished the thought as arrant old lady nonsense. Mo did not subscribe to any thought that even hinted at religious belief however alternative, she had quite enough of that in her own childhood, thank you very much.

'Well, Franny, my Daddy was called James MacIntosh, and he was only twenty-six when he died.'

Franny screwed up her face in concentration, counting on her fingers. 'Is that really *very* young, Nana?' It seemed like a lot older than her, having just celebrated her seventh birthday.

'It's a very young age to die, Franny. So, I called your Daddy after him, James MacIntosh Brooke. I guess people do that to make up for losing people that they shouldn't have lost.'

'How did he die, Nana?'

'He was ill with something that people in those days called quinsy – his tonsils had gone bad. People couldn't have their tonsils out like you did last year, and they didn't have that medicine you had last winter to stop infections.'

'Peni…. Pencil…'

'Yes, penicillin. That's a hard word, well done for remembering it, Franny'.

'So he just died?'

'My mother said the doctor made a mistake. Gave him too much of a pain medicine called morphia.'

Mo noticed that Franny's eyes were becoming round and troubled. 'But don't worry, Franny, that was before doctors were properly trained. They don't make mistakes like that now.'

'What was your Daddy like, Nana?'

Mo sighed. 'I don't remember. I was told that I look like him. We both had red hair. My mother said he was clever, and that he was quiet and thoughtful.'

'But your hair isn't red like Joanne's - it's grey.'

Mo remembered Joanne, Franny's new best friend; she had come to the recent birthday party. Franny had announced last week that she wanted red hair like Joanne. In fact, Mo thought, Franny wanted to *be* like Joanne and Joanne's older sister, who, in Mo's opinion, were allowed to wear dresses that were far too short and "adult."

'It is now, Franny. But your blonde is nicer, I think. You wouldn't like to be called "Carrots" by other children all through your childhood, now, would you?'

Franny giggled. Then her face set back into earnest, serious lines again. The child is going to persist, thought Mo, with a mixture of amusement and pride- as she always does.

'Where did your Daddy go when he died, Nana?'

'No one knows, Franny,' replied Mo, considering the child too young to be told that his life had been snuffed out by a fool of a doctor. 'He just wasn't with us anymore.'

'You're not going to go there soon, are you Nana?' asked Franny; deep concern in her voice. 'Joanne says old people die.'

'I'm not that old. And anyway, I'm going to live to 90-something like Aunt Bea,' replied Mo. Indestructible old battle-axe, she thought to herself.

'How many more years is that, then?'

'Oh, fifteen, maybe twenty? You'll be a big girl by then.'

'Like Charlie!' Charlie, Mo's oldest granddaughter Charlotte, and Franny's 'big cousin' was another of Franny's heroes; Charlie had been very kind to Franny when she had come for an extended visit two years ago, having recently finished university in California. In Franny's imagination, Charlie looked like the glamourous mini-skirted models and pop stars in the newspapers and magazines that her father sold downstairs in the shop.

No, please not like Charlie, thought Mo, recalling her shock and concern at the letter she had received from her daughter Adi, Charlie's mother, shortly after Christmas.

ON TIME

'Yes,' she said.

'And if I ever have a little boy like Charlie had last week, I'll call him James MacIntosh too, so no one *ever* forgets your Daddy.'

Mo felt tears rising behind her eyes. All these lives that start and end in ways that none of us would ever have chosen, she thought. 'Come on Franny, let's make some cakes for tea.' She held out her hand.

'Hurrah!' shouted Franny, running towards the kitchen.

'Wait, Franny, let's find your pinny……'

Five minutes later, Franny was covered in flour. Quinsy, morphia and the silly doctor were all quite forgotten for that afternoon.

DESCENDANTS

Jamie: London, March 2025

'So I think that's the best idea, then, Jamie,' said Annamarie decidedly. 'You ask Fran to come and give us some help. We're stabbing in the dark here and we need some help from a historian. And under the circumstances, I think she's the only candidate.'

Jamie looked around the plastic and steel laboratory, imagining how out of place his mother would be in such an environment with her dusty books and historical artefacts.

'But you don't know my mum. She's…'

'Got a PhD, historical creds and we could pass her off as a data cruncher,' Christian interjected. 'She's perfect.'

'But she's like…weird. She's just as likely to start carrying on about whether NAMIS is happy or not, and start quoting *I, Robot* or some other variation of fantastical shit to us.'

As Christian and Annamarie dissolved into giggles, NAMIS booted up.

'Working.'

Jamie looked towards it. Like a Sat Nav, it could sometimes sound as though it was channelling human thought. Annamarie had even given it a name that it answered to, based on its original designation, the Navigation And Movement In Space computer. Jamie could have sworn it sounded keen for them to talk to it, to involve it in all their decisions. But even though it was in

ON TIME

some ways a member of their very close-knit research team, in the end, like a Sat Nav, it was a navigation robot, albeit a highly sophisticated one that could talk back to you and offer original opinions in its own, very limited sphere.

'Stand down, NAMIS, we're talking about you, not to you.'

The light on the console flicked off. And, also like a Sat Nav, thought Jamie, it directed us into a river that we weren't expecting to be there. The only thing was, in this case it was the river of time; Einstein's fourth dimension.

Christian frowned. 'Jamie, you know she is not going to do that. She's got exactly the right skills for the job, and she would never split on us. She's family. And you also know that she would be completely aware of how high the stakes are here.'

Jamie sighed. 'It will take a while. First of all I will have to explain in terminology that she can understand how that thing over there came into being and then I will have to explain how none of us have yet fully worked out how it can do what it is doing, and then she'll go all "oh Jamie" and "do you realise the implications of this, Jamie" on me, because she still thinks I am about five years old, and then…'

'You won't be able to stop her coming here and doing exactly what we want her to do,' declared Annamarie.

'We could sign her on as an hourly paid data-cruncher,' mused Christian. 'I'm sure she'd do it for free. But to make it all look tidy – she's supplementing her pension with a bit of pocket money and keeping her mind active, all the usual old bugger clichés. We'll say we didn't get any offers from the grad students because it was too irregular and there was too little cash on offer. It's perfect.'

Jamie sighed again. 'I just know it's not going to be as straightforward as that. You really, really don't know my mum.'

'I know she's very good at what she does' said Annamarie. 'My Grandma Rachel was absolutely thrilled when Fran so kindly wrote that summary of Kindertransport evidence for her. Said that it really helped her to make a bit more sense of her childhood, all these years later'.

'She's good at that I know, but...'

Christian grinned. 'She's a clever lady who made you a clever boy, but the pair of you *are* both a little bit Aspie. Big deal. She's the person we need for this job, and who knows, it might even result in a bit of mother-son bonding. She's got her head stuck up her history of childhood and you've got yours stuck up your equations. Neither of you could ever understand the other's obsessions, but now you've got an opportunity to put what you know and can do together. Dr Anderson, meet Dr Anderson. You're going to be colleagues. Now let's be professional and get on with it.'

They sat in silence for a moment, looking around their austere laboratory, low winter sunshine glinting on NAMIS' metal fascia. Jamie reflected on the momentous events that he and the team had lived through over the last three months. When the calculations that were coming back from NAMIS indicated that the objects they were transporting were not only moving through space, but also unexpectedly through time, the team's initial rejoicing had been swiftly infiltrated by a gnawing anxiety. So they had agreed to keep the knowledge of the discovery strictly between the team for a while: Jamie, Annamarie, Christian and Ellie, Annamarie's PhD student who worked as their lab assistant.

Then when Jamie, the only one in the group with an established partner, had found it difficult to explain why he needed to take certain precautions such as having his phone almost permanently turned off, it was agreed that his wife Suzi could be allowed into the secret. Suzi also worked at the university as a postdoctoral researcher in the linguistics faculty and her skills would become extremely useful if the team managed to record speech in different

ON TIME

historical eras.

'We've been through this umpteen times Jamie,' Christian continued. 'We just can't risk this leaking anywhere at the moment. The whole thing would be weaponised by those bastards in Parliament and the Senate; we'd end up being forcibly conscripted by them.'

Jamie frowned. 'You sound like my mum.'

'If that is what she would say, I think she would be right,' said Annamarie, fretfully.

Jamie scuffed thoughtfully at a spot on the worn beige linoleum with the toe of his old lab shoe, contemplating the likely response from their Anglo-American government-backed funding sponsors. 'They wouldn't leave it entirely up to us anymore, and that's for sure. I guess we might get a lot more cash…'

'But do you think we'd be running it *at all*, Jamie?' asked Annamarie.

Jamie had never cared for politics, and certainly not with the same passion as his mother, but he was not entirely bereft of political imagination. He shuddered at the thought of the British and American governments unleashing MI5 and CIA operatives with hard eyes and sharp suits into his laboratory, once they had calculated which points in history could most usefully be tweaked in the pursuit of reducing enormous national debts, and to quash a few niggling international annoyances.

'OK then' he said, somewhat reluctantly. 'I'll ask my mum to come to London for a visit.'

~

At home later that evening, Jamie asked Suzi: 'What do you think about my mum coming to work on the project? Annamarie and Christian suggested it. We're getting to the point where we need some historical advice. It would mean that she would find out what's going on, though.'

Suzi looked at him quizzically. 'What do you think about it?'

'I'm really not sure.'

Suzi looked at her phone, making sure that it was turned off. She knew that Jamie's would be off already; he was obsessive about ensuring that it was turned off before he started such conversations. Everyone in the know about the project had their mobiles switched off more often than they had them switched on nowadays. Fran had already remarked on this to both Jamie and Suzi, that both of their phones always seemed to be on message. Suzi half-smiled, thinking about Fran with her phone always beeping away. She would have to change that, then.

'So, are you going to move on from sending stuff to remote areas then? If so, it's probably a good idea, Jamie. If you need a historian, who else could you trust?'

'Yes. We were thinking about dropping some tiny cameras here and there and then bringing them back to see what they had recorded. Nothing terribly sophisticated. But we need to know what is happening where and when to target times and locations effectively, and we need a bit more nuance on that than Google can offer. None of us studied history past GCSE at school.'

'Do you mean what was happening?'

'Yes – and no. From the data that is coming back from NAMIS, it probably makes more sense to say *is*.'

Suzi decided not to ask for the full explanation; she knew that she would quickly get lost in one of Jamie's detailed technical analyses. 'Are you going to record speech?'

Jamie smiled. 'Only incidentally. To do that with any intention, we'd have to send a person back. And we're not prepared to risk that quite yet. Besides, NAMIS is at such an early stage of mapping. We can only go back about 150 years at the moment. And it can't seem to work out how to go forwards at all. We can't even guess at why so far.'

Suzi had thought that setting up her own home after all these years of paying enormous rents would be an all-absorbing adventure. She and Jamie had only just managed to raise the mortgage to buy their tiny mews house with

ON TIME

Fran's help, and because their landlord was desperate to sell to pay off some debts. But following Jamie's momentous discovery, which had happened shortly after they moved in, they had done very little. They didn't talk about the stress that his work was creating, but it was always there, sitting with them in the room like an interloper. In some ways, thought Suzi, it might even help to have Fran around a bit more whilst in on the secret. Who knew, it might reduce the intensity.

'We *will* get around to recording speech,' promised Jamie, breaking her out of her thoughts. 'And when we do, we will know which expert to call on. I guess I'm lucky, having all these experts in the family.'

'It would be amazing to analyse Latin actually spoken by a Roman, to track English from 1066 to Chaucer, to Shakespeare…'

'Well, all in good time, literally, I guess. NAMIS is constantly learning. At the moment it's constructed maps covering a century and a half after only five months, and we think it might speed up. If only we didn't have this pressure of secrecy on us, it would be absolutely amazing.'

As a Trans-Atlantic couple, Suzi and Jamie had been learning about the problems of being between a rock and a hard place for the past decade. It had started slowly, with the Brexit referendum, which had made little impression on them at first. Suzi's country of birth, where Jamie also had family and friendship connections was always beckoning. Then came the 2016 election, after which Suzi cried for a week. Suzi's parents, who had entered the US from combat-weary Vietnam in the mid-1970s, expressed the fear that they had seen such rising societal division before, and its lethal consequences. And then of course, this prediction had played out further, following the subsequent election.

To say that it had been a helter-skelter ride in both nations since that time would be an understatement. Austerity had impacted on the infrastructure of all western nations since the world emerged from various degrees of lockdown, following the wide availability of the Corona Virus vaccine. The bullish days of pre-pandemic still seemed like a different era.

Jamie had therefore been relieved when his grant to develop an experimental matter transporter, in partnership with Artificial Intelligence expert Annamarie Simons, had been confirmed through the new Anglo-American research alliance, formed to facilitate Trans-Atlantic technological innovation. As one of the UK's up and coming physicists, Jamie was well placed to benefit.

The funding bought him and Annamarie out of their faculty duties for half of their allocated work hours, and a few months later, when they had enough success with inanimate objects to move on to transporting simple plant matter, they had been able to buy out Christian Novak, Jamie's old undergraduate roommate, for a few hours a week from his work as a post-doctoral researcher in the university's biology faculty. And then they had discovered that their prototype machine was moving its freight not only through space but also through time, and their lives had changed forever.

The light was fading outside. Suzi rose from her chair, turned on the lamp and drew the damask curtains. The shabby red and white sitting room always began to look cosy as the light faded to evening. She lit the candles she had placed on the old marble fireplace that had always struck them as over-ornate for such a tiny room. The comforting smell of lavender began to permeate the air. She picked up the TV remote. 'What about a bit of Netflix, forget about it all for an hour?'

Jamie turned on his phone. 'OK. In a sec. I'll just text my mum and ask if she and Kylie can come for a visit.'

Suzi browsed the Netflix offerings, wincing at the new dramatization of *The Time Machine*. She flipped to the old Hollywood musicals, and began scrolling.

ON TIME

Freddie: Sittingbourne, April 2025

'Here we are Freddie,' said Granny Fran.

Freddie stared into the window of the shop. Mizzling rain dribbled down the windows.

'Not flowers before,' he muttered.

'Eh?' replied Granny.

Freddie did not respond.

'Come on, let's go in,' she urged, taking his hand.

Freddie felt a flash of emotion. Had he been older, he would have described it as a sense of 'foreboding'. At the moment, his mind was a jumble of feelings that he couldn't find the words to articulate, of pictures that he could not properly decipher and words that were beyond his ability to elicit.

As his grandmother took hold of his hand, he could feel things; relentless curiosity, a compulsion to delve beneath surfaces and simmering impatience. Suddenly a flash bulb picture appeared in his mind's eye of a little girl. Granny… Fran… Franny- big, intense blue eyes, light blonde hair, a dirty face and scabby knees, always rushing into things that were not her business. He briefly felt that it was him who somehow had to be responsible for her, rather than vice versa. He felt a rush of affection that overrode his previous concerns. He smiled up at her.

Granny was leading him into the shop. As they crossed the threshold, Freddie felt a rush of yet another emotion he could not fully comprehend; a sweet ache he would one day learn was called "nostalgia."

'We had fun here sometimes, granny.'

'What do you mean, Freddie?'

'Me and Mummy played here. Jack came over to play, too, sometimes. You weren't born, though'.

Fran looked into Freddie's eyes, dark and distant. It was happening again. 'What are you seeing, Freddie?'

Freddie didn't reply immediately, struggling for words. 'I played here' he said eventually.

'No, you've never been here before, Freddie. This was where my granny lived when she was little and we've come down here to see it. We're staying with Jamie and Suzi for a few days, do you remember, while Mummy is at home with baby Jack? We're on our way to the seaside; I wanted to pop in here for a few minutes. Were you making up a story? For baby Jack, maybe?'

'What is Jack doing?'

'Well, we can FaceTime mummy in a minute and find out. I expect he's asleep.'

'But will he wake up?' urged Freddie, with rising agitation. 'There were fireworks, and stones before, and he wouldn't wake up.'

'Is that part of your story, Freddie? Because it sounds like rather a scary one. Jack's fine. We'll FaceTime in a minute and you can see him, I promise.'

Freddie's eyes began to clear. 'Do you think he will play soldiers with me?'

'When he's old enough, Freds. He's a bit little for that at the moment, isn't he? You can always play with Dylan. We'll take a trip to Cardiff in a few weeks, to see Aunt Rae and Dylan.'

Freddie was looking at the flowers. 'Are we going to buy some for Mummy?'

But Granny didn't hear. She was talking to the lady in the shop, boring grown-up stuff.

Freddie wandered over to look up the steep staircase that ran down the middle of the building. As he imagined the rooms that might be up there, vivid pictures danced through his mind. He didn't like that staircase, because… but it was no good, the reason wouldn't pop up in his mind.

Granny said he was *magin'tive* and that was where his mind-pictures came from. She told him that she had been 'very much the same' when she was a little girl, and that she had loved the stories that her Granny, who she called "Nana Mo" had told her. Nana Mo could remember all the way back to Queen… Freddie couldn't remember the name, but it had begun with a 'vuh' sound, and she had died when Nana Mo was a little girl.

'Come on Freds, we're going now,' said Granny. She had bought a bunch of floppy white roses.

'Mummy won't like those.'

'We're not taking these to Mummy, Freds. We are going to take them to my great- grandfather.'

Freddie looked at her, puzzled.

'He died Freddie, a long time ago now. Like your daddy's Uncle Bob did in January. Do you remember, you took Bob some flowers with your mummy and daddy?'

Freddie nodded.

'Well, that's what we're doing now. It won't take long. Then we'll drive on to the beach.'

Freddie took hold of Granny's hand. Like most four-year olds, he was used to being swept along in incomprehensible adult agendas. He knew his grandmother well enough to know that there would probably be ice cream at the end of this sequence of events, and not just for Freddie but for Fran, too. It was one of those delicious grandparent-grandchild secrets that they shared, because his mummy was *very* convinced that too much ice cream was not good for either Freddie or Fran.

As they walked down the road, Freddie was aware of Granny talking into her phone: '…FaceTime later when the baby is awake… he had one of his moments, some story about soldiers and wanting to play with Jack…well, I expect he wants to be the older one in the playfighting now. He's always the little one with Dylan. Yes, I can take him to Cardiff next month if you want…'

Suddenly, Freddie saw a monster puddle. 'Can I splash in that one, please Granny?' he asked. He had given up asking mummy, because he knew what the answer would be. Granny was a bit more… persuadable. Freddie would not have been able to construct the word 'persuadable' but as a bright, sensitive four year old, he was familiar with the concept.

'Oh, go on, then.'

He smiled and jumped.

Later on, when he was sitting in the back of Granny's funny little yellow car, Freddie wondered why Granny never bothered about his muddy shoes like his mummy and Aunt Rae did. Granny's car was full of all sorts of interesting things, like books (although they seldom had pictures in) that she had thrown onto the back seat and forgotten, shoes, empty water bottles, sweets (which usually ended up being eaten by Dylan and Freddie) and forgotten cardigans which were usually to be found in the back footwells. Every so often, Granny would tut-tut when she was getting Freddie out of the car, pick up a shoe or a cardigan and say, 'oh that's where it went.' Then more often than not, she would be distracted by fiddling with his seat belt or her phone bleeping and drop it back where it had been before.

If Freddie could have conjured up the word, he would have proposed that there was something *random* about Granny that he both liked and worried about at the same time. She seemed to live in her own head a lot more than the other adults he knew. But when she invited him into her thoughts it could be like riding on a magic broom.

'Can I have Bagpuss, please, Granny?'

Fran took the tiny soft toy from the dashboard and passed it back to him. 'Be kind to him Freds.'

That was another thing about Granny. She had a way of making magic seem real, actually in the everyday world, not only in a story. When she had given him her old teddy bear, she explained how he had become real, and why that meant Freddie had to treat him with the utmost respect.

'He's been really loved, Freddie,' she had said, *'and that gives us the responsibility to treat him like a real person. You know, like Kylie the dog? She can't tell you if you have hurt her, or hurt her feelings, but you can certainly do that, so you have to make an*

ON TIME

especially hard effort to be kind to her?'

Freddie had nodded. He got the idea. The bear sat at the bottom of Freddie's bed at home and got patted every night. Freddie hoped his mother was giving Old Ted his daily pat. She had promised that she would. When Granny gave Old Ted to Freddie, she had promised she would read Freddie a story about how toys become real. She said that it was something about a rabbit, but he would need to be a bit older first.

'Granny, am I old enough to know that story about the rabbit?'

'Rabbit? What, Peter Rabbit?'

'No, the real one.'

'Not *Watership Down*, surely?'

'The one that children make real.'

'Oh, the *Velveteen Rabbit*! Gosh, you have got a good memory. Yes, I would think so. I've got the book at home. We can read it when we get back.'

'Is Bagpuss real, Granny?'

'Kind of. I got him to sit in my car to remind me how important stories are to children. I wrote a book about that, Freds. You can read it when you are older. Bagpuss was on an old TV show, and he told children stories.

'He was real?'

'Yes… and no… he was a puppet. We can watch his video on my iPad tonight if you want.'

The flowers on the seat next to Freddie were radiating a sickly sweet scent that he didn't like. He usually liked the smell of Granny's car because it smelt like Granny, a delicate ice-creamy odour of perfume and soap, with a faint whiff of old paper.

'I don't like these flowers, Granny.'

The car slowed and came to a halt. 'It's OK, Freddie. We're going to get rid of them now.'

As Granny helped Freddie out of the car, he looked around. He didn't like this place either; it felt sad. The rain had stopped, and a watery sun was peeping through the clouds, but the day still seemed... dark, somehow. There was an old church and a huge area of grass around it, peppered with big stones. Freddie had seen a similar place like this before, in Leeds, when he had taken flowers to Great Uncle Bob with his mummy and daddy.

Granny tucked the flowers under her arm, took his hand, and they crossed the road.

'This is where my great-granddad is, Freddie. We won't be long. We'll leave him some flowers and then be on our way to the seaside.'

Freddie noticed that she had a sheet of paper in her other hand. She bent down to show him.

'This is a map of all the graves in this churchyard, Freds. And my great-granddad is here. We'll find him, leave the flowers and go.'

Freddie looked doubtful. He knew Granny wasn't good at finding her way with a map, or even with the Sat Nav. As she was showing him the map, a man came out of the church.

'Which one are you looking for?'

Fran showed him the map.

'It's over there, in the Victorian bit. Who are you looking for?'

'My great-grandfather, James MacIntosh.'

'I think there are two stones with that name on. They've fallen over now, they're so old.'

Granny took Freddie's hand, said 'thank you' to the man, and they walked over to the area that he had indicated.

Freddie was glad that they had found the stones they were looking for. Granny rubbed off some moss from the stones so that she could read the writing. Then she gasped. 'Oh, so you lost your daughter, too. I didn't know that. And you are all here together, all four of you.' She stood silently for a few seconds.

Freddie looked up at her, catching her sadness. 'Granny?'

ON TIME

She looked down at him, her eyes a little damp, marvelling that such a young child could be such an acute empath.

'It's OK, Freds. It all happened such a long time ago, long before I was born, and there's nothing we can do to change it. I didn't know that my great-great grandfather James lost his daughter when she was 18 besides losing my great-grandfather when he was still a young man. And they probably both died of things we could cure with a few pills nowadays. But look, James senior lived to a good old age in those days, just into his 80s.'

Granny pointed out some numbers etched on the stones. 'This says James MacIntosh 1831-1911; this says Mary MacIntosh 1831-1895; this says Katherine MacIntosh 1863-1881 and this one is my great-grandfather, James MacIntosh 1867-1893. 1893 is more than 130 years ago. That's a very long time. Shall we give them the flowers now?'

Freddie nodded.

As they laid the flowers, Granny said, 'It's too little too late, isn't it? I'm so sorry.'

"What?' replied Freddie.

'It's OK, Freds, I wasn't talking to you. Come on, let's go. Only half an hour more and we'll be at the seaside. Bucket, spade, fish, chips and ice cream. Sound good?'

Freddie cheered.

And to make things even better, he had seen an excellent splashing puddle on the rickety old path.

~

Later that evening, Granny tucked Freddie into his cosy ready bed in her room in Jamie's house in London, gently shooing Kylie off. Kylie grunted and moved grumpily down to the end. Freddie giggled. He liked being with Kylie. He knew she would jump onto his granny's bed later on. 'Jamie…is like James, isn't it, Granny, those people we saw today.'

'Yes, that's right, Freddie. That's Jamie's real name, we

just call him Jamie. His full name is James MacIntosh Anderson. We've always had a James MacIntosh in the family, ever since my daddy. We call them that after that man we visited today.'

'But now there's me and Dylan and Jack…'

Fran smiled. 'I think maybe it's getting too long ago, now, Freddie. My great-granddad would be over 150 years old now. Maybe his name has gone on for long enough? Anyway, look what I found on the internet.' She showed him a picture of a rabbit on her phone. 'It's the *Velveteen Rabbit*. Do you want me to read it to you?'

Freddie nodded. His eyes were drooping.

Granny began to read…

…"What is REAL?" asked the Rabbit one day, when they were lying side by side near the nursery fender, before Nana came to tidy the room. "Does it mean having things that buzz inside you and a stick-out handle?"

"Real isn't how you are made," said the Skin Horse. "It's a thing that happens to you. When a child loves you for a long, long time, not just to play with, but REALLY loves you, then you become Real."

Freddie slept, and as he fell into the deepest cycle of slumber, he became more like the 'real Freddie'. The biggest problem for the conscious Freddie was that there were so many missing *words*. There were many things that Freddie knew that he knew, but it was a type of knowing that he could not fully communicate, however hard he tried.

When he did manage to push some of what was inside out, it usually emerged in the form of a story that just popped into his head. Freddie thought that Granny was usually the best at listening to these and taking them seriously- she was never too busy like some of the other grown-ups- but even she would sometimes ask silly questions, like 'what were the names of the soldiers' which of course he didn't know, and moreover, didn't interest him. He saw the moving pictures and narrated what was going on as best as he could. But it was more than seeing- he knew how the people *felt*. And that was the most important thing for Freddie; how the people felt.

The other problem was that he didn't always remember what he had said when he was trying to narrate the pictures. They arrived, moved, and vanished quickly, more vivid when he was tired, sleepy or bored, fading away when he was happy and absorbed in play. He got feelings about people, not only about who they were *now* but who they were *then*. He had a strong sense of his grandmother as a child of his own age 'and she was no different then' was the phrase that kept coming into this mind. He thought of her as a splash of bright colours, sky blue for cleverness, sunshine yellow for funniness and off the wall eccentricity, but also a sharp electric red for impetuosity and deep vermillion for impatience. Freddie did not have the words to describe even a small percentage of these thoughts at the moment, but he saw the colours vividly. He sensed that it was the reds in his grandmother's palette that led her into trouble. And on this trip to London, he had a strong sense of these coming to the top.

He had once tried to talk to his grandmother about his colours, but she had come up with a long word – 'synny-feesia'- and then went on and on at his mother about it, how it was an indication Freddie might be 'very crate-ive later on'. Mother had nodded and smiled. Freddie wasn't sure what 'crate-ive' meant, but it sounded like a good thing.

The problem for Freddie now was that he couldn't find the right words to tell his grandmother about her reds boiling to the top. And, although he didn't have such an acute sense of his Uncle Jamie, something about his colours bothered Freddie too. Jamie was different- his colours were deeper, richer, somehow more sophisticated than Granny's. He had the clever blue, too, but it was a different shade, a rich azure blue, like a deep ocean. Freddie intuited that this had recently become stronger.

But there was also something…rusty orange in there too. Jamie was not sure about something, and it was worrying him.

Freddie half woke and tried to listen to the adult voices outside. They sounded excited about something. But they were speaking very quietly. Granny said: '….amazing' and then Jamie said, 'but only at the beginning….'

Thunder rumbled outside. Freddie twitched anxiously. He didn't like thunder. Thunder meant lightening and lightening meant… but it was no good, he couldn't remember. And it had been a busy day. Kylie was snoring softly. Granny sometimes snored loudly. Freddie's last thought before he drifted off into a dreamless sleep was 'I hope she doesn't do that tonight.'

TRAVELLERS

Annamarie: London, September 2025

'How are you finding it, Fran?' Annamarie asked.

'Surreal,' replied Fran.

They both laughed.

'I just wish I knew how it does what it does,' continued Fran. 'I'm not used to working on projects where I don't get most of what is going on.'

'Well, we'd like to know how it does what it does. The problem is, it's a kind of combination of what I know and what Jamie knows, and that makes it a lot smarter than both of us.'

'Ah, that I understand. NAMIS is like your child.'

Annamarie thought for a moment. 'That's a great way to look at it, Fran. I never really thought about it like that.'

'I guess I would, wouldn't I? My whole adult life has been about childhood. First of all, Jamie and his sisters, then teaching history in school for a while, then my thesis about children's stories and myths. This is sort of…different. It's not my project.'

'Yeah, but you've really helped us. That idea about the Krakatoa eruption was inspired.'

Fran smiled. 'It was a big bang, wasn't it? It's a shame we can't share the data with the geologists. How did you do with the London smog?'

'That was a bit more difficult; working out where to drop the equipment. But yes, we've got some good data on that, too.'

'When I was a little girl, the buildings in London were still all very dirty, you know. They cleaned them up over the late 1960s and early 1970s. So, you got back to 1883 for Krakatoa. When are we likely to get back to Pompeii?'

'Maybe not as soon as we thought. We are only at 200 years at the moment.'

'Not long before we'll be able to look at the American and French Revolutions. And soon, we'll be getting into the zone where we will be able to find out what people we've only seen in paintings actually look like.'

'That might be difficult with a static drone.'

'When are you going to send people back?'

'Oooh, the million-dollar question. We already did the animal tests. Christian said there was nothing wrong with any of them when they came back, he checked it down to the atomic level. They got a bit hot or a bit cold, depending on whether we had sent them to desert or polar areas. We chose the species to suit of course.'

'Didn't they wander off?'

Annamarie picked up what looked like a bulky plastic plaster from the bench. 'Of course. But we put the mobile pad on them. It picks up the signal and brings them back. We had to be able to do that before we could do anything with something non-static.'

'So why can't you send a person back?' said Fran.

'Well…what if it went wrong? We'd never be able to explain that, would we?'

'Why should it go wrong? A person would be safer than an animal, surely. I mean what if the pad had fallen off the animal? Or if it had unexpectedly encountered a person?'

'I guess… we took that risk. We only sent them to uninhabited areas.'

'But would you have sent a person back to get the animal if the pad had fallen off?'

Christian wandered into the lab, stirring a malodourous instant noodle. He sat at the bench shovelling it into his mouth. 'Yes, I'd go and get it. We can't leave anything in the past. Might do something weird to the timeline.'

'How do you know?' asked Fran.

'We don't. But you've seen all those movies, haven't you, when people go back and kill their granddad or whatever? We have to work on the basis that it would create a problem.'

Fran looked at him, smiling faintly. 'And what about the Quantum Leap hypothesis?'

'What the hell is that?'

'Oh, it was this old TV programme... over thirty years ago, now. This bloke used to jump around in time, "putting things right that had gone wrong." That was what the intro voiceover said, anyway.'

'Who said it had gone wrong?' asked Annamarie.

Fran thought for a moment. 'I suppose that was a bit vague.'

Christian grinned. 'It always is.'

'There was one episode,' Fran continued, 'where he went back in time to save President Kennedy.'

'So did he?' asked Annamarie, intrigued.

'No, he couldn't in the end. But he saved the President's wife, Jackie. He was the man who lent over her in the car to protect her after the shooting started.'

'Did Jackie die, then in real life?'

Fran began to feel old. 'No. She was beautiful, elegant and sort of wistful. She went on to marry someone else. It didn't work out that well, though. She's dead now.'

'So, it was like – the jumper caused a disturbance in the Force?' asked Christian.

'No, it was nothing like *Star Wars*. The thing about *Quantum Leap* was that what the jumper made happen then became part of the historical reality that exists in the real world. The world sort of moved onto a different timeline and the only person who knew about that was the jumper and his computer.'

Christian scraped up the last dregs of his instant

noodle. 'Shit. Oh well, if we're doing something like that, I guess we'll never know about it.'

He wandered out of the laboratory, throwing the empty noodle cup in the bin. Annamarie took it out and rinsed it under the tap over the tiny sink. She dried it carefully on a paper towel and put it into the recyclable waste.

Jamie walked in. 'So how are you planning to move this project forward then, you two?' asked Fran.

'We're doing it,' replied Jamie, tersely. 'And I'm not your PhD student.'

'But if you sent a person back,' Fran persisted, 'you could find out so much more. I was talking to Suzi yesterday. She's got so many ideas about what you could do if you recorded language, even in Victorian or Regency times. And once we get back another couple of hundred years, we could go and see a Shakespeare play at the original Globe. That would be amazing.'

'And dangerous. Not only in terms of the risk to the timeline, but of all the things you wouldn't know about interacting with people in that society. Come on, mum. You're the one who knows about all that cultural stuff.'

'But imagine. You could see history, interact with it… obviously you'd have to be aware of the timeline, not talk about anything important with anyone, leave anything behind or do anything silly like that. But you could watch… it would be incredible. And you know what, Jamie? To move this project on, you are going to have to bite that bullet pretty soon.'

She picked up the papers she had come to collect and walked towards the door. 'I'm off back to the house then.'

Jamie glowered after her. He was getting that sulky teenager look that was becoming familiar to his workmates since his mother had joined the team.

Annamarie picked at her fingernail. 'She's probably right, Jamie. We're doing brilliantly with the drones, but all we're getting is videos and data, and it's data that we can't share with people who could do useful things with it. OK, so we're keeping Christian busy with bits of plant life, but that's not moving us on significantly. And yes, NAMIS is learning and moving gradually backwards in time, but we haven't made many inroads into *how* it's doing that, or why it can't seem to go forward; Ellie's working on that. The only way we could significantly add to what we know right now is to take the next step and let a person take the trip.'

'But we can't spare any one of us. What if something happened to us? We're all such integral parts of the team. If one of us didn't come back, it would kill the project stone dead. Maybe we could send Ellie, but what if something happened to her? She's our student, our responsibility…'

Annamarie sighed. 'It's a problem. I'd love to go… and Ellie can do nine-tenths of what I can do now. In fact, she's coming up with some amazing ideas of her own that I would never have thought of.'

'Well, you can't. Got to go now… masters group to teach, over in Physics.'

Annamarie was left in the lab alone. She tried to work on data spreadsheets, but her mind began to wander. He tried to save the President, but he couldn't, she thought. But he managed to save Jackie. She googled *Quantum Leap*, becoming fascinated with the hapless explorer, being catapulted around the recent past "righting what went wrong." Maybe, she mused idly, he could have been the blond stranger who lifted her Grandmother Rachel onto the Kindertransport train just before it left, and thereby saved her life. If he hadn't done that, then Annamarie's mother, Linda would never have been born, and then of course, no Annamarie.

Rachel Rosenberg Bialystock was going to be 94 next month, still living in her own flat in Hampstead, her body crumbling relentlessly, but her mind as sharp as ever. Annamarie had heard the story of Rachel's narrow escape from Prague many times. Rachel had never gone back, or ever spoken Czech to Annamarie, nor even to Linda. '*I never wanted to be reminded of that time again,*' she had said. She told Annamarie that she couldn't speak Czech anymore, anyway. Annamarie wasn't sure that was entirely true.

Rachel had a few pictures of her mother Anna, of other people in her family and a letter that Anna had written for Rachel's foster family to give to her when she was older, should she and Anna not be reunited by that time. Annamarie knew that Rachel had written an English translation of that letter, many years ago. She found the yellowing pages one day in an old box in her grandmother's wardrobe. She read the translation quickly, guiltily, then put the papers back, feeling remorseful that she had opened the box at all.

Anna's letter was written in a beautiful curving script that, according to the scribbled English translation clipped to it, apologised to Rachel for sending her away, and explained why this had been the best opportunity for Rachel at the time. It expressed a hope that Anna and Rachel would meet again as soon as Anna found a way to escape the Nazi vice that was slowly closing around Jewish families in the Prague of 1939. But this never came to be. Rachel had never been never able to trace any record relating to her mother at all, apart from her birth in Prague in 1900.

When Rachel narrated the story, she seemed to slip back into the mind of the seven-year-old she had been, describing what happened simply and clearly, with little embellishment:

'I knew that all sorts of things were wrong. Children do, you know. I guessed that my father had gone away because he was doing work he had to hide from the Nazis, even though everyone told me that he was working in Ostrava and would be back soon. I just felt it. I knew that my mother and my grandmother were worried. They tried to smile and laugh with me, but they couldn't hide their fear. My mother packed my bag, and she took me to the station. When we got there, a lady urgently wanted to speak to her. My mother went over to speak to her, and then never came back. The train was ready

ON TIME

to leave. And then there was a man – he looked like a German, tall, blond… he arrived a few minutes before the whistle blew. He spoke to me in a language I couldn't understand; I think now it was probably English. He clearly said my name, 'Rachel.' He picked me up and put me on the train. The train pulled out, and I never saw my mother again. She never even said goodbye. I wish I knew what had happened to her.'

Annamarie, Linda and Rachel had made extensive searches for Anna Rosenberg in every archive they were able to access over the years. Rachel's father had been executed by the Nazis in 1940, whilst Rachel's grandmother had been gassed in Auschwitz in 1942, along with most of her extended family. But Anna's name didn't appear on any such record.

'I spent seven years expecting her to come and find me after the war,' Rachel explained. *'I tried to find her and the rest of my family through the Kindertransport people. That's how I found out what had happened to everyone else. In the end, I said to my foster mother on my 21st birthday, now I have to let her go and believe that she's dead. But who knows, maybe she had another family after the war and wanted to forget? Who could blame her?'*

When Annamarie was fourteen, Linda had reminisced about a hot summer day when she was about eight, when she and Rachel had been returning from the park on a crowded bus. A lady in a pretty, sleeveless summer frock stood next to them, hanging onto the bar next to where Linda was sitting. Linda had seen a number written on the lady's arm and asked her mother what it was for. The bus was noisy with chatter, and the lady hadn't heard, but Rachel had gone red, then white and told Linda to shush. When they got home, Rachel told her the story of Anna and her family for the first time.

'That must have been awful,' Annamarie had commented.

'It was. But you know, it didn't seem real to me. It was just…too horrible.'

Annamarie had felt a strange sense of knowing wash over her, that Anna had died not long after Rachel left

Prague. She pushed the thought away, bemused. She had decided the previous year that she was an atheist, and that she was going to be a scientist. There was no way that anyone could mysteriously "know" such a thing.

'Do you think that Anna was alive after the war?' she'd asked Linda.

'I don't think so. I just hope that whatever happened to her, she didn't suffer. I've never known what to say to Grandma about that – whether it would have been better for her to believe that her mother was dead, or whether it was better to hope she was alive and out there somewhere.'

Rachel had often spoken of Anna to Annamarie, who had been named in honour of her great-grandmother. *'You look so much like her,'* she frequently commented. *'And you have her spirit, somehow.'*

Of course, she didn't elaborate on the story of what had happened to her family until Annamarie was in the top class in Primary School. Then once she'd told Annamarie, she came to school and talked about her childhood to all the children in Annamarie's class. Mostly, she talked about arriving in London, how lucky she had been to find a kind family who had always longed for a little daughter, and how she had lived with them in Cornwall during the war, where they took her away from the worst of the bombing. They had returned to London after the war, and then when Rachel was sixteen she had started her training as a nurse in the brand new National Health Service. *'I wanted to give something back to the country that saved my life,'* she said.

Then in 1960, she'd married Joe, one of the doctors at the hospital, and two years later, Linda was born. Joe had died following a stroke when Annamarie was doing her GCSEs. One day, shortly before Annamarie left for university, she was brushing her long, dark hair in front of the mirror when she'd caught her grandmother staring at her. *'Sometimes, I think you get more and more like her,'* Rachel had said *'and other times, I think I am just telling myself a story; one that brings her back somehow. I can't really remember her face, or her voice anymore.'*

'That must be so sad, Grandma.'

'Sometimes. But I was one of the lucky ones. I'm here, now and so are you and your Mama. We must be grateful for what we have. We can't go back.'

But now, thought Annamarie, we can.

Jamie: London, September 2025

They've both got that face on, thought Suzi. Here we go.

'I don't see why not, Jamie,' urged Fran. It's the perfect solution. Works for me, works for you, gives us a project within a project that we can also publish when we finally unveil this thing to the world.'

'Have you turned your phone off?'

'What do you think? Of course I have. And you know I would never touch the bloody automated assistant with a barge pole.'

Jamie had no reason to doubt her. Annamarie said a couple of weeks ago that she was so glad that Fran was one of the paranoid variety of over 60s when it came to phones and social media.

'Annamarie thinks it's a good idea.'

'She would.'

'And Christian said it would probably be a good development.'

'What if something happened to you? How do you think I would feel?'

'Christian said you'd done all the experiments with animals. He couldn't find anything wrong with any of them. Jamie, you know some Victorians thought people would explode if they travelled at over 20 miles an hour?'

Jamie snorted. He turned to Suzi: 'What do you think, then? Do you still want to take a trip to the Globe with her to see the premiere of *Romeo and Juliet* in maybe about six month's time?'

'It's your project, Jamie. Don't bring me into it.'

'You're going to have to try it with a human being at some point, Jamie,' Fran insisted. 'And as Annamarie said, you can only keep it under wraps for so long. You have to make regular reports to the funding body, and if it seems like nothing is happening, they will start asking questions. Christian said he reckoned you had about six months.'

Jamie felt the walls closing in around him. Fran always argued like this. He went to the fridge and took out a beer. Their tiny kitchen seemed so ordinary, so normal. The fading wallpaper printed with strawberries that he had to change at some point, the cracked green paisley patterned tiles over the sink and the view out of the patio doors onto the tiny courtyard where Kylie was sitting by the climbing ivy, warming her old bones in the last beams of Autumn sunlight. He remembered a snatch of a haunting song that Fran used to play in the car when he was little, that compared the fading of summer to the sadness of losing loved ones.

He felt tears prickle at the back of his eyes. So here they were now then, talking about time machines, and making his elderly mother the first passenger in one. Hadn't the family lost enough people in the last few years? He went back into the living room. Fran was sitting on the sofa. Suzi was nowhere to be seen. Jamie knew she had probably retreated to the desk in their bedroom and would later claim that she had urgent emails to send before tomorrow morning. She didn't like what the Anderson family called "discussions."

'You act like those Terminators in the movie, smashing each other through walls,' she once commented. *'We don't hit one another,'* Jamie had replied, startled. *'No,'* Suzi had agreed, thoughtfully. *'But it's what you and Fran do intellectually. You're both so calm and so...ruthless.'*

Characteristically, Fran now persisted. 'Jamie, you've got to try a person in that time machine before your six months are up. And wouldn't an *old* person be the best choice within the small group available? If anything goes wrong, I'm only going to lose about 15 useful years at most, that we can only be optimistic about if the 'Rona doesn't outwit the medics again. And it wouldn't really impact on the project, anyway. I can leave you a list of good times and places to drop your drones.'

Jamie stared morosely at his beer bottle. 'If this *was* a possibility... and I emphasise *was*...where and when would you go?'

'Oh, that's easy. Sittingbourne 1890-91, to find out what happened when Nana Mo was born.'

Jamie's head jerked upwards in surprise. 'I thought you were going to say somewhere historically significant – you know, like the day the first world war began, or to see Churchill do one of his speeches, or Queen Victoria's coronation or something.'

'No, that would be daft. We're all aware of the dangers of accidentally interfering in history. That would be far more likely if I went somewhere- somewhen – that was historically significant.'

Jamie didn't reply. But he was listening more closely now. Perhaps I've been too hard on her, he thought. She actually does seem to get it.

'Look, Jamie,' she continued, 'I went to Sittingbourne with Freddie when we were down in April. It's a little high street on the way to the seaside. It's pretty, but it has that air of "nothing ever happens here" and I bet nothing ever has. My great-grandparents were ordinary people. I would observe them and their lives as an ordinary person. I already know quite a lot about them, and I've been studying the everyday things such as late Victorian middle-class manners and dress conventions. I'll turn up as a new member of the congregation in their Presbyterian church and observe them from there. We can record speech on one of those super-sensitive mini recording devices that Suzi's team recently piloted. Can you imagine the type of data I would collect? When and if you decide to go public, I could name my price on the book deal. We would all get something out of it, and nothing is likely to go wrong.'

Jamie picked at the label on his beer bottle, looking thoughtful. 'You'd also go down in history yourself as the first person to travel in time. You'd be sort of like Neil Armstrong.'

Fran grinned. 'A 60 something *female* Neil Armstrong- an old sista doing it for herself.'

Jamie picked at the threads in the arm of the old armchair, which had been in his parents' living room when he was still an undergrad. 'No, an old sista doing it for her son.'

There was a short silence.

'So, can I do it, Jamie?'

Jamie looked at his mother in amusement. She had the same "pleeeease" face on that Dylan used when he wanted to stay up to play on his X-squared box war games.

'You know,' she continued, 'I always knew you would invent some kind of amazing machine. I would be so honoured to be your first human passenger.'

Jamie grinned impishly. 'Don't try the flattery now. I've heard your idea. It's better than I thought it might be. I'll discuss it with Christian and Annamarie tomorrow, and we'll make a logical, considered decision together. Now that's it. No more debating.'

Pompous little git, thought Fran. But for once she held her tongue. She knew Jamie well enough to know when she was winning.

Fran: Sittingbourne, April 1890

'Pleased to meet you,' said the young man. 'James MacIntosh. But everyone calls me Jim.'

Fran looked at him, smiling politely, trying to keep the turmoil within her mind from showing in her face. Decades of dealing with capricious students had helped her to appear calm when mentally paddling hard under the surface. Beautiful auburn hair, sweet smile, nice face, but more friendly-looking than handsome, she thought. The relationship to Nana Mo showed in his face, most particularly his distinctive hazel-green eyes. And strangely, there was something of Jamie about him; the way that he stood and moved, the expressions that crossed his face, but it wasn't overt. Jim was shorter and of course, had different colouring. It *was* a distant relationship, after all.

'Frances Anderson,' she replied, extending her hand in the way that she had studied so carefully. He inclined his head, and the sun shone brightly on his hair through the cracked, smeared window, sparking flashes of rusty light. Burning embers, thought Fran melancholically. She watched the dust motes dancing in the sunbeams, contemplating why church halls were always so dusty, and why they always smelled the same – dust and old paper. Nothing much changed there in over a century.

'I hear that you recently lost your husband, Mrs Anderson. I'm so sorry.'

As he touched her hand, she felt a flash of powerful emotion, the family connection that they shared rushing to the surface. She saw his eyelids flicker. So, you feel it too, she thought.

As a history researcher for over thirty-five years, Fran had studied intently for this visit. As the pioneer historian to go on a field trip of this nature, she was determined not to be found wanting. She had meticulously investigated clothing, food, manners, language, accent…it was surprising how Americanised English speech was becoming in the twenty-first century. She'd even had her hair dyed back to grey, which she absolutely hated; no respectable bottle blondes in this environment. But there were still some things she was learning on the hoof. A tall, well-built woman in her own time, the first thing she had noticed when she emerged into 1890, after the strange odours assailing her nose, was that she felt like an interloper from the land of the giants. It was a good thing that the local population were far too polite to remark on anything of such a personal nature.

'And what do you do for a living?' she asked, already knowing the answer.

'I'm an engineer. Just finishing off my time as a journeyman. I work with my father.'

Fran became aware of the older man sauntering up behind Jim's shoulder and her heart fluttered again. Even though the older man had a bushy red and white beard, the likeness made it obvious that they were father and son. I've read so much about you, she thought. You were so much easier to find in the records, all that work you did for the town council after you retired, the speeches you gave, the street lighting you fought for… but most of what she had read was still in the future for these people.

'James MacIntosh,' said the older man with a sharp Clydeside inflection, inclining his head politely and offering his hand. 'But everyone here calls me Mac.' Fran barely stopped herself from blurting out 'yes I know!'

Instead she replied primly, remembering her Victorian manners. 'Pleased to meet you, Mr MacIntosh. Frances Anderson.'

'Was your husband Scottish, Mrs Anderson? Being that it's a Scottish name and all?'

'I don't think so, Mr MacIntosh. But I think maybe his grandfather might have been.'

'Ah, there's so many of us down here now. Was no work there when we left.'

But you never forgot, did you, thought Fran, because when you finally manage to buy your own house with your son-in-law, shortly after you retire, you are going to call it 'Renfrew.'

She became aware of some girls milling around at the table, giggling, pouring tea and passing around sandwiches. An older woman extracted herself from the group and took hold of Mac's arm. 'Do introduce me to our new member.'

'Mrs Anderson, this is my wife, Mary. Mary, this is Mrs

ON TIME

Frances Anderson.'

'So pleased to meet you, Mrs Anderson,' smiled Mary in the same strong Scottish burr as her husband. 'Do come and have some tea. And let me introduce you to my friend Polly Burns.'

Three great-great grandparents in rapid succession thought Fran, covering her churning emotions with a polite smile.

Polly looked maybe fifteen years younger than Mary. Fran began mentally calculating. I think Polly's forty-two, she thought, while Mary's just coming up to sixty. Even without her access to birth records, Fran would have found it easier to tell their ages in the period she now found herself in. No modern face creams, no subtle modern hair dyes, primitive dentistry. Fran presumed that the locals must think that she was a few years younger than she actually was.

'Lovely to meet you Mrs Anderson,' said Polly. She had the local old Kentish accent. 'Where are you from?'

Fran had decided that becoming a Victorian Londoner meant slightly exaggerating her own original accent, which was the easiest option. 'London. Pleased to meet you, Mrs Burns.'

Fran met the eyes of her two great-great-grandmothers, a feeling of unreality washing over her. She was fast beginning to realise that before she had arrived here, she had constructed these people in her mind rather like fading figures in an old sepia photograph. Now they were real, living, in three dimensions and full colour, she was finding the experience quite overwhelming. And suddenly there he was – the man that Fran had long suspected of being the villain of the piece, her other great-great-grandfather in this branch of the family, William Burns. He was a decade younger than Mac, harder and smoother looking. And, she remembered, Burns was already a local Town Councillor. She moved forward to be introduced to him, surreptitiously observing the body language between the two men.

You don't like each other even now, do you, she thought, as she bowed and smiled. *You* think he's a jumped-up Glaswegian oik, and *he* thinks you are an up your own arse, pseudo-posh Edinburgh pillock, pretending to be something you're not.

Burns was explaining to her that he was one of the church elders, the local master jeweller, and that he had left Edinburgh for England with his master many years ago, when he was a journeyman. He went on to explain, as Fran already knew, that he owned a double fronted shop in the middle of the high street which was a jewellers on one side and a sweet shop/ tobacconist on the other, his wife and older daughters helping him to serve the customers during busy periods. 'It's very convenient,' he explained, 'because we live over the shop.' So that's why Nana Mo bought the shop in London after the war, thought Fran. It was like coming home.

'My parents had a shop in London,' she said out loud. 'It was my grandmother's originally, she bought it after… her husband died. We lived over it, too. My parents are both dead now.'

Nearly said 'after the war' she thought. That was a near miss. Did people buy shops after the Crimean War? She didn't immediately know what effect that had on the economy. Although she remembered, a generation earlier Napoleon had sneered at the English as 'a nation of shopkeepers.'

Pay attention, she reminded herself. Don't say anything that might cause consternation. Maybe don't tell them so much that is rooted in reality? Perhaps it would be easier to come up with, and memorise a complete fabrication? She needed to go over her notes when she got back. And out of this corset, which was only loosely tied. She shifted on her feet in a vain attempt to try and stop it digging into her. Bloody hell, they all wear these things she thought. And don't say bloody hell here, ever. She thought of the austere, sin-obsessed sermon with which the sallow faced minister had exhorted the congregation.

Mary was smiling kindly at her. 'And you've not long been a widow, hen, have you?'

You've got that kind smile and way of talking, like Nana Mo, thought Fran. She felt tears rising.

'Come on now,' urged Polly, catching Fran's mood, 'let's leave the men to their chatter and have a cup of tea.' She took Fran's arm and guided her over to the refreshments table.

'Thank you,' Fran replied, weakly. She was hoping that she wouldn't have to actually drink the liquid in the cup that would be offered. Having been induced to spend considerable sums of money in faux Victorian tea shoppes over the years, naturally one of the first things she did on arrival in 1890 was to find an authentic one. She quickly learned that the idea of 'things tasting better in the old days,' was a complete myth. The tea in particular was horrid. It reminded her of the tea that was not uncommonly served in the US, made with hot water that had not been properly boiled.

A young lady in a white dress handed her the dreaded cup of tea.

'Thank you Izza,' said Polly. 'This is my eldest daughter Isabella, Mrs Anderson. She's going to be nineteen next week.'

For the first time, Fran glanced into the living face of Izza Burns-MacIntosh, her fierce, managerial great-grandmother. Mo had frequently passed the opinion that her mother was a strait-laced Victorian prude. Fran's father James had described his grandmother as a harsh disciplinarian who despised grubby little boys. Fran's Aunt Adi had recounted hilarious tales of Isabella terrorising the maids in the hotel that she owned with her second husband in Portsmouth in the 1920s. But what Fran saw was a mop of shiny, dark curls escaping from an untidy knot at the back of the girl's neck, merry, dancing brown eyes and a pretty little mouth that seemed permanently turned up at the corners.

Isabella beamed at her. 'Pleased to meet you, Mrs Anderson.'

Fran had a sepia photograph of this girl when she was a woman maybe twenty years older, a stiff collar, tightly piled hair and stern dark eyes glaring out at the viewer. Good heavens, what happened to you she thought.

Mary and Polly were talking softly beside her. As she listened to the soft rise and fall of the conversation, she realised that the awkwardness that existed between the two men was completely absent between the women. Their chatter rose and fell, the Scottish and Kentish burrs creating a quaint harmony, all so domestic and tranquil, the work of the church, the bad weather for the time of year, what the children were doing. And, Fran remembered, as she smiled and nodded, that they both had a lot of children. Polly's were younger and, from the tone of the conversation, she seemed to be finding things difficult. She glanced briefly at Polly's face; anxious, watchful brown eyes and a prominent worry line between the eyebrows.

Oh dear, thought Fran. And you are probably already just pregnant with the youngest one now. But never mind, it's going to be a boy, your only son. Maybe that'll make up for it. Gosh, I'm so glad I wasn't born in the nineteenth century. Did they wear these corsets when they were *pregnant?* She bit her lip.

Out of the corner of her eye, she noticed that Jim had approached the tea table. As he took the cup from Izza, his hand brushed hers. She looked up into his eyes and smiled. They spoke softly to one another, becoming more animated; both now clearly had a lot more to say. He touched her hand again. This time it was clearly intentional. She beamed at him, and his hazel-green eyes danced.

Fran looked over towards the two mothers. You would have managed it between you in the end, she thought. But you're both going to die unexpectedly and too soon; seems to be the curse of our bloody family. She looked back at Jim. The expression on his face now somehow reminded Fran of Jamie as a sweet little boy, giggling with his sisters in the garden.

And it was at that precise moment that the seditious thought first popped into her head: I'm not going to let *you* die.

FAMILY BUSINESS

Fran: London, November 2025

'What's "meet the ancestors" like from your perspective, Fran?' asked Annamarie.

Fran pondered for a moment, looking around the now familiar grey and white lab, the low sun filtering in through the window, sparking light off the metal surfaces. It was almost impossible to describe the mass of conflicting emotions that had been through her mind during her excursions in time over the past month. Wonder and awe, certainly, but also some painful emotions triggered by meeting with members of her family of whose ultimate fates she was already aware. She was beginning to think that maybe she should not have mixed the personal so intricately with the professional.

'I really don't know. I know this sounds a bit wishy-washy, but I think I need more time to *process* than I thought I would before I started. On the one hand, actually being in a culture that is so similar, yet so different from your own gives you so much more nuance as a historian... how things actually looked in three dimensions, how they sounded, even how they *smelt*... it's amazing. But at the end of the day, I'm meeting members of my own family who look, act, even express themselves similarly to people I have lived with all my life... and that's difficult at times.'

Jamie raised his head from his PC screen. 'Difficult? How?'

ON TIME

'Well… it's like their problems are your problems. For example, I see the difficulties that Mary and Polly have with the children, and I want to… I don't know, talk to them in a way that might seem too… familiar. Like I might talk to Niamh or Rae. So, I have to keep stopping myself. For one thing, I've presented myself as a childless widow, and for another, it would seem extremely odd. And of course, if I got too far into it, I might let my guard down and start passing twenty-first century opinions that would sound totally off the wall. I don't think any of those temptations would have come up if they had been perfect strangers.'

Christian turned away from the 3-D plant rotating on his computer screen. 'How are they familiar?'

'Mary is very like my Nana Mo. Not in looks, but she's got this kind but still commonsense way of talking – she can sympathise while she's telling you to be sensible about something, all at the same time. And Jim…there's so much about him that reminds me of…' she stopped abruptly.

Annamarie smiled. 'I think I know what you are going to say Fran. Jamie. Jim sounds like Jamie.'

'No, he doesn't,' Jamie exclaimed. 'He's got that sort of countrified accent that Suzi calls "old Kentish." I don't know what you are all on about. Suzi said something about she could "hear the relationship" when she listened to the audio file yesterday.'

'Oh, is she working on that already, Jamie?' asked Annamarie, concern in her voice. 'I don't think we can buy her out for those hours like Christian or put her on an hourly wage like Fran and Ellie, though. We couldn't explain on the project accounts what a linguist working full time in another faculty of the university was doing for us.'

'Don't worry about it. I can't keep her away. She's having a whale of a time.'

'And that's something else I'm worrying about,' continued Fran. 'How ethical is it to record people who have absolutely no idea of voice recording technology at all, let alone the fact that I have a miniscule device packed with electronics in my pocket that can capture everything they say? And then I'm sharing it with a bunch of other people, with no ethical clearance from the university at all.'

Jamie and Annamarie caught each other's eyes and smiled.

'Oh, bloody hell, they've been dead for years, Fran,' laughed Christian. 'Besides which they never really *say* anything at those ghastly church hall gatherings, anyway, do they? "Oooh, more tea, vicar?"'

Fran groaned, half laughing. 'No vicars in the non-conformist, double-predestinationist, Presbyterian church, mate. They are *ministers*. And everyone is equally hell-bound. Although, sitting through those services is probably penance enough. But yes, I know; I am not hugely bothered at the moment. They are public conversations at the end of the day. And sharing them amongst ourselves doesn't feel that terrible. But if we ever went public… that might feel a bit different.'

'That's a problem for the future,' replied Jamie. 'We've got to take the attitude that whoever these people were, and however real they seem when you interact with them, that their time is over.'

'We are the dead,' mused Fran.

'Eh?' said Christian.

'It's a line from *1984*. About people whose time is over. Different context. Didn't you say, Jamie, that as far as your calculations are concerned, what is happening in time when we are doing this doesn't clearly distinguish between the past and the present?'

'It's hard to explain in basic terms, but yes, sort of.'

'In which case, who are the dead here? The people in our past, who are dead in our time, or us, the people in their future, who are not yet born?'

Jamie grinned at Annamarie 'told you!'

'Oh, shut up Jamie,' replied Fran, smiling ruefully. 'I am just asking the question.'

ON TIME

'That's what I told Annamarie: that you *would* ask the question.'

'This is because all they ever do in the humanities is talk,' interjected Christian, 'talk, talk, talk. Whilst we get on and *do* things.'

'Like Zuckerberg,' said Fran, 'move fast and break things. And that worked out well, didn't it?'

Jamie looked troubled. 'We haven't broken anything.'

'Not yet,' replied Fran, archly.

'So, that's in your hands then, mum, as the solitary time-traveller, isn't it?'

Annamarie and Christian grinned at one another. They had learned that watching Fran and Jamie skirmish was an excellent spectator sport.

'There haven't been any tech problems that you haven't mentioned, have there?' Jamie added.

'No. If I make sure my phone is fully charged and set to silent before leaving, I can hide it in my bag, and use files I've loaded on it for reference if I need to. I just go and lock myself in a cubicle in the Ladies for a minute or two if I want to do that. And because the local time of arrival in the past is set on NAMIS, I set the counter on my phone when I arrive, so I can keep an eye on the time. But it hasn't really been necessary; there's a big clock in the church meeting hall.'

'Oh, that's good then' said Jamie, turning back to his computer screen.

Fran let out a large shuddering sigh, making a soft humming sound. She picked up her laptop and left the lab. She walked slowly down the dark beige and brown corridor, deep in thought. This was the oldest building of the university, which had been home to over a century of experimental science. She was sure that if she came to visit the building in 1890 (and actually gained permission to enter, being female) she would find it little different to the way it was today. Presumably, they would have decorated a few times since then, she mused. But it certainly hadn't seen a lick of paint for a while. Christian had told her, only half joking, that the university put all their non-prestigious, speculative projects here.

Fran wondered how many brilliant scientific minds had walked down this corridor before her, and what triumphs and regrets they had been contemplating as they had done so. Whatever they'd done, and whatever they discovered, she thought, I bet I am the first one here wishing that I'd thought things through more carefully before placing my long dead relatives into the very first historical petri dish.

Rachel: Prague, 1st August 1939

Rachel felt a horrible knot forming in her tummy as Mama explained that she was going to have to move yet again. It might have been exciting if Papa was coming home and they were going somewhere nicer with Mama and Bubbe, but that wasn't what was going to happen. Instead, Mama was telling her that she would be taken to the train station tomorrow morning and then she was going to have to get on a train without Mama, Papa or Bubbe.

Mama was doing that adult thing that Rachel had experienced so often recently, trying to make something awful sound exciting, telling her there would be lots of other children and some grown-ups on the train who would look after them, taking them to a faraway place called 'England' where there were lots of nice things to eat, and people who would be kind to them. But Rachel was seven, nearly eight, and she wasn't anyone's fool.

She started to cry. 'I don't want to go, Mama.' It was happening again; this was the next horrible thing. First of all, Papa had gone away. Then Rachel and Mama had to leave their lovely house to live with Bubbe in her tiny apartment. And not long after, the bad men had arrived in Praha with their guns and their shiny, scary cars. Now this.

Mama had tears in her eyes. 'I don't want to send you, drahoušku, but I have to. I will try to explain to you again.

ON TIME

I am trying to keep you safe from the bad men who have come to Praha.'

'So why don't you come with me, Mama, you and Bubbe? Then you would both be safe, too. Papa won't mind. He's always away in Ostrava. He won't miss us.'

'Papa does miss us, Rachel. When you are older, you will understand why he has to be away so much now. Bubbe and I have to wait here, until he comes home. Then we will come to England to be with you.'

Rachel felt her bottom lip wobbling. 'Don't want to go to England.'

'You will go on the train with all the other children, and you can have fun together.'

Mama turned towards Rachel's new suitcase, opening it. She held up an envelope for Rachel to see. 'Give this to the people you stay with in England. It's got some things in it for them to read, and a letter for you that I'm asking them to keep. And some pictures of me, Bubbe and Papa, so you know we are still thinking about you, and you can think about us.'

'Why do the people in England have to keep them, Mama?'

'Because it might be a while before we see you again, drahoušku. We will be with you as soon as we can, I promise. You can have fun playing with the other children until then.'

She opened the curtains on the tiny eves window. 'Rachel, do you see those stars out there?'

Rachel stood on the bed and followed her gaze. 'Of course, Mama.'

'Those are the same stars that the children in England see, too. So, when you look at the stars in England, remember I will be looking at the same stars here, and I will be thinking about you.'

She lifted Rachel into bed and tucked her in.

'I can't go to sleep, Mama.'

Mama smiled. And then she started singing the lullaby

she had sung to Rachel since she was a tiny baby. Rachel's eyelids began to droop…

Spi děťátko spi, zavři očka svý,
Pánbůh bude s tebou spáti,
andělíčci kolébati,
spi andílku, spi.

Spi, děťátko, spi, zamkni očka svý,
dám ti buben a housličky,
nedám tě za svět celičký,
spi, dítě spi.

Rachel: London, November 2025

Sleep my child, sleep, close your eyes,
God will sleep with You,
angels will jiggle You,
sleep, angel, sleep.

Sleep my child, sleep, lock your eyes,
I will give you drum and violin,
I will not give you even for a whole world,
sleep, baby, sleep.

…Rachel slept. Her eyes twitched behind her eyelids. The voice sang.

That was what it *meant*, and Rachel knew what it meant, but the words were different. And then as so many times before, she heard the boots marching, caught a flash of bright cold sunshine sparking on armoured vehicles, felt the scratchy string from the label hung around her neck, and then as always, saw the sad, blue eyes of the tall stranger who picked her up and put her on the train. She woke with the customary thought: 'why didn't Mama say goodbye?'

She looked at her bedside clock. 3.14am. She struggled

to sit up in bed, breathing heavily. No more 'Rona, hopefully-she'd recently had her yearly vaccination. But presumably, she was starting with a cold – again. She got a lot more of those nowadays, and every time, it seemed that it took her longer to feel properly well again. She moved her legs around and carefully placed her feet on the floor. She pulled the cord to turn on the light, caught a firm hold on her walking frame, heaved herself to her feet and moved slowly to her little blue and white kitchen a few feet away to put the electric kettle onto boil. She stood by the window and waited, twitching the bright gingham curtain aside to look out at the stars. It was a clear, cold night and even with the lights of the West End beaming up into the night sky a few miles away, there were plenty of stars to see. At least she knew that her mother, Anna could not be looking at the same stars from somewhere else in the world now. Whatever had happened to her, too many years had gone by; she would be long dead.

Rachel poured the water onto a teabag, put a teaspoon of honey into the cup ('still a European at heart Mama,' her daughter Linda would laugh), put the cup on the tray on the front of her walking frame and carefully walked the few steps into the living room.

Annamarie had decorated for her, a nice, clean magnolia. The room was too small for anything else. Rachel looked at the picture over the tiny mantlepiece, a view of Parliament Hill Fields with small figures flying kites, and the skyline of London in the distance. Annamarie had pointed to the skyline.

'You can think of me at work in the lab there, Grandma.'

Rachel smiled at the thought of her beautiful, clever granddaughter. But maybe she worked too hard? Was she ever going to marry and have children? The thought of Annamarie as a mother brought a vision of her own mother Anna close, and for a moment, Rachel thought she could remember the shape of her face, the sound of her voice and the touch of her hands. The older Annamarie got, the more she reminded Rachel of Anna.

Rachel sunk down into her chair and turned on the lamp on the table beside her. Waiting for the tea to cool, she closed her eyes. A tableau she had seen so many times in her mind's eye began to play behind her closed eyelids.

The platform at Prague station was full. Rachel stood in a crowd of wailing children, some throwing tantrums in a manner that would have horrified her very proper Bubbe, parents crying, and ladies running around with clipboards, speaking to each other in a strange language and trying to shepherd children onto the train. All the parents remained on the platform. Some of them were hanging onto children through the open windows. Some of the children were struggling to get off, and parents kept pushing them back into the train again, and some of the mothers were putting the children onto the train, then wailing and taking them off again. Rachel clutched tightly onto Mama's hand.

Then a lady walked out of the crowd and asked Mama to step aside from the crowd to talk for a moment. And when Rachel had looked around, Mama and the lady were gone. Rachel began to cry. Then she saw a man making his way briskly through the crowd, walking directly towards her. He crouched down and spoke kindly to Rachel in a foreign language she couldn't understand, clearly calling her by name. Then he picked her up and handed her to an older girl, standing by the open window of the nearest train door. Rachel looked back into his eyes and saw a deep sadness within them. Even now I'm 94, thought Rachel, mentally straddling eighty-six years, I don't think I've ever seen such sad eyes as those.

The whistle blew, and the train began to pull away. The older girl clutched Rachel more tightly as the train gathered speed; she could not wriggle away. And Mama was nowhere to be seen. Impulsively, Rachel waved at the sad, kind stranger, and saw, through tears, that he was waving back, although he did not smile. And then she left Prague forever. Apart from in her dreams, of course.

Rachel's head started to nod, and her tea grew cold. Her eyes began to flick behind her eyelids again.

nedám tě za svět celičký,
spi, dítě spi.
'I will not give you even for a whole world,
sleep, baby, sleep'.

But she did give me away, thought Rachel, drifting downwards into sleep. And she didn't even say goodbye.

Fran: Salem, Mass., December 2025

'If you had a time machine, would you go back in time and kill Hitler, Rob?' Fran asked her cousin, sitting in his cosy living room. They were warming up after the long drive from Logan. Fran had been comforted by the Christmas lights shining below as the plane came into land, as if the 'Rona had never swept through the people and places that she loved. But then she noticed a new picture of Charlie on the mantlepiece, probably taken at Woodstock. She was wearing a floppy straw hat and flowery t-shirt, making a peace sign whilst beaming into the camera. Stung by the reminder that nothing could ever be quite the same again, Fran looked down at the flames flickering on the authentic-looking logs in the familiar gas fire. The snow fell thickly outside.

'I don't know, Franny,' Rob replied. 'You're the university professor now. What do you think?'

'Ha. *Jamie* is the university professor now. I'm the hired help.' They watched the football game on TV for a moment, the New England Patriots vs the Toronto Argonauts. However many times Rob had explained through the years, Fran had never really managed to grasp the rules of American football.

'It's just something that bubbled up in the ancestry research,' she added. 'What do you think?'

Rob, a keen ancestry researcher himself, looked thoughtful. 'What wrong would you be looking to right, in the dim and distant past of our family then, Franny?'

Fran jumped, caught herself, and managed to smile. 'Well... it seemed like a terrible shame that Nana Mo's dad died so young. Of something that a simple course of antibiotics would cure nowadays.'

'Yes. But that must have happened in so many families. Look at all the people who died of TB.'

'I guess. But it's different when it's your family, isn't it?'

Rob thought for a while. 'I guess so....' He looked out of the window. 'Snow starting to blizzard again.'

For a moment Fran felt a flash of annoyance at his lack of interest. But then she reminded herself, Rob had never met their ancestors in person. Be careful, she thought. Of course, it's different for him, like it was different for you before. They are still all two-dimensional dead people in old sepia photos for him.

'I guess it is what it is, Franny. All the things that happened between then and the 1940s are the reason that you and I are here today aren't they? If someone killed Hitler before the Allies came into the war, my mum and dad would never have met. And maybe your mum and dad wouldn't have ended up where they met in 1948, either.'

Fran smiled at him. Good old Rob, the only person who still called her 'Franny' and spoke good commonsense to her... like Mary and Mo, she mused. It was why Fran had decided to return yet again to this beautiful, sleepy seaside town that she had loved for most of her life. It was all still as she remembered. The cute little town hall, the fire station, the town square, the 'Bewitched' hotel and the statue of Roger Conant. Just as it had been when she spent those long hot summers with Aunt Adi and took those magical teenage trips on the Greyhound to see Charlie in New York... all so long ago. Now no more Charlie, and no more itching to get on the I95. Too many painful memories... Charlie taking her to the top of the South Tower not long after the Twin Towers were built, the notification of Charlie's death in New York as the news got worse and worse, the city locked down with greater numbers of COVID-19 deaths than some small countries. Fran tried not to wish anyone ill, but she sometimes hoped *that* President would burn in hell for what his ignorant, callous mismanagement had done to Charlie and all those others, in a city that had already seen far too much tragedy.

Fran moved her thoughts to happier memories, the wheel turning on Coney Island, the Empire State, Grand Central Station, the trips to Brooklyn, Liberty and Statton Islands, shopping at Macys, the Broadway shows. *Grease*, *Hair*, *A Chorus Line*… she still had the programs in a drawer at home. A drawer at home… and then she saw, in her mind's eye, the pink packet of antibiotics, the pills all neatly encased in their foil and plastic bubbles, waiting for her three thousand miles away across the ocean, in her bedside table at home. The ones she got when she went to the doctor with an infected ingrown toenail, but then decided instead to go on dabbing her toe with antiseptic because the pills might come in useful for….

She had tried but failed to think of Jim as a person who was already dead. She knew that applied to all the people in the world to which NAMIS had transported her, but it was somehow different with the ones she knew were going to live to a reasonable age. And the illness that had taken Jim's life was so trivial, a minor illness in her own time. She wondered if she might have taken a different attitude to the situation, had she been time travelling in the time before the 'Rona. It had been an uncomfortable culture shift for Fran, and humankind in general to get their heads around the fact that there was now a communicable, deadly disease rampaging around the world.

Perhaps, after all the recent deaths in the family, she wasn't ready to lose Jim. But she knew all too well the dangerous territory into which she was heading. Jim had, in fact, died over a century ago. There was just something about him that triggered a type of *maternal* feeling in her;

that she had to protect him, keep him safe. And she was old enough to *be* his mother, after all. But then, he was nearly a century older than her in real time.

'Timey-wimey stuff,' she said out loud.

'Eh?' replied Rob.

Fran grinned. 'Oh, something they say on the TV sci-fi shows. Don't you feel close to all those daughter-of-the-revolution ancestors you traced back to your dad's family?'

Rob laughed. 'You know perfectly well I never found any. Only Irish carpenters, who threw our other ancestors' tea into the Atlantic.'

They had this conversation at least once whenever they met.

Fran nodded. 'Yep, all mad revolutionaries. Scottish Covenantors and dissenting Huguenots for the pair of us, with a tiny bit of Kentish mixed in. And then more Scots and Kentish for me, with a splash of Viking, and Irish for you.'

'And that's why we're all such mad bastards,' they said together.

'None so mad as Charlie,' mused Fran. 'God, I wish I'd been old enough to go to Woodstock and to San Fran for the Summer of Love with her. And go on all those protest marches.'

Rob grinned. 'What did Nana Mo say when she found out she'd had the baby?'

'I don't know. They didn't tell me much about that, I was only little. And then by the time Charlie married and they all came over to see us, Nana Mo was dead.'

They both fell silent.

'Split families,' said Rob, reflectively. 'It's hard, sometimes.'

'But great holidays. Lots of places to visit and to feel at home.' Fran bit her lip. She had nearly said something about Sittingbourne… not the Sittingbourne of now, the Sittingbourne of *then*.

'Do you think I'd be a mad enough bastard to kill

ON TIME

Hitler, Rob?'

Rob smiled and raised his beer. 'Hell, yeah.'

Suzi: London, December 2025

Suzi turned off her laptop and took her earbuds out. The house was quiet apart from the sound of the television downstairs, interspersed by faint snoring. Jamie had gone to sleep on the sofa again. He slept fitfully at night now, but frequently nodded off when he managed to become absorbed in a television programme. Suzi was increasingly worried about his stress levels but felt unable to do anything to change the situation.

And it was principally for this reason that she felt a little guilty for her joy in the opportunities Jamie's work was bringing to her; research material she had never in her wildest dreams thought to be a possibility. What linguist wouldn't jump at the chance to hear crystal clear recordings of English as it was spoken by ordinary people in ordinary conversations at the end of the nineteenth century? And through serendipity, Fran's family offered some unusual riches in this respect. West and East Coast Scots, and the Old Kentish burr. The words they used, their inflections, the customary ways that they addressed people in their families, and the more formal ways that they addressed their church acquaintances; potentially years of research ahead in the few short conversations Fran had so far captured on file. At the moment, Suzi was principally focused on helping Fran to sound even more authentic in the relevant time period, but she found herself listening to the conversations over and over again, each time finding something different to pore over.

Sometimes, Suzi wondered what it would be like to meet an ancestor from her own family from that time period, how difficult she might find it to understand what they were saying, and to extract the nuance from their conversations. Her Vietnamese was somewhat rusty and

American accented, and the culture in which she had been raised was light years away from the culture that her nineteenth century ancestors would have inhabited. If she had been offered the chance to do what Fran was doing now, she would find it extremely difficult to achieve the same level of authenticity. And would she have found an ancestor who sounded as much like her as Jamie's great-great-grandfather Jim sounded like him? The rise and fall of the voice, the ways their thoughts were expressed? She doubted it.

These were all ideas that had not occurred to her before, growing up in Boston at the turn of the twentieth century. Her situation might be worth an academic paper in itself; reflecting on ancestral issues for diaspora peoples in a world where time travel had become a reality. But that future seemed distant at the moment. Jamie, Annamarie and Christian had come no closer to deciding what they were going to do as the project report deadline drifted closer. Fran, of course, was too fascinated with her "family business" to pay attention to such matters. But to be fair, she hadn't forgotten the interests that she and Suzi shared.

A couple of weeks ago, they had all been present in the lab, a few days before Fran travelled to the US. Fran, with her customary enthusiasm, asked Annamarie for an estimate of when she and Suzi would be able to take a trip to see a Shakespeare or Marlowe premiere. Annamarie thought it would be early in the new year- maybe late January or early February. NAMIS was still slowly reaching further and further back into the past.

'I really need you to come with me,' Fran said to Suzi. *'I'm going to start struggling with the language at that point.'*

'I guess both of us can only read it at the moment Fran,' replied Suzi. *'We're making our best guesses at the way that it was actually spoken. As you know, I am finding a few minor surprises even in late Victorian English!'*

'Yes, I know. But you'll pick it up so much more quickly than

ON TIME

me. You have a better ear.'

Suzi had to admit that was true. And she *did* want to help. But she wasn't sure that Fran quite grasped the situation in which Suzi would find herself. Fran would frequently talk about her Flemish and Scottish ancestors, particularly when references to Brexit cropped up, and chunter about 'not being English, but European.' But the thing that was never discussed, although it was obvious to Suzi, was that Fran didn't *look* different to the majority population, and that made a big difference to the way that she experienced the world, compared to someone from a minority ethnic heritage.

The COVID-19 Pandemic had created a prejudice that bubbled up in both the UK and US towards people of Far Eastern heritage. And those who were ignorant enough to espouse such views were also typically unable to grasp the differences between people from Chinese, Japanese, Korean and Vietnamese origins. Not, thought Suzi, that this changed anything. Ignorance was ignorance, and prejudice was prejudice, whoever it was aimed at, it was not acceptable and that was that. Although this wasn't an issue that she personally met that frequently on a day-to-day basis, in her daily round within her comfortable, middle class, multi-ethnic circle of friends and family. But still, it was always *there*, like Pennywise the Clown in the drains in *It*, lurking under the surface to rise up unexpectedly in a tactless remark, or the lack of make up for certain skin tones in the drug store, or an offensively unfunny joke on social media.

And now, with the advent of the time portal, yet more questions arose. How would these issues translate to time travelling? Fran had already made the point that London had been an international port between the middle ages and the dawn of the twentieth century, and given Britain's history as a seafaring nation, it would have been host to people travelling from all over the world. And while it was a far smaller city prior to industrialisation, and diversity would not have been anywhere near twenty first century levels, the population around the Thames would have certainly had contact with people from a wide range of ethnic backgrounds.

'How violent would people have been in the sixteenth century, Fran?' Suzi had asked.

'Probably more casually so than now. Wearing of swords was fairly routine. Not a great idea to go out after dark, I guess. But Shakespeare ran a lot of his plays in the afternoons. The apprentice boys used to bunk off work to see them. We could also wear scarves that obscure our faces, you know. It wasn't that unusual for ladies in those days. But maybe we should send the lads in beforehand, you know, just to check it out.' Fran had grinned, winking at the two other women.

Christian had risen to the bait. *'Jesus, Fran! Am I going to have to start taking fencing lessons? Although, I might be tempted. I always wanted to see those rotting heads on the spikes on London Bridge.'*

Fran had wrinkled her nose. *'Ewwww.'*

'We need to think this through carefully,' Jamie had said, seriously. *'For the moment, however far into the past NAMIS is able to reach, the only travelling people are going to do is mum visiting Sittingbourne in the 1890s. OK?'*

Fran had nodded. *'Yes, agreed. But wouldn't it be great to engage in a bit of Tudor audience participation in the premiere of A Midsummer Night's Dream, and then throw some rotten fruit at the blokes in the stocks on your way out?'*

Christian's expression had also changed to deadly serious. *'You can't take fruit, just like you can't take seeds or whatever abroad. You could blow the ecology apart. It was far more homogenous in those days.'*

Like people, thought Suzi, standing up to roll down the blind on the tiny eves window. I'd be entering an homogenous ecology. And while Fran says that it's not entirely so, for her that's always going to be in theory, whereas for me, it's always going to be in practice. She took one of Fran's battered old books of Shakespeare plays from the shelf and turned the pages to the beginning of *A Midsummer Night's Dream*. Then wistfully, she began to read aloud, in the best Elizabethan English pronunciation she could muster.

Annamarie: London, 30th December 2025

Annamarie put her phone down on her desk, frowning. It seemed that Grandma Rachel really wasn't well, then. She'd admitted to being 'a bit chesty' over Christmas, but now Linda had rung with the news that Rachel had been admitted to hospital.

Annamarie opened the online Czech language programme file on her PC with the exercises she had completed during the past six months. She sighed. She'd expected to get a better handle on the language by now, but it was so difficult. And languages had never been her strong point at school, either. She'd given them up as soon as she could to focus on maths and science. But she'd probably scraped into 'tourist' level Czech now, and that was good enough for what she needed. She could always put the notes in a file on her phone-just in case she needed them.

She envied Christian, who had a basic and relatively unaccented grasp of Czech from the holidays that he had spent with his father's family after the Berlin Wall had fallen. Christian's father was a minor hero of the Prague Spring in his own country. He had been welcomed back in early 1990, shortly after the Velvet Revolution. But by that time, he had made a life in England with his British wife and family. The Czech Republic was a nice place to go for the summer, Christian had told Annamarie. His father's sister lived in a semi-rural area, near Prague; a slower pace of life than London. He'd invited Annamarie to go and stay with his aunt the following summer, to look around some of the places that Rachel would have known as a small child.

Annamarie's feelings towards the Czech Republic were conflicted. On the one hand, she yearned to go to visit the town in which her grandmother's family had lived for generations. On the other, she felt a creeping unease. So last month she had gone for a long weekend in a Prague hotel, alone. Walking through the cobbled streets, she admired the ancient beauty of the city, whilst at the same time feeling an aching sadness that she could not shake. In the end, she had not actually visited Prague Station. She had taken the tram there, but then she stood outside, unable to bring herself to go in. She hadn't told anyone of her visit, not Linda, not Rachel and definitely not the people at work. Such a beautiful country; such a tragic history.

Christian saw it differently, of course. His father had been one of the youngest student protest organisers in the late 1960s. Then when the Russians came after him, he managed to sneak across the Austrian border, and finally ended up in England, where he met Christian's mother. Christian, born in Bristol in the late 1980s, was the youngest of their four children. Annamarie hadn't met Christian's father, but she presumed Christian was like him. She could imagine Christian having what Rachel would call the 'chutzpah' to smuggle himself across the Austrian border, and then onto the autobahn to thumb a lift into Vienna.

Annamarie's thoughts turned again to her Grandmother Rachel. She had also been studying the history of the Kindertransport over the last few months. Rachel had told her little, but Annamarie had started with the account that Fran had written for Rachel and the letters in Rachel's Prague box, which she had accessed again. Rachel had been staying with Linda since the second week in December, and Annamarie had gone over to Rachel's flat to pick up some clean clothes. This time, she had taken pictures of all the Prague documents on her phone.

ON TIME

Once she had carefully read through all the information, she accessed the historical record herself through the university library and realised that Rachel had been on one of the most historic Kindertransport trains of all – the last one that left Prague station on 2nd August 1939. By that time, the Czechs had been living under Nazi rule for nearly six months, in Hitler's so-called Protectorate of Bohemia and Moravia. Whilst Annamarie already knew the fate of her great-grandfather – he had been executed as a member of the resistance in early 1940 – she had to go more deeply into the records to track Rachel's grandmother and extended family. They had been transported to Theresienstadt in 1940, and thence to Auschwitz in early 1942, where they had all eventually died. Rachel's grandmother, who had been in her mid-60s by that time, was sent to the gas chambers on arrival.

But where did Rachel's mother, Anna, go? She had just disappeared. There was no record of her at all, other than of her birth, and the few photographs and letters she had given to Rachel. When Rachel was dead, then all living memory of Anna would die too. And whilst this did not completely hand a victory to the Nazis and their vile regime, because Anna's granddaughter and great-granddaughter would live on, Annamarie still burned for all the memories that Rachel had lost, time that should have been spent with her mother and grandmother, things that had belonged to them that she should have inherited, a settled life that could have been lived in one place, if that was what the family had chosen to do, a chance to say goodbye when natural death occurred, and graves to visit. Annamarie knew that she could not get any of this back for her grandmother. But maybe, just maybe, she would be able to steal a chance for that final goodbye with Anna.

Annamarie sat in the deserted university, all the staff and students still absent, due to the Christmas break. She looked across the room at the machine sitting in the corner humming faintly, waiting for an instruction. 'NAMIS' she said, her voice echoing in the empty room.

The light on the console flicked on. 'Working.'

'Can you help me?'

'Coordinates?'

Annamarie took a memory stick from her PC and slotted it into one of NAMIS' many portals. The main screen went blue for a second. And then, the rows of data began to appear.

MISSING

Fran: London, Tuesday 6th January 2026, 10am

'Have you seen or heard from Annamarie, Fran?' asked Ellie, as Fran walked into the lab.

'No. Should I have?'

'Not necessarily, but it was supposed to be the first day back for all of us yesterday, and we'd agreed to do some routine maintenance on NAMIS - make sure it's all working as it should after the break. But Annamarie wasn't in. She didn't ring or text to explain. I texted her a couple of times yesterday, and I've tried ringing her early this morning, but it's going to voicemail, and she hasn't rung back.'

'I'm sure there's a simple explanation. Has she contacted Jamie?'

'Not yesterday.'

Jamie walked into the lab. 'Where's Annamarie?'

'We don't know.' replied Ellie.

Jamie frowned. 'She's not contacted you? I thought she must have done. She's not contacted me, either. I wondered if she had been over in the IT faculty yesterday for meetings or something, so I've just been over to check, but they haven't seen her, either. They thought that she must be with us or marking student assignments at home or something. Have you started the maintenance checks yet?'

'No. I was waiting for her.'

'Do you think you could make a start on it, please

Ellie? I can help you with some of it tomorrow, if necessary.'

'What do you want me to do about contacting Annamarie?'

'We'll sort it out today, don't worry.'

As Ellie bent over the console, Jamie caught Fran's eye and moved to the door. She followed him out into the corridor, shutting the door behind her. She could see Ellie's shadow through the frosted pane at the top of the door, which for some reason always reminded her of the old 1950s bathroom doors that were still common when she was a small child. This whole building is like a trip in time in itself, she thought.

Fran and Jamie walked without speaking to the little kitchen that they shared with the other rooms on the same floor. Jamie glanced around to ensure that they were alone.

'I think that means your next scheduled trip will have to be postponed. We'll have to find out what's up with Annamarie. You're feeling OK, right?'

'Yes.'

Fran knew that Jamie and Christian were paranoid about spreading modern diseases into the past. All living samples that made even the briefest of trips were carefully checked over for infectious illness before they travelled, and that included Fran. Fran had to take PCR tests the same day she travelled to be completely sure. All time travelling biological organisms were also checked for diseases *from* the past when they arrived back in the present, even though they didn't travel unless they were up-to-date with all possible vaccinations. Fran had been to her GP and requested boosters for a potential research expedition to Brazil. She also took precautions, familiar to her from the pandemic period, to avoid direct physical contact with people in the past as much as possible. She wore white cotton gloves for most of the time (fortunately in keeping with the fashions of the day) and discreetly wiped any utensil she had used with an antiseptic wipe that

ON TIME

looked from a distance like a small ladies' handkerchief. It had also been useful that nineteenth century people were more formal about social distancing.

Even so Jamie and Christian were constantly on edge in case of the advent of some new type of illness, that they would be unable to detect. Every so often, they rationalized this between themselves: the general pattern was a century between pandemics, and the twenty-first century had already had its lumps in that respect. Fran was vaccinated, and therefore, shouldn't be a problem. But they were also aware that nothing was ever certain, either in epidemiology or in time travel. Especially in time travel, thought Fran.

'It's probably nothing,' said Jamie. 'She's maybe gone to a conference and forgot to mention it to anyone, or got a huge pile of marking she's staying at home to bottom. She might even be unwell, and her phone has stopped working; there are so many possibilities. You off home soon?'

'I guess so. I'd popped in to discuss the next trip, do some planning, but if Annamarie isn't here, then I suppose we can't do that.'

'Could you do me a favour, please, then? Go round to Annamarie's and see if she's OK? I'll text you the address.'

—

Fifteen minutes later, Fran was pressing one of the buzzers on a large front door that belonged to what she thought of as a 'big old London house,' like the one her maternal grandparents had once owned. Nowadays though, such buildings were principally converted into rented flats, for childless professionals like Annamarie, Suzi and Jamie. Fran caught a glimpse of a large, somewhat neglected garden at the back. She sighed, thinking of her maternal grandmother in a floppy hat and gardening gloves that were too big for her, carefully pruning her roses.

'Hello?' said a female voice.

'Annamarie?' replied Fran uncertainly. It didn't sound like Annamarie.

'Who is this?'

'Fran. From the lab.'

'Oh, Fran, Jamie's mum?'

'Yes.'

'It's Linda, Annamarie's mum. Come on up'.

The door buzzed. Fran walked up the polished wood stairs to the first floor, to find a woman of approximately her own age peering worriedly around the door.

'Annamarie's not been in work, then?' asked Linda, concern etched in her tone.

'We don't think so. That's why I came round, to see if she wasn't well. She hasn't called us.'

'That's not like her. I got here a few minutes ago. I was worried because I hadn't heard from her since Friday. She usually calls or texts every few days. I wasn't so worried over the weekend because I thought she might have been busy with something, but when she didn't answer any calls or texts yesterday, I decided to come round this morning. She's been here recently, look.' Linda gestured towards an unwashed cup and plate on the draining board.

Fran looked around. The flat, although sparsely furnished with few ornaments or pictures, and anonymous cream and beige decor throughout, did indeed look occupied. There was a paperback book, academic journals and a TV control on the coffee table, and an iPad and a pile of loose papers on the dining table. A pair of Doc Martens stood by the armchair, and there was a hoodie draped across the back of one of the two dining chairs. A solitary poster had been stuck above the dining table. It looked like an academic conference poster to Fran; a blue and white design headed 'How AI will change the world' with a picture of a robotic head superimposed on a globe.

Fran walked over to the draining board and looked into the cup. 'The stain is dried on and the teabag has dried out, so she can't have been here for a day or so.'

ON TIME

Linda took the cup and looked into it, pulling out the teabag until it ripped, the tea leaves spilling across the floor. 'Oh, dear, where on earth can she be?' She picked up a sponge from the draining board and dabbed distractedly at the mess.

'Once, when Jamie was a second-year undergrad, he and Christian went for a long weekend to Prague and stayed with Christian's aunt. They got crazy cheap flights or something. He didn't tell us until they got back. I was quite cross. His excuse was that the plane company had a passenger list, so I'd find out if anything happened to him. Which is true enough, I suppose. But I was still annoyed.'

'Annamarie has never done anything like that. And definitely not when her grandma is so ill. That's what I was ringing to talk to her about yesterday.'

'Rachel is ill? Oh, I'm sorry.'

Linda raised her eyebrows in surprise. 'You know my mother?'

'No, we've never met. But I wrote something for her once.'

'Oh yes. That's right, you're the Fran who wrote the Kindertransport history notes for Mama. Thank you so much for that. She knew so little of where she'd come from. She was so young when she left, she couldn't remember most of it.'

'It was interesting to do, I enjoyed it.'

There was a short silence.

'I don't know what to do,' faltered Linda, dabbing at her eyes. 'Annamarie is my only child, you know. And after my husband died in the pandemic….'

'Oh, I'm so sorry. Mine died not long after the pandemic finally tailed off… Look, don't cry, I am sure there will turn out to be a simple explanation for this. It can be so hard to keep tabs on academics over the non-teaching periods; the students aren't back in till the week after next. Perhaps she booked herself onto a conference somewhere at the last minute, and just forgot to tell us and the people in the IT faculty.'

Fran walked over to the dining table and looked at the top sheet on the pile of papers. 'Prague. Look, this is a bill for a flight to Prague... oh, but it's from November.'

Linda stared at Fran, her eyes expanding in shock. 'We've never been to Prague. *She's* never been to Prague... because of...' she tailed off, picked up the sheet and looked at it. 'She *did* go to Prague. And she didn't tell me.'

Linda sat down heavily in the armchair and began dabbing at her eyes again.

Fran, never the most tactile of people even in normal circumstances, stood silently. The item now at the top of the pile attracted her attention. It was some type of transport ticket, printed in a language which looked likely to be Czech. So, thought Fran, Annamarie went to Prague and she didn't tell us, and she didn't tell her mother. The pink packet of antibiotics, still in the drawer in Leeds, popped into Fran's mind's eye. A sinking feeling began in her stomach, and her mind began to race, a single ominous thought bubbling to the top: so why didn't you say anything to us, or to your mother, Annamarie?

Yesterday evening, Fran had decided that the antibiotics would stay in the drawer in Leeds. She had already contemplated on the plane back from the US that the consequences of interfering in time would be likely to outweigh the benefits. And she had given her word to Jamie that she would do everything she could to avoid meddling in the past; that she would behave in a professional manner, retired or not. Now a question that she had been trying to avoid for the past hour broke through and raced to the front of her mind: What had *Annamarie* decided?

Five minutes later, she was walking down the street back to the laboratory, hoping that the polite 'goodbye and I'm sure everything will be fine' that she had said to Linda had sounded convincing, because Fran was no longer sure that anything was going to be fine. If Annamarie had taken a trip to Prague in the past, why had she not returned? She would have been travelling into extreme danger. Fran looked down at the pavement, idly attempting not to stand on the cracks as she remembered doing as a child, skipping along, holding onto Nana Mo's hand. Mo's voice played in her mind, laughing as she recited a funny poem that warned children to beware of bears who lurked, waiting to eat children who trod on the lines.

Oh Annamarie, thought Fran, did you leap into a bear pit? What lines did you tread on? With every step that she took, the feeling of dread intensified, dark tendrils of fear winding ever more tightly around her throat.

Jamie: London, Wednesday 7th January 2026, 10.30am

Jamie, Fran, Christian and Ellie sat dejectedly around the table in the laboratory. They were discussing the issue of Annamarie's Prague trip again, for the umpteenth time since yesterday lunchtime, when Fran had shared her suspicions with them.

'Annamarie's mother rang this morning,' said Jamie, worriedly. 'She wants to go to the police. I've managed to persuade her not to do that until tomorrow. She asked me all sorts of questions about "the types of people that Annamarie was friendly with at work". I told her truthfully that Annamarie works 10 to 12 hour days and most of that here with us. It seems that the mother went through all the travel documents relating to Prague and found out that Annamarie definitely travelled alone. So at least she was reassured on that front.'

There was a heavy silence.

'Jamie,' said Fran, 'I've always arrived back at the time portal about thirty seconds after I left…'

'Yes. That's how it's set up to work.'

'But when you've checked my tele-thingies…' continued Fran.

Christian grinned. 'Telomeres. Amongst other things.'

'...they indicate that I've aged for whatever time I have spent in the past.'

'Yes, that's right. You have moved in spacetime, but your body keeps on ticking like clockwork. There's a lot of further research to do on that one.'

'So, if, and I stress if, Annamarie had taken a trip through the time machine, she ought to have arrived back shortly after she left. But what if something had happened to prevent her return?'

Jamie frowned. 'Well, that wouldn't happen unless something went very wrong.'

Jamie had spent all night lying awake worrying that the time machine might be at the bottom of the mystery as his mother had suggested, but they had agreed to wait to see if Annamarie was in today before speculating further. And when they arrived this morning, and she was still absent, he still wasn't ready to fully admit that even to himself. That would open a whole nest of further problems. He sighed. He turned to Ellie 'Have you checked the logs on NAMIS?'

Ellie looked back, an uncertain expression on her face. Annamarie always checked the logs on NAMIS. She had shown Ellie how to do it, and Ellie had full access, and sometimes assisted. But now, although it had not been openly stated, she was being asked to check up on Annamarie. It felt uncomfortable.

Jamie perceived and understood her hesitance. 'Do you want me to help you?'

'Yes please.'

They moved over to the machine and began to work on the console.

Christian looked pensive. 'Do you really think Annamarie went through the time portal, Fran?'

'It's just a hunch.'

'I was beginning to think the same myself. Ever since you told us about the mystery trip to Prague, to be honest. She could have gone to my aunt's; I told her that she would be welcome anytime. But she obviously didn't want any of us to know. She didn't even tell her mum.'

Fran took the ticket that had been on Annamarie's dining table out of her pocket. 'Where is this to, Christian?'

Christian glanced at it. 'It's a tram ticket to Praha hlavní nádraží. Prague train station.'

Fran felt her stomach turn. The Kindertransport.

'Jamie,' said Ellie from the other side of the room, tears in her voice. 'Someone used NAMIS when we weren't here.'

'To go to Prague on 2nd August 1939,' replied Fran, bleakly. The others turned to her, shocked.

Jamie stared at her incredulously. 'How do you know?'

'That was the day that Annamarie's grandmother Rachel took the Kindertransport to England. It's a significant historical event. It was the last Kindertransport that left Czechoslovakia. By early September, Britain and Germany were at war.'

There was a brief stunned silence. Then Jamie slammed his fist onto the console. 'Fuck, fuck, fuck. What the *fuck* is wrong with her? She should have known.'

Fran looked back at him, sorrowfully. 'Jamie, we all *think* we know. We are all academics here, aren't we, going about our research with professional objectivity. But once you get into that thing, you start to realise what it can do to you psychologically. It can scramble your emotions. And that's something I've struggled with, believe me.'

'But you've never…'

'And Annamarie probably hasn't. We're all still here, and as we were, as far as we know. So that would indicate that she hasn't meddled in time. But the question remains: where is she?'

Jamie was staring into space. When he was younger, his sisters had sometimes accused him of having no imagination. But that wasn't true. While he wasn't good at what he thought of as the 'sparkly unicorn' type of thing that his mother wrote about, he had an excellent imagination for logical and technological progression, and multiple scenarios were running through his mind at a rate of knots. 'What if she got arrested by the Nazis?' he said, bleakly.

Christian frowned. 'Hang on, that's jumping to the worst possibility, and I think she'd be smart enough to avoid that unless she was very unlucky.'

Fran nodded. 'They hadn't got around to mass round ups at that point. I think it's more likely she's lost or damaged the return pad. I dropped mine on the floor in the church hall once. Luckily, I felt it fall and managed to scoop it back into my pocket before anyone noticed.'

Jamie raised his eyebrows in exasperation. Fran wrinkled her nose at him. 'Like you've never lost anything.'

Christian grinned. 'Children, children.'

'I agree, the lost return pad is probably the most likely explanation' said Ellie, quickly, keeping the conversation on topic.

Christian nodded. 'And no one else could use it. From their perspective, it would just be a strange lump of inert material. It would have been set to her DNA; she would have to have done that.'

'So,' continued Ellie 'what we need is someone to take her another one to where she is now. And our best guess is that she's going to try and intersect with her relatives at the station at the time that the train leaves for England. That's the place we need to start looking, anyway. But how would the return be managed?'

'I am guessing that Annamarie should come through a minute or so after the person who goes with the rescue device,' said Jamie. 'It shouldn't have any effect on either of them if they come through separately; theoretically. So, I have to go and look for her.'

'No, you don't,' Christian replied. 'I do. We can't lose both you and Annamarie, besides, I can navigate Prague like the back of my hand, and I speak fluent Czech. Neither of which you can do. It's a no-brainer. You don't

ON TIME

fit the person specification, mate.'

Fran opened her mouth to agree, but then checked herself, realizing she was hardly an unbiased commentator.

'He's right, Jamie,' agreed Ellie. 'It would be crazy for you to go instead of him. I can sort out things like fake passports and money.'

Jamie nodded. 'OK then, but not right now. Let's plan this thing, to the extent that we can. We can put you through early tomorrow. We have that much time, and the past will still be waiting for you whenever we do it. We can get you some suitable clothes, like mum got for herself, we can go through what happened on that day and take a bit of time deciding where we put you down, and when, exactly. I've said that I will ring Annamarie's mum tomorrow if she didn't turn up by then.'

Fran stood up. 'I can already tell you a lot of what is known about what happened that day. I'll have to revisit that account I wrote of the Kindertransport for Annamarie's Grandma Rachel. Then we can do some more research, look at the pictures that exist, maps etc. We can easily get everything done today.'

She looked intently into her phone, tapping briskly for a few seconds. 'Right then, so there's several vintage shops within easy walking distance. Christian, come with me. We'll go and get you some baggy trousers, braces and a knitted cardi. You'll have to leave your sweatshirt and chinos in 2026. And you'll have to get rid of that designer stubble. Then we'll come back and have a look at the Prague you are going to. Believe me, it will be *very* different to the one that you know.'

Christian raised his eyebrows at the other two and followed her out of the lab. Ellie managed a weak smile. 'We'll be able to get her back, Jamie, won't we?'

Jamie moved over to his desk. 'I'm cautiously optimistic. We know where she's gone, and there's been no impact on the present, so I think we might be able to pull it off.'

It was the most likely explanation, he thought, that Annamarie was stuck in the past, having lost the return pad, or the return pad had been broken or was somehow malfunctioning. But what a past to be stuck in. It would have been so much easier to cope with this situation if the location had been the sleepy Sittingbourne of the 1890s, rather than Nazi-occupied Prague. What a stupid, stupid thing to do. He took a screwdriver from his top drawer and headed over to Annamarie's desk.

'What are you doing, Jamie?' asked Ellie, uneasily.

'Breaking in. We need all the evidence we can get'.

He popped the lock on the desk and rifled through the drawers. Pens, paperclips, envelopes, spritz perfume, sellotape, hand cream in the top drawer, and a pair of jeans, a jumper and a pair of trainers in the bottom drawer. And an old, battered looking fork in a plastic specimen bag, with cake crumbs still clinging to it. Jamie grinned ruefully. How like Annamarie to bag an item that she didn't have time to wash, rather than just throw it unwashed into her drawer. She had a habit of only remembering to eat lunch a few minutes before she had to leave the lab to teach.

Then, in the middle drawer, at the side of a pile of heavily annotated data print-outs, he found a small recording device, of the type Fran had taken through the portal to Sittingbourne. He took it back to his desk and plugged it into his PC. It was Annamarie and an unknown male voice speaking, in a foreign language. He looked at Ellie.

She shrugged. 'It's Annamarie. But I can't catch even one word of that language.'

'Neither can I.'

Jamie took out his phone, and dialled Suzi.

Suzi: London, Wednesday 7th January 2026, 11am

Suzi sat at Jamie's desk and turned on the recording

ON TIME

device. She listened for a moment and turned it off. 'It's Annamarie. And she's speaking fluent Czech. I'm sorry, Jamie, that's not one of my languages. We'll have to wait for Christian to get back.'

Twenty minutes later, Fran and Christian arrived back in the lab, carrying several bags from the nearby vintage shops.

'Hello Suzi,' said Fran, 'what are you doing here?'

'We found a recording device,' explained Jamie, 'and we need Christian's help. Suzi says the language on it is Czech.'

'OK,' said Christian.

Jamie turned the voice file to 'play'. Christian listened carefully to it for few minutes and then turned it off. 'This makes no sense.'

'Why?' asked Suzi.

'Because it's Annamarie, speaking fluent Czech.'

'Isn't her grandmother Czech?'

'Yes,' replied Fran, 'but Rachel, the grandmother, left Prague for England on the last Kindertransport to leave Czechoslovakia. She was only seven, and by the time she had been in England for a few years with her foster family, she couldn't speak Czech anymore. I think she got a sort of mental block, due to the trauma. It wasn't unusual for children who went through that experience. People weren't offered mental health support like they would be nowadays. And anyway, there were so many of them after the war.'

'Annamarie was learning Czech,' explained Christian. 'She said it was for when she came to Prague with me in the summer. I'd said we could go to stay with my aunt. She did one of those correspondence courses, and she asked me for help with some of it. But she was… well, hopeless. English accent you could cut with a knife, and she couldn't get her head around a lot of the grammar, either. That's her voice, yeah. But it's speaking fluent Czech, with a Prague accent. Never in a million years.'

Fran looked thoughtful. 'Perhaps she was kidding you? You know, she'd come out with it, when you got there? Make up for all those times you kidded around with her?'

Christian smiled ruefully. 'Fran. I have a slight English accent in my Czech, and I started learning odd words and phrases from my dad from the time I was born. And then from being about three, I had to speak it with cousins who hardly spoke any English, when we were in Prague in the summer. Believe me, someone who'd only started learning Czech six months ago wouldn't speak it like that, even if they were an accomplished linguist. And she really wasn't. She was terrible.'

Jamie frowned. 'Maybe she was planning this for longer and didn't tell anyone the whole truth. I'd be surprised and disappointed if so, but...' he trailed off.

'Have you got a recording of Annamarie's voice anywhere, Jamie?' asked Suzi.

'I know where to find one,' answered Ellie. 'She did a load of online lectures during the lockdowns; I saw some as an undergrad. I'll find you a URL.'

'Thanks. I've got some voiceprint software I can run the two files through. That will tell us if it definitely *is* Annamarie on both files.'

Fran looked up from scrolling through files on her phone. 'It certainly sounds like her.'

'What are they talking about on the file, Christian?' asked Suzi. 'I made out that it was about a child and a train, but not much else.'

'It's a mother explaining to a man who speaks Czech with a heavy English accent that she wants her daughter to go to England on the children's train because her husband is on the run from the Nazis somewhere in the Sudetenland. She implies that he's working for the resistance.'

'The Sudetenland?' said Fran. 'That was the area that the Nazis occupied initially. But surely it would be Rachel's mother making these arrangements, not Annamarie?'

ON TIME

'The fact that the recording device is here and has that file on it indicates that she's made other trips, not only the most recent one,' replied Jamie. 'Ellie, what did it say in the logs?'

'Only that one came up. But she programs NAMIS. Well, we both do, but she's in charge of it. She could have erased the others from the log on return.'

'Would NAMIS have a memory in its deeper program in what passes for its "mind"?' asked Jamie.

'It's possible. We've never properly explored that… it's all so new. We're still trying to work out how it is doing what it is doing, as you know. It's state of the art AI. It can learn, and that means it can remember, in a manner of speaking.'

She turned to the machine. 'NAMIS?'

'Working.'

'How many trips to Prague did Annamarie Simons make?'

'Three.'

Jamie let out a long sigh. 'Dates, NAMIS?'

'30 December 2025, 31 December 2025, 2 January 2026.'

Jamie felt his stomach turn. So then, Annamarie had carefully planned this to pan out over the holiday period when no one else was around. 'OK NAMIS,' said Jamie, tersely: 'where is Annamarie Simons?' He was aware that all present, including himself, were holding their breath.

'Not in time.'

They all exhaled and looked at each other, puzzled.

'Do you have her DNA in your memory, NAMIS?' Jamie continued.

'Affirmative.'

'Can you get her back then, without the pad?'

'Negative.'

'Can you give us her coordinates?'

'Negative.'

'Why?'

'Not in time.'

Jamie turned to Ellie. 'Is this thing malfunctioning?'

Ellie took a quick look across the console. 'Checked out fine yesterday. And no problems I can immediately see now.'

'And the calculations all checked out fine, too,' agreed Jamie. 'It's like she was there, and then she wasn't.'

'Correct,' said the machine.

They all jumped. It was always strange when the machine interjected without being directly asked.

Jamie sighed, looked down at the desk and inhaled sharply. 'Is Annamarie Simons dead, NAMIS?'

Ellie's lips began to tremble.

'Outside parameters.'

'It's a simple enough question,' snapped Jamie. 'If she's not dead, she must be in time. So where in time is she?'

'Not in time.'

Fran was reminded of one of those telephone answering robots that took you round in a circle and never put you through to a human being. For a second, she felt an insane urge to laugh. 'What's going on with it, Jamie?'

Jamie ran his hand through his hair. 'I don't know. Don't you think I wish that I did? For fuck's sake, the whole idea was that we worked all this type of thing out on the lowest pressure situation that we possibly could, and you going to and from a little country town in peace time was ideal. And now I'm having to find someone missing in a war zone. It's probably a missing return pad that's the problem. The link NAMIS uses for travellers with a biology is between the DNA recorded on the machine and the corresponding record on the return pad. So maybe, following the logic, it thinks she isn't anywhere now. That would be why she drops out of the calculations directly after she went through. I just don't think I can work that out for sure before tomorrow morning, though.'

'Don't fret Jamie,' said Christian. 'I'll have her back early tomorrow morning.'

ON TIME

Jamie took a shuddering breath. 'I hope you're right.'

'Let me run those voice files through my software, Jamie,' said Suzi. 'It may turn up something.'

She left the lab and headed back to her own office in the adjacent building. She sat at her desk, accessed the link that Ellie had emailed to her of Annamarie's lecture, and plugged the recording device into her PC. She downloaded the two files into her voiceprint software and waited for the analysis to load. The blue line snaked slowly across the screen.

If it is Annamarie's great grandmother speaking, she thought, it's not beyond the bounds of possibility that they have very similar voices. Granted, it's a distant relationship, but these things can happen, look at Jim and Jamie. What had her twelfth-grade biology teacher said? 'Genetics is not a mixing bowl, but a pack of cards.'

The blue line reached the end of the box, and the analysis screen popped up. Exact match, 100%. Suzi gasped. So, it had to be Annamarie speaking on both files. It was the only way that result could have been obtained. She took the recording device out of her PC and headed back to Jamie's lab. Some news could only be delivered in person, she thought.

She popped her head into the lab, and saw Jamie and Ellie were still there. 'It's Annamarie speaking, 100% positive. I've never had a match of that magnitude without it being the same person speaking. Voiceprints are like fingerprints, specific to that individual. We developed the software when we were working on an unlocking device for smartphones. It would have worked, definitely. But in the end the company went with face recognition because that's more precise. Voices carry, and people might unlock their phone without meaning to.'

Jamie put his head in his hands. Suzi sat down next to him.

Ellie looked at him in concern. 'Annamarie can't be doing anything sinister, Jamie. I've known her for nearly seven years. Three years as an undergrad, one as a master's student and now nearly three years on my PhD. She volunteers on a lot of student welfare initiatives and she's done some brilliant stuff on the LGBTQ society, one of the masters students was telling me only last week. She's a brave, honest, caring person.'

Ellie accessed a page on her laptop. Jamie glanced at the image of Annamarie addressing a meeting against a backdrop of a rainbow flag and the Black Lives Matter logo, under the headline 'Leading Information Technology specialist Dr Annamarie Simons leads university seminar in the wake of new government anti-demonstration legislation.'

'Everything I know, and feel, tells me that you're right, Ellie. I've known her for three years; she was recommended to me when I started writing the bid for the NAMIS project. Trusted her from the beginning, knew she was the person I wanted to work with. But this is all so weird. Why was she sneaking around like that? What the hell is going on?'

'Whatever it was, it must have started very recently,' said Ellie. 'Because remember; you never intended to create a time machine. I don't know what's going on here, but I do know it will have a simple explanation in the end. There is no way that she would have been playing us.'

Fran and Christian had walked into the lab whilst Jamie was speaking. At any other time, Ellie, Jamie and Suzi would have burst into a fit of giggles at Christian's appearance. He was wearing a style of trousers that were only nowadays seen in period movies, braces, and a cardigan of a type that only men over 80 would volunteer to wear. His face was immaculately clean shaven. I hope she didn't make him do that with a cut-throat razor, thought Suzi, smiling faintly.

Fran looked troubled. 'I can't answer the Czech question, Jamie. But I can enlighten you on the rest of it. I know how it is to get obsessed with the past.'

ON TIME

'This isn't a history project!'

'No, I know that, Jamie. Listen. It's about family. I went from seeing my ancestors as grumpy two-dimensional figures in old sepia photographs to meeting them as real, live people who laugh, fall in love, have everyday problems, gossip. You get drawn in. And Annamarie's Grandma Rachel is still alive, here, now. There isn't even that element of separation. If you can do something to help, and there is a lot that you *could* do, once you have access to that time portal, it starts to seem simple. And then it becomes an obsession.'

Jamie looked at her in horror. 'Oh my God, what did you do?'

'I didn't *do* anything, Jamie. I just thought about it. A lot. I went to the doctors, got some antibiotics and kept them in a drawer rather than taking them. Jim died from septic tonsillitis. He wouldn't have a trace of the antibiotic resistance we have nowadays. He probably wouldn't even need to take the whole course. It preyed on my mind… But the pills never even got as far as London. They're still sitting in my drawer at home. And I'm going to throw them away as soon as I can, now. But what if someone you loved was dying of something you could easily cure? Can you imagine how tempting that would be?'

'Why would you even do that? This is an academic research project. We all agreed!'

'And I stuck to it… in the end. But I'm telling you, it was hard. To know that a young father-a close relative-is going to be… was snuffed out by an illness that I could cure for him like that…' Fran snapped her fingers. 'Well, it's like playing God, isn't it? These are all things that we should have discussed… that *I* should have discussed before. I'm thinking that some of this is my fault.'

'No, Fran,' said Suzi, softly, 'it's not.'

'Then it's mine,' said Jamie, grimly, 'for dreaming up that thing over there.'

Suzi put her hand on Jamie's arm. 'No, it's not yours

either, Jamie. Unless it's shared equally with Annamarie. And anyway, do you think that Hiroshima and Nagasaki were all Oppenheimer's fault?'

'No. If that team hadn't got there first, someone else would have, it was only a matter of time. And it could have been someone on the other side.'

Suzi nodded.

Fran frowned. 'Now I am become Death, the destroyer of worlds.' She suddenly remembered a snatch of an old song focusing on the pilot who dropped the World War II atom bomb. He had named his Boeing B-29 Superfortress bomber after his mother, Enola Gay, and the lyrics asked whether she was proud of his accomplishments. Fran bit her lip.

'And' continued Suzi 'If it's partly your fault and partly Annamarie's, and partly Fran's, well, it's also probably partly mine.'

'How?' replied Fran and Jamie in unison, turning towards her with identical baffled expressions on their faces.

Suzi smiled faintly. 'Because... I should have guessed a little of what she was feeling, not only about the fate of one relative, but about the fate of her people as a whole. It is the way that it is for diaspora populations. Do you remember that trip to the Globe you wanted to take, Fran?'

'I wanted *us* to go. Not just me.'

'Yes, I know. And I wanted to go. But did you think it would have been different for me than it would have been for you, Fran?'

'No... well, yes, I can see it might have been a bit different because...'

'I'm Asian. I look Asian; I look different. Oh yes, I speak English as a first language, like you, well, not quite like you, but like an American... and I've been raised in an American-Anglo culture. So that makes Shakespeare part of my linguistic heritage, too. But the majority population doesn't necessarily see it that way. Because I look different. And a lot of them judge me on that, whether you, or I, like that or not.'

Fran looked pained and faintly embarrassed. 'It's so unfair.'

'Yes, it is. And I know a lot of people from all backgrounds truly believe that, and that they want society to change. But the majority have never done enough about it, have they? I'm not blaming any of you personally; I know you'd like it to be different. But collectively, Europeans and Americans of European heritage haven't done enough to challenge the status quo, have they? And *of course*, I would be wary of entering a culture where no one has any idea of human rights, let alone civil rights.

'But that doesn't immediately occur to you, does it? Because you've never had to think about it. But Annamarie has. Granted, she looks more like you. But she will have had to deal with the casual asides, the unfunny jokes, ghastly things said online or in graffiti, careless remarks made when she will go through the "should I say something about this or should I let it go?" routine. And like me, when she thinks about the recent history of her family, she finds people catapulted out of the place that they called home, having to settle somewhere else. And a somewhere else that is not always welcoming, although some people may be kind. In the end, she is part of a people who were placed in a situation where they were forced to rely on the hospitality of others. And the persecution her ancestors experienced has inevitable echoes for subsequent generations.

'Do you remember when you showed me your great-grandmother's china tea set, Fran? My family has nothing like that, and nor will Annamarie's Grandma Rachel. All of these things left behind in the place that they had to run from. What if I had the chance to travel in time like you Fran, to meet my ancestors? How many common points of reference do you think I would have with them?

Neither Annamarie nor I even share a common first language with our great grandparents.'

There was a brief silence.

'And' continued Suzi, 'So, Fran was tempted to rescue her great-grandfather because he died from what is now an easily curable illness. That's eminently understandable. But how tempted do you think you might be to pull your ancestor out of the inferno of the twentieth century, if you had that chance, and you knew that she had disappeared into it without leaving a trace?'

Fran blinked. 'That reminds me. Annamarie told me that she'd done her DNA on one of those ancestry websites, like I did. She told me she didn't find anyone from Rachel's lineage, even though she searched copiously for them.'

'She couldn't tell only from her own DNA, Fran,' replied Christian. 'But I'm betting she did Rachel's too. Asked her to spit in a test tube and told her that it was for some other reason.'

'You didn't tell me,' said Jamie to Suzi. 'You didn't tell me all that.'

'It's not something that would generally come up. But I was thinking of extending it to a piece of academic commentary once your project was in the public domain. *Diaspora peoples in the age of time travel*, something like that.'

Fran's face lit up. 'That would be fabulous, Suzi. There's this social history journal that…'

Jamie groaned. 'Oh, God. The report. It's due in six weeks' time. What the hell are we going to do?'

'Stall them,' said Christian, 'if you have to. I'll have Annamarie back tomorrow, and then we'll all sit down and decide together. Sounds like we've got a lot that we could put in it. *If* of course, we are going to go down the rocky road into qualitative,' he grinned at Fran. 'Meanwhile,' he continued, 'can I say for the record, that *none* of this is my fault, it's something some bloke got me into. And now I am going to have to pull the fat out of the fire wearing this pair of nasty clown trousers.'

Jamie looked stricken. 'I'll go, Christian. It's my problem, not yours, I should go.'

Christian grinned impishly. 'No, you won't. You'll fuck it up, and you know it. I'm the one for this job. And then we'll all be sitting round here this time tomorrow thinking about what to put in the sodding report.'

'And you are not going to be angry with Annamarie, Jamie,' said Suzi, firmly.

Jamie made a small humming noise, similar to his mother's. 'As long as she promises not to do it again.'

'Oh, she will, Jamie,' exclaimed Fran. 'She will have learnt her lesson, I'm sure. Those antibiotics are toast. And I'm not even the one lost in time.'

She turned to Christian. 'Come on, let's get onto those maps again.' Christian sighed, grimaced comically, and followed her out of the lab.

Suzi stood up. 'I'd better go, too, Jamie. Things to do'.

Ellie stared admiringly after her. 'That was brilliant, what Suzi just said, Jamie. When the time comes for her to go public with her article, she can interview my mum, too. She could certainly expand on that perspective from an Afro-Caribbean heritage.'

Jamie nodded. 'Yes, most certainly. It's certainly been a learning experience far beyond what any of us expected it to be when we first started. And in many ways, that's a good thing.'

'Embrace complexity. That's what Annamarie used to say to me when I was struggling with my data.'

'Absolutely. I just do so wish we were discussing this with her now, here, safe with us.'

There was a brief silence.

'Do you think Christian will get Annamarie back, Jamie?'

Jamie thought of some of the student exploits that he had been on with Christian, him the cautious, sensible one, and Christian the one who would always push a situation a bit further and end up getting away with it.

'If he can't, I don't think anyone can. And if, after all, if it's only that Annamarie is stranded in time without the return pad, we're pretty sure where and when she went. So, there's a good chance it will work out OK.'

They fell silent, trying to get on as usual, to think of everyday things. But the flat, sad atmosphere remained. It was still a ship with a missing crew member, thought Jamie. And again and again, he hoped that Annamarie had fallen into a calm eddy amidst the tempest.

Rachel: London, Wednesday 7th January 2026, 10pm

Rachel was aware of a rising consciousness. Linda had taken her to the hospital, she remembered. She had been struggling to breathe. The nurses had taken her to a ward, and then a doctor explained he was going to give her something to make her feel more relaxed. 'Then you will be able to breathe more easily,' he explained. Rachel didn't remember anything after that.

She looked around and saw that she was in a tiny white room. The light from the window was dazzling. What a beautiful day, she thought. Then she noticed a little boy standing by the window. What a handsome, serious little chap, she mused. She smiled at him. So tiny, but with piercing eyes that looked… too old, somehow.

The boy spoke in a high, clear voice. 'It will be OK. He saved you. But you have to take another journey now.'

Rachel stared at him, a distant memory beginning to surface. 'I'm dreaming this, aren't I? I remember you. You were on the platform at Praha hlavní nádraží.'

The boy smiled. 'We helped you to get on the train; I will make sure that Jamie comes to save you. But you have to travel again now. It will be OK.'

Rachel started to ask him why his tenses were so mixed. The man- called Jamie, apparently- had saved her eighty-six years ago. But the light from the window had been growing brighter as he spoke, and the little boy had disappeared into the glare.

A lady walked out of the light. She had long dark hair and…

'What are you doing here, Annamarie?'

'I've come to take you home, drahoušku.'

'How do you know that word? Ah, this is a strange, mixed up dream.'

'Not a dream, Rachel,' smiled the lady, taking hold of Rachel's hand. And then she began to sing: *"'nedám tě za svět celičký,..*" Anna really wouldn't have given you for the whole world, Rachel. And she gave you, Linda and Annamarie your lives. Let me explain.'

'Mama,' exclaimed Rachel, wondering why in the midst of a dream, she should be feeling more and more awake.

The light intensified.

LOST AND FOUND

Dylan: Cardiff, Wednesday 7th January 2026, 4pm

Dylan sighed. Just home from school, and now he had to look after his little cousin and 'show him how to play on the X-squared box.' That was what his mother had instructed him to do, anyway. She was downstairs with Aunt Niamh, cooing over baby Jack.

Dylan liked Freddie; as much as any just-twelve-year-old could like a nearly five-year-old, anyway. If he had a little brother, he wouldn't have minded if it had been Freddie. Freddie was very clever for such a little boy, funny and sort of thoughtful. And he seemed to know a lot about soldiers, the last time they had played (although Dylan was getting too old for that, of course, he'd only played because Freddie had wanted to). Freddie seemed to *know* things, like he had actually been a soldier. Their grandmother, Fran, had once said jokingly, '*so perhaps he was a soldier in a previous life.*'

'*Don't be so ridiculous,*' Dylan had replied. Granny had just laughed. Dylan was going to be a soldier, he had decided. Or a pilot, or something like that. He liked things that *worked*, and things that you could think about scientifically; things that added up and made sense, not silly superstitious stuff, like the girls at school telling one another's fortunes. What a load of bull. He looked at Freddie. He'd better not say words like that in front of *him* again. He'd already got into trouble for…

Freddie was staring at the screen, which was showing

the entry portal for *Peace Keeper: Pandemic*. Dylan was fairly sure this wasn't what his mother had in mind when she had issued the instruction to 'show Freddie how to play on the X-squared box.' But she hadn't said he *couldn't*...

'Let me do it, Freds.'

He wasn't worried about Freddie looking at the screen. He wasn't old enough to notice that Dylan and his friends had found a way to get into the mainstream, worldwide game online. And they'd beaten some older American kids yesterday. That was a whole load of new swear words, put together in interesting ways. Dylan wished he could ask his Aunt Suzi to explain what all of it meant, but he wouldn't be able to do that without getting into trouble and getting the whole lot of them banned for a month by their mothers. And have all the passwords changed again, which was a total pain in the arse.

Dylan took the controller, gently. 'You see, Freddie, this is the new game. It's based on some riots that happened a few years ago, when the schools kept shutting down because old people were getting sick. Have you heard granny talking about the 'Rona? You weren't born yet.'

Freddie looked at him, uncertainly.

'So, this game is about that sort of situation,' continued Dylan. 'You're a soldier and you have to get through the crowds to HQ without killing anyone. Do you want a go? I'll help.' We'll stick to the kids' version today, he thought, tapping out a message to his friends.

'Without killing anyone?' asked Freddie. He seemed unsure.

'Yes. That's why it's harder than *Soldier: Pandemic*. We can use reasonable force, but we mustn't kill anyone. We're peacekeepers, look. Blue helmets.' He showed Freddie his avatar.

'But... that's not what being a soldier... *is*,' replied Freddie, slowly.

Dylan sighed. The pesky kid was at it again, and it

wasn't only about playing make believe soldiers this time. It was *Peace Keeper: Pandemic*, for fuck's sake (don't say that out loud, he checked himself) and Dylan was the expert. He'd just beaten a bunch of big kids. He looked at Freddie, frowning. You could do more about younger brothers than cousins, he mused. If it was only you and your little brother, all you got was your mum shouting at you. Things like wedgies, Chinese burns… just enough to show them who was boss. But cousins were tricky. He wouldn't only get his mother shouting at him, but his aunt looking annoyed and sometimes even Granny would pitch in. But Granny wasn't here today. She wasn't downstairs but in America, or London or something. She went to a lot of places for an old lady. And now she was working for Jamie. He had heard his mother and aunt laughing about that. He couldn't imagine that would work out for long. Granny was too bossy, like his mum. Lost in thought for a moment, he hadn't noticed that Freddie had sort of stopped. His eyes had gone dark. Then he clutched Dylan's arm, tightly.

'They always shoot at you. The fireworks keep going off. And there was one man who was too close to the fireworks, and he died. His friend was with him and he didn't die, but he was so sad, he had to go to the hospital to get better. There was sand and mud and stones all around, flying in the air. And the fireworks, they kept going off. Jack… you… both of you. And the man.'

'What man?' said Dylan, genuinely frightened.

'THE MAN. He was so sad he had to talk to the doctors, but they couldn't make him better. Not really.'

'Shut up, you little weirdo' said Dylan, pushing Freddie's hand off his arm. But Freddie didn't notice.

'So then next time, the man went to sea before they made him a soldier, because,' Freddie looked straight at Dylan with his deep, dark eyes, 'you don't want to be a soldier.'

'Fuck off.'

Freddie looked down and paused for a moment. When he looked up, he was Freddie again. His blue eyes were dancing with mischief.

'Ooooh, you said…'

'Shut up, shut up, I didn't.'

'I'm telling.'

Dylan caught Freddie by the collar. 'No, you're not.'

'Am. Let go.'

'I'll let you pick the weapons if you stay.'

Freddie looked at the screen, on which a variety of tasers, batons and armoured vehicles were rotating.

'Don't want any of those, I want a motorbike.'

'But that'll cost loads,' groaned Dylan.

Freddie looked at him and shrugged.

'Alright, alright,' sighed Dylan, letting go of Freddie's collar. They could hear the baby crying downstairs, so with any luck, no one would have heard. 'We'll get a motorbike. Which one?'

'I want to choose,' Freddie insisted, taking the controller.

'What did you mean about the fireworks?' asked Dylan, gently retrieving the controller. 'Look, you turn it around like this.'

'What fireworks? Can you get fireworks?'

'Oh, yes,' replied Dylan, flicking the screen onto stun grenades.

Freddie: Cardiff, Wednesday 7th January 2026, 10.05pm

Freddie was having one of those dreams again, when he knew he was asleep, and he knew he knew things that he didn't know when he was awake, and his lack of words to explain and describe what was going on didn't matter; he could *think* more clearly. He could hear a song in a language that he'd never heard before, but somehow, he knew what all the words meant. He was talking to an old lady, but she was also a little girl. In his dream, that didn't seem strange at all. He often had dreams where he was grown up, and sometimes even where he was old. When that happened, the words seemed to come, but then they'd completely escape him again by the time he woke up.

The old lady had to get on a train and somehow Jamie was there. Freddie was standing on the platform, watching Jamie. Jamie was panting, because he'd been running, and he was looking for the old lady, but when she was a little girl. Freddie saw her first, standing alone on the platform. She looked so frightened. Then she turned and stared directly at him. As their eyes locked, an awful emotion started to build inside Freddie, stronger than he had ever felt before. He felt that he was drowning in tears, drowning, drowning, drowning. He couldn't breathe.

He sped up, up into wakefulness, realising that his face was wet, his nose was running and he was screaming as loudly as he could. His mother, Aunt Rae and Dylan were looking at him, wide-eyed. 'You're awake now, Freddie,' said his mother. 'Come out of it. You're here with us. Everything is fine. You must have been having a very bad dream.'

Freddie couldn't properly remember; it was already slipping away from him. All he was left with was the colours. Like a huge smoking bonfire, black and grey and orange and yellow and red. He winced. His eyes went dark. 'Tell Franny that it can't be her, it has to be Jamie. She can't run fast enough.'

'You mean Granny? Granny Fran?'

'She can't RUN fast enough,' urged Freddie, beginning to cry again.

'OK, OK,' soothed Aunt Rae. 'We'll tell her.'

'TELL HER NOW!'

Niamh and Rae looked at one another. 'What's the time?' asked Rae.

'Ten past ten.'

Rae took out her phone. 'It's not too late. You know

she'll still be up. She never goes to bed till after midnight. Let's ring her. It'll help him to settle.' She walked out of the room.

Freddie sat on his mother's lap. He felt his breathing begin to slow. When he'd woken up, he'd felt like his chest was going to burst.

He could hear his aunt talking softly, just outside the door. Dylan had turned away and picked up his own phone, taking the chance to flick through YouTube whilst no one was paying any attention.

'He had a nightmare,' Rae was saying. 'Something about you and Jamie… and running.'

Freddie's eyes began to darken. He rose from his mother's lap, walked out of the room and stood next to his aunt. He saw her jump when she looked at him. He held out his hand for the phone. Rae passed it over without a word.

'You can't run fast enough, Franny,' he said into the phone. 'Do you remember? The boys were running, and you couldn't run fast enough. Let Jamie do it.'

'OK, Freddie,' he could hear Granny's 'careful' voice on the other end of the phone. 'But why?'

'Jamie has to run, Franny. You can't do it. You've got to remember that. Do you promise?'

There was a brief silence. Then Fran replied simply: 'Yes Freddie. I'll remember. I promise.'

Freddie's eyes began to clear. He handed the phone back to his aunt and went to sit back on his mother's lap. He could hear Aunt Rae talking softly into the phone outside, but he wasn't listening. It didn't matter what they were saying anymore. Granny had promised.

'What did you mean, Freddie?' asked his mother. But Freddie's eyes had closed, and his breathing was soft and regular. He was deeply asleep.

Dylan looked up from his phone. 'He is one weird little kid.'

Then he realised that both his mother and his aunt

were frowning at him. 'Just saying.'

'He had a nightmare, Dylan,' replied his mother. 'The drama's over. Go back to sleep.'

'I can't. Jeez.'

'Put the phone down and read your book. And keep the light low. Don't wake him up. And try to go to sleep.'

Dylan picked up his book from the bedside cupboard.

'Are you OK, Dylan?' asked Aunt Niamh.

'Yeah. He had a bad dream, OK. But you do know he has them when he's awake, too, don't you? Talks about soldiers.'

'Yes, I know,' sighed Aunt Niamh. 'I've heard that one, too. I think he makes it up in his imagination.'

'He *is* a funny little guy,' said Rae. 'But he'll grow out of it. You weren't showing him some type of horrible war game today, were you Dylan?'

'No,' replied Dylan, innocently. His mother frowned. But all she said was, 'School tomorrow.'

'Yep,' said Dylan, looking at his book.

His mother and aunt left the room. Dylan put his book down, picked up his phone again and put in his earbuds. He could hear his mother and Aunt Niamh walking down the stairs, talking.

'…just obsessed with soldiers.'

'Thank goodness the baby slept through.'

'Very imaginative. Mum was right about that.'

'Why running?'

Fran: London, Wednesday 7th January 2026, 10.25pm

Can anything else disturbing happen on this most surreal of days, thought Fran, putting down the phone. She was alone in her tiny room at Jamie's, trying to watch a film on her iPad. She knew she wouldn't sleep properly tonight. She kept replaying the plans for tomorrow in her mind. She was worried about how quickly they had had to plan everything. She had taken weeks over finding the right clothes for her own trips in time, and studying manners, the culture of the Presbyterian religion her ancestors had belonged to, everything. But, she thought, for the umpteenth time, Christian was going to a later era, the outfit they'd found and the issues that they had discussed should see him through. She had revised the notes she'd written for Rachel and done some further research. Then they'd all met together for a final time to thrash out where to put Christian down, how he would get to the station and what he might find. But she still felt uneasy. The stakes were so much higher than for a social trip to a peaceful little town like Sittingbourne. And this time, if she'd got anything wrong, it wouldn't only impact upon her. And now, Freddie.

Fran had already decided that her middle grandson was some type of "sensitive." She wasn't comfortable with the concept of "psychic" but there was no doubt that Freddie seemed to know things that he shouldn't know. However, she'd put that down to being receptive to adult mood, some degree of synaesthesia (which she had studied on the internet, after Freddie had first mentioned his 'colours' to her) and a lively, active mind which picked up on everything in the world around him and filtered it thorough a huge imagination. But really, after all the weird things that had happened today, this last episode possibly rated the highest.

Suzi and Jamie were already asleep, worn out from the stress of the day. Fran knew that if she were still awake between 3 and 4am, she would hear Jamie get up and walk down to the living room. He wouldn't be able to go on much longer like this, she thought. Kylie the dog was snoring on the bed beside her. Fran patted her head. Lucky Kylie, who knew nothing about time travel, and would probably have a lovely time running around some fields in the past if she was sent back through the time portal. Fran thought back to a day long ago, when she had been running around carelessly… the day that she bust her lip.

She stroked the scar, still faintly discernible after nearly sixty years.

The soundtrack to the incident was always the same; an old song called *Waterloo Sunset* playing scratchily on an old transistor radio, which the teenagers in those days called a "tranny"- which meant something quite different now, mused Fran. The boy in the song had the same name as her older brother, Terry. Terry had volunteered to take her to the park that day. It was a hot, sunny afternoon, at the beginning of the summer holidays. When they arrived, some friends of his were already there, lying on the grass, eating ice cream and listening to someone's "tranny". They were nice to Fran, giving her ice cream and calling her 'little sister.' One of the girls had plaited daisies into Fran's hair, and lent her the cowbell that she was wearing around her neck to wear for a while. Fran was in heaven. She felt like a real teenager. Not as cool as Charlie of course, but then Charlie wasn't a teenager anymore. She was off in San Francisco for the Summer of Love, and she was going to change the world. Photographs of her had arrived that morning, looking impossibly cool in a tiny mini skirt. Nana Mo had tutted over them, and then left them on the table in the living room. Fran had picked them up and looked intently through them when everyone else was busy.

The tinny strains of *Waterloo Sunset* had carried across the park. Terry was running around with some of the boys. Fran had wandered over. She decided to join in. But the boys were running much faster than she could. She'd tried and tried to catch up. Then she'd heard one of the girls shout, 'be careful!' But it was too late. Fran had tripped and fallen head-first onto the pole upon which the park regulations were displayed. She'd sat up, feeling that her mouth was wet. Then she'd seen the pool of blood on the path.

That evening, after the lip had been stitched, and Terry had been thoroughly assured that it wasn't his fault, Fran's father James had looked at Fran's face and grinned.

ON TIME

'Wounded soldier, then? Never mind, Franny. No permanent damage done. But that's what's going to happen if you try to run with the big boys.'

Fran had tried to smile, but her lip was still a bit frozen. *'I know daddy. But I can try, can't I?'*

James had smiled. *'Yes, Franny. And I think you always will. And that's not such a bad thing. But try to be a bit more careful.'*

Nearly 60 years later, Fran sat in bed and frowned. Why did Freddie say 'remember?' He might be a "sensitive," but wasn't that a bit *specific*? She shook herself. She was tired and spooked and seeing patterns where none existed. It had been that sort of day. There was no such context to the message. She had no plans to run anywhere, and neither did Jamie. If there was any running to be done, Christian would be doing it. And Christian was usually very good at talking himself out of situations before he had to run.

Freddie can just catch my feelings sometimes, thought Fran. Seems like he can do it even when he's miles away. She smiled at how Jamie would scoff even at that idea. But he hadn't seen Freddie's eyes darken as his 'feelings' took over, and she was convinced that there was something – what was that Shakespeare quotation that her father James used to use- "more in heaven and earth"- about it.

I've been upset today, thought Fran, rationalising. Freddie has "caught"' that somehow, and he's probably heard the girls talking about me being with Jamie, so he's had a nightmare about it. Nothing to worry about. She turned on the film again but found that she couldn't concentrate. She accessed YouTube and typed "Waterloo Sunset" into the search box. She smiled as the comfortable old song flooded her ear buds. Kylie snuggled into the crook of her elbow. Fran rested her head on the plump spelt pillow she had brought with her from Leeds a few weeks ago and closed her eyes.

Pam Jarvis

Annamarie: Prague, June 1939

Annamarie settled back into a plush chair in the café, feeling impossibly glamourous in her 1930s outfit, especially the hat. And the blonde wig, of course. She glanced furtively at her great-grandmother, 3 tables away. Rachel had been right. The resemblance between Annamarie and Anna was so obvious that Annamarie had decided that the blonde wig was a necessary addition after the first time she caught sight of her great-grandmother. So, she'd acquired it before making the second trip, today.

Annamarie had initially arrived in the Prague of the past on a cold grey day in early April 1939 and made her way to the nearest tram stop to the tiny apartment building where Anna, Rachel and Anna's mother lived. The papers in Rachel's Prague box had revealed the address. She didn't have to wait too long. Anna came out with a little girl, who Annamarie realised with a pang, had to be Rachel. Annamarie had followed them discreetly down the cobbled street, across Náměstí Republiky, where she'd nearly lost them in a crowd, through the Prasna Brana. Then Anna and Rachel had stopped to wait by a tram stop on the other side of the road. Annamarie had found the tram stop for trams travelling in the opposite direction and stood near to the kerb, pulling the brim of her hat low over her eyes. She didn't want either Rachel or Anna to get a full-face view of her. She'd been ready to leave at that point, anyway. She'd fulfilled the objective of that particular visit; to locate Anna and get a brief look at her.

Annamarie had initially imagined that it would be great fun to travel in time, to have all the experiences that Fran had described: the sights, the smells, the unexpected similarities and differences. Fran had described the brightness of the stars in a world less polluted with artificial light, for example. But Annamarie felt none of this. While Prague in 2025 had made her feel sad and flat, Prague in 1939 actively frightened her. The moment that

ON TIME

she had stepped into this reality, she felt like she needed to run, to flee, to go home, to be anywhere but here. The anguish and anticipation amongst the people hung like a tangible presence over the city. In this Prague, Annamarie felt as though she had been penned up, like a caged animal- but even worse than being caged, there was an additional overtone of being corralled, in an arena crowded with other animals, waiting to be slaughtered.

Presumably, thought Annamarie, this is intensified for me because I know what is going to happen. She shivered. But she had got through that initial short mission, and now here she was again, waiting to collect the final pieces of information she needed to turn up on time to meet her objective. She wasn't able to hear the conversation between the Englishman and her great-grandmother; they were too far away. But she did have a state-of-the-art, directionally sensitive recording device at the top of her handbag, set to max, that would pick it up. She would be able to select and enhance the required conversation on return. And then a combination of her inexpert Czech, the university's online foreign language dictionary and the much-acclaimed new online translation program that Jamie's wife had worked on would give her enough to extract the information that she needed: exactly what time the train was leaving and from what platform. And anything else she could get from this eavesdropping exercise would be a bonus.

Annamarie's heart ached for her great-grandmother. Rachel was not with her today. Annamarie had now painstakingly patched together the run-up to Rachel's transportation to England, using the account Fran had written for Rachel as her starting point. Anna would have given this man a photograph of Rachel that was sent to England to be circulated amongst prospective foster parents. A family then picked her from a portfolio of children's photographs. This would have been the kind people with whom Rachel lived from her arrival in

England until she was sixteen, when she left to live in the nurses' home while she was training.

Now Anna was meeting with the organisers of the transport to arrange the final details. The man and his female assistant were meeting people in turn. Annamarie sat there as people came and went for a while, fearing that she had got the wrong date, somehow. She'd had to dig a long way into the historical record to find it. But then Anna walked in. Annamarie turned her face away as Anna drew near, tilting the brim of her hat to obscure Anna's view. Anna was wearing a small hat, so Annamarie managed to get a good look at her face as she walked past. A tall, elegant woman; long, thick, dark hair braided into an upsweep, and delicate tapering hands with well-manicured nails. She should, by rights, be beautiful, thought Annamarie. But Anna's face was so etched with worry, and her eyes so haunted by anxiety that she seemed prematurely aged. 'Grey and drained' was the description that came to mind.

Annamarie stole another furtive glance as Anna sat at the table, talking to the charity workers. Where did you go after Rachel left? thought Annamarie. Did you try to get out of the country by another route, and that went wrong somehow? I'm almost certain that you never had another child. No search I ever did through ancestry DNA analysis ever turned up a living relative for Rachel, apart from me and Linda. And somehow, I just know that you didn't live for a significant amount of time after Rachel was gone. For as long as she had known Rachel's story, Annamarie had felt this to be true, even though she wasn't generally given to 'feelings' about things. And after the unsuccessful DNA matching search, she decided that she had enough confirmation to formulate a plan.

If someone was going to die very soon anyway, she'd calculated, what would be the harm in pulling them out of their natural time and taking them to a place where they could live out the rest of their lifespan in peace? And not only would this give Anna a second chance, transporting her to 2026 would also give Rachel the chance to say the goodbye that had been stolen from her by the Third Reich, along with so much else that could never be recouped.

Annamarie knew that her grandmother did not have much longer to live. She was ninety-four years old, and her health was failing. But if Anna could be taken to see her, they would be granted however many months Rachel had left to say their goodbyes. Yes, thought Annamarie, it was certainly beyond bizarre to take a thirty-nine-year old mother to meet her ninety-four-year-old daughter. But it was the only remedy Annamarie could offer that would keep the timeline intact, so she had decided to go for it.

The university site reopened the day after tomorrow in Annamarie's present, following the New Year bank holiday. But the buildings would still be deserted due to the Christmas holidays. So, she'd planned to return through the time portal to Prague 1939, to intersect with Anna at Praha hlavní nádraží on 2nd August. Then when Rachel was safely on the train, Annamarie intended to take Anna back through the time portal with her, to 2nd January 2026. Once Anna had recovered from the initial shock, Annamarie intended to use the university language translation technology to explain more fully to her what was going on.

Annamarie had calculated that it would be possible for herself and Rachel to help Anna to integrate herself into twenty-first century society. And there might even eventually be, through Christian's family, a chance for her to do that in the Czech Republic, in a place where the ancient streets would still look familiar, and where she could speak the language. Annamarie hadn't yet worked out what she was going to do about Linda. Probably swear Rachel to silence and tell Linda that Anna was a distant relative she had tracked down through an ancestry website. Linda tended to panic when presented with disturbing information. But all of this could come later.

Annamarie had been working for a few weeks to develop a more flexible time travel activation pad when she was alone in the laboratory; one that could transport DNA in the opposite direction, from the past into the present. It had been hard without any help from Jamie and Christian, but now it was reliably working on plant life. She hadn't managed to test it on animals. But she had calculated that there was a good chance that it would work with animate creatures; the technology was identical to that used to create the original return pad. And what did Anna have to lose that she hadn't lost (wasn't going to lose) already? So now, Annamarie had to acquire the specific DNA that she needed to work with.

The conversation between Anna and the charity workers was winding up. A man was waiting for Anna to leave so he could sit down in her place.

Annamarie picked up her bag and carefully placed a sterile wipe in the palm of her right hand. She rose from her seat, and moved over towards the charity workers' table, hiding her face behind the brim of her hat again. As she got within two steps, she stumbled and caught the table to stop herself from falling. 'Prominte,' she said, closing her hand around the handle of the fork that Anna had used. She moved quickly to hide it in the folds of her skirt, walking towards the ladies' room. Once in a cubicle, she carefully placed the fork into one of Christian's sterile specimen bags, making very sure not to touch it directly, to avoid contamination with her own DNA. She zipped the specimen bag tightly then dropped it into the bottom of her handbag. It was done. Time to go home.

—

The lab was cold and silent, as she had left it. She stripped off her glamorous outfit, folding it carefully into the bottom drawer of her desk. She put on her sweatpants, hoodie and Docs. She glanced out of the window at grey sleet falling on the rooftops. She washed her hands thoroughly and put on a pair of sterile surgical gloves. Then she removed the specimen bag from her handbag, carefully extracted the fork and, after throwing the bag into the bin, placed the fork prong end into the relevant aperture on NAMIS's console.

'NAMIS.'

'Working.'

'Make a return pad for this DNA.'

The light flashed above the aperture and the machine hummed faintly. Annamarie held her breath.

The pad dropped into the empty slot next to the aperture.

Annamarie let out her breath in a sigh. 'You're coming home to us, Anna. You're coming to say goodbye.'

Before removing her gloves, she placed the fork into a clean specimen bag and tucked it beneath her travelling clothes in her bottom desk drawer, just in case she might need it again.

It wasn't perfect, but it would have to do. They were on their way.

Christian: Prague, 2nd August 1939, 3am

Christian dropped gently into the grass, and immediately laid flat on his stomach, looking around cautiously. He was alone; it would seem that Fran had guessed correctly. The first problem they'd had to solve was where to put him down from the time portal. They always tried to avoid travellers being observed popping into or out of time; it was something that they had to do to avoid causing a stir amongst the people in the area. This was relatively easy to accomplish in a peaceful area surrounded by countryside like Sittingbourne. Whilst Prague was also surrounded by some open green areas, Fran had said that that there might be people hanging around anywhere, day or night, in an occupied country, and of course there was a curfew. Their best bet, they decided, would be to put Christian down in an unpopulated area in the middle of the night, and then for him to sit it out until daylight.

So far, so good.

Christian moved to the cover of a small copse of trees. He sat down underneath them, looking up at the stars between the leaves. Fran was right, without the bright streetlights of the twenty-first century, they were magnificent. So here he was, at 3am on 2nd August 1939, in Klánovice-Čihadla, a nature park on the edge of the city, with several hours to wait and keep himself out of trouble. Christian peered into the darkness. He was already familiar with this park, from summers spent with his father's family, but he'd never been here when it was dark. And August or not, it was a bit chilly. He was glad Fran had managed to find him a coat to go with the baggy trousers. He tucked his hands into the sleeves.

He'd never had a conscious sense of the struggles that his father's nation had been through across the entire twentieth century. It hadn't been on the history curriculum at school, and he hadn't been that interested in history, either. His father, Matt, told the story of his brief student activism and his flight from Prague to Vienna like an isolated episode in an adventure story. Matt had only been eighteen at the time and found asylum in the UK at a time when the public attitude to asylum seekers had been far more welcoming. He'd now spent fifty-six of his seventy-five years in England; Christian and his siblings, all born into the UK and their mother's English family, had felt no conflicts in describing themselves as British. 'Novak' was an easy name to say and spell; the other side of their heritage seldom came up. Except of course, the European base opportunity, which was useful. Christian wasn't old enough to remember a time when the family couldn't travel freely between the UK and the Czech Republic.

But sitting here under the stars in a different time, in a country that had been invaded and subjugated, Christian felt the stirring of his Czech identity. The land of his

ON TIME

fathers was being trashed, and there was nothing he could do about it. And it felt... wrong. It was a good thing we didn't go shopping for a gun, too, he thought. Christian shook himself, and grinned. This could turn into the type of obsession that Fran had been talking about if he didn't watch himself. He prided himself on his lack of sentimentality. He had to frame this experience like being an extra in an old movie. The script had been written, and what was going to happen was inevitable. The fact that Annamarie couldn't deal with that situation was the reason for the mess that they were in now. He fingered the two return pads in his pocket, one for him, one for her. They used the DNA profile for Annamarie that was in NAMIS' memory to make the new pad. It should work. It would be a first trial, however. Fran's DNA had been re-entered every time she made the trip.

Christian dozed for a while. Then he saw the light beginning to creep along the horizon. He hunkered down further into the trees. He had about an hour's walk into town, to Praha hlavní nádraží, the train station. He'd planned to get there about 8.30 am – an hour before Rachel was to board her train. The details had been clear on the voice file they had found in Annamarie's desk. He also planned to get some breakfast on the way. He wanted to take the opportunity to see a few sights on what he expected to be his last trip into the past for a while. He waited until the countdown on his phone, hidden deep in his coat pocket, indicated that it was 6.30 am, and then set off on his way.

This is surreal, thought Christian, as he walked through the familiar, ancient cobbled streets; the same but not the same. The sights, the sounds and the smells, just as Fran had described. And she wasn't familiar with Sittingbourne in the way that Christian was familiar with Prague. He watched the quaint old trams going up and down the streets. Then a Nazi patrol car glided slowly past, which gave him the creeps. Ignore them; stay out of their way he thought. Ellie had not only managed to make him an authentic looking 1930s British passport, she had also managed to create a few sheets of paper money that would pass for authentic, given that no one would be looking for the quality of image capture and printing that could be achieved with twenty-first century technology.

He looked around. He would stop for a quick breakfast, then he would be on his way. He ducked into a small, somewhat run-down café a few streets away from the station, after seeing through the window that it was crowded with men dressed similarly to himself. That way, he would blend into the background. He fingered the packet of sterilizing wipes in his pocket, with which he would discretely wipe the crockery and utensils before leaving.

He took a stool by the counter and ordered coffee – turecká káva- and rye bread with salami. There wasn't as much on offer as there was in his own time, he mused. 'Obvs,' he thought and grinned, amused by the incongruity of the twenty-first century expression in the current environment.

A man walked in and looked quizzically at him. 'Jan, what are you doing here?'

Christian stared back, nonplussed. 'Sorry?'

'Oh,' said the stranger, moving closer. 'Not Jan, sorry. You look like my brother. It's uncanny, in fact. But he's a bit younger than you, I think.'

Christian was thinking. His paternal grandfather had been called Jan, but he had never met him. He died before Christian was born. In fact, Jan never met any of his England-based grandchildren, because Matt had not been able to travel back to Czechoslovakia before the Velvet Revolution at the end of 1989.

Christian blinked. 'Oh? Well, they say everyone has a double somewhere in the world, don't they?'

He was thinking, my grandfather's brother. So, this guy is my great-uncle. What a head-fuck. He's definitely ten, maybe twelve years younger than me now, by the look of him.

'I'm Christian Barnett,' he continued, clicking into his rehearsed cover story. This was his mother's family name; everyone had agreed that a British name and nationality would be the best option for his faux 1930s passport in case he was required to show it anywhere. Britain would be a neutral country for another month yet.

'Matyas Novak. Are you English? You speak good Czech. Only a bit of an accent there.'

'My father is English, my mother is Czech. I live in England. I'm here on a visit.'

'Better get back there, then. Nothing to stay here for now'.

Christian was running family stories through his mind. His father's name was Matyas- long anglicised to Matt. And he had been called Matyas because...this guy had died in the war, early on. He'd been involved in something famous; it seemed to be a family trait. It had a strange name. Operation Anthropoid? Christian stared at his great uncle. Three years hence, before he even got close to the age that Christian was now, this guy was going to help the men who killed Hitler's chief general in Prague, Reinhard Heydrich, and he was going to die in the process. Christian swallowed. He was starting to be consumed by the feelings that Fran had described to him, and that had presumably led Annamarie to jump into a war zone. He struggled to contain them.

'Yes. I know what you mean.'

'That bastard Hitler. We've got no chance. You'll be better off on your little island. They're not going to help us.'

'I'm sorry. They might at some point. You never know.'

'It's too late. We're all on our own in this. No one gives a shit.'

Christian looked at Matyas. Beyond the sadness, he felt

a rising pride in his family, and in his father's nation, its refusal to acquiesce, despite being so much smaller than an overbearing enemy, not once, but several times in its history, and the part that his own family had played across generations in the fight against tyranny.

'I give a shit,' he said, passionately, 'I really, really do. That's why I'm here. To help make it OK in the end – at least for some people. Never give up.'

He put his hand briefly on Matyas' arm.

Matyas smiled grimly. 'Then it's too late for both of us. But never mind, we'll keep trying.'

'Yes, we will,' replied Christian, feeling his eyes beginning to fill. 'We absolutely will.'

A man sitting at the back of the café waved urgently at Matyas.

Matyas waved back. 'Got to go. Good luck, then.'

He stuck out his hand. Christian shook it bare-handed, forgetting the time traveller's social distancing code. He swallowed the huge lump that was coalescing in his throat. 'Good luck, Matyas Novak.'

Matyas walked across the café to talk to his friend. Christian cuffed discreetly at his eyes and looked down into his pocket at his phone, counting down the seconds. It was time to go, to find Annamarie. She was the only one he could rescue here.

As he walked swiftly down the street towards the station, he realised that he had to cuff his eyes again. Ridiculous, he thought. It was a *movie*. A movie that starred Matyas, with Christian as an extra in the opening scene. He repeated this to himself several times. But he wasn't feeling like an actor anymore.

Annamarie: Prague, 2nd August, 1939, 8.55 am

Annamarie walked onto the platform at Praha hlavní nádraží. She had steeled herself for the scene she was about to witness, but still found that her distress nearly

ON TIME

overwhelmed her. Fran had once told her about Jamie's sister's little boy, who seemed to feel things for other people. Annamarie had found this strange, at the time. She had always had a sense of herself as a practical person, who was able to avoid becoming emotionally overwhelmed like her mother, Linda, frequently did. But this? This was like nothing she had ever experienced before. She stood for a moment amongst the mayhem and realised how lucky she was to be born into a peaceful nation, and for it to generally remain that way, despite the tremors of the past few years, up to this point in her life.

Everyone on the platform, apart from the harassed adults running around with clipboards, was crying. Mothers, fathers, children. Some of the children were screaming, and some of the mothers were close to hysteria. The children were being put onto the train, jumping off, and then being pushed back on again by the adults. Annamarie watched in horror as a sobbing mother pulled a child of around three or four years old off the train, and the father snatched him from her and put him back on again through one of the open windows. Annamarie tried to put an emotional barrier around herself. All I have to do, she thought, is to find Anna and Rachel. I need a few moments to explain to Anna what I'm here for – to help her, a passage to England for one adult only, later today – we will make sure that Rachel leaves on the train, and then I'll explain the details. Which might be difficult, but we will have time.

Annamarie had thought about trying to catch up with Anna at an earlier point in time, to explain the whole situation, but she'd decided that if she took that approach, it might be impossible to persuade Anna to put Rachel on the train at all. She had guessed that the most likely outcome of that strategy would be an insistence from Anna that she and Rachel must remain together. But the huge anomaly that would cause in the timeline could not be risked. Rachel's fate would change, and potentially create a whole series of paradoxes, many of which would lead to Annamarie and Linda never existing at all. So, Annamarie had decided her only possible strategy would be to intervene today. She had formulated a plan to speak to Anna on the platform before she put Rachel on the train, impart the information that there was one passage to England waiting for Anna later today. Then Annamarie would remain with Anna to make completely sure that she said a reassuring goodbye to Rachel, and they would both wave her off on the train, which would only change only one, very minor detail in Rachel's life, but one that would hopefully make a small positive difference to her. Only then would Annamarie reveal the exact nature of the passage she was offering and get herself and Anna to a secluded area where they could activate the pads.

Annamarie shouldered her way through the crowd as gently as she could. Getting people *not* to pay attention to what we are doing today might not prove as difficult as I thought, she mused.

And then, there they were. Anna and Rachel, making their way through the crowd towards the front of the platform. Annamarie's heart began to race. She approached Anna, shielding her face under the brim of her hat.

'Paní Rosenberg? Excuse me. Can I talk to you for a moment?' Her Czech sounded broken even to her own ears as she remembered the phrases she had practiced carefully. But she was encouraged to hear English voices around her from the Kindertransport social workers. At least she didn't stick out like a sore thumb. They were speaking similarly fractured Czech to the children and parents.

Anna looked up. Annamarie instinctively pulled her false blonde hair around her face to avoid a reaction from Anna to the similarity of their appearance. But then she realised that she hadn't needed to bother. She saw from the expression on Anna's face that she was not really seeing anything. She looked utterly broken.

'I can help you,' said Annamarie gently, hoping that she was being understood. 'Please let me explain…'

'Promiňte?' said Anna. The noise around them was deafening.

Annamarie's Czech ran out and she replied in English 'let's just move back out of all this noise.' She mimed putting her hands over her ears and shrugged, gesturing to the back of the platform, approximately three metres away.

Anna spoke to Rachel in rapid Czech. She's asking Rachel to wait there for a moment, thought Annamarie. I think I have been able to make my meaning clear.

Anna turned to Annamarie and followed her to the back of the platform, whilst keeping a close eye on Rachel. The two women stood by the wall. Annamarie felt tears rising in her eyes. Looking at Anna, she saw her expression mirrored in her great-grandmother's face. She reached out and took Anna's hand, flesh meeting flesh. Then there was a flash of white light and …nothing.

Christian: Prague 2nd August 1939, 8.45am

Christian walked swiftly into the station. He was later than he intended, due to his conversation in the café, and then, the closer he got to Praha hlavní nádraží, the more crowded the streets seemed to become. Now he was pushing his way through groups of people, crying and arguing and shouting at one another. He glanced into his pocket, checking the countdown on his phone. He was still comfortably on time. He walked onto the platform and sat on a bench for about 10 minutes, waiting for Annamarie to turn up. He wondered if he might spot the great-grandmother, if she looked anything like Annamarie. He would certainly have noticed Matyas in a crowd, given his likeness to his namesake. The number of people on the platform was beginning to build, as was the noise and confusion. He stood up and looked around. It didn't help that the women all wore hats, some of which partially obscured their faces.

He felt the stress build within him as he watched the tableau of human misery that was growing around him. He'd had about all the emotion he could take for one day, he thought, even before he had arrived at this fragment of Hades. He just wanted to find Annamarie and go. His defences were now in tatters. He had never felt such despair in his life. Any joy or wonder that he had felt about travelling in time was gone. When they got back to the lab, he was going to go home, he decided. All the talking could wait until tomorrow. He would leave Annamarie to the others to deal with. He was done.

Then he spotted Annamarie. She was leading a child across the platform. What was Annamarie doing with a child? And then, another woman emerged from the crowd, and began to speak to her. And suddenly he realised that no, *that* was Annamarie. But she was wearing a hat, and a blonde wig. A blonde wig, for fuck's sake, what was that about? No wonder he hadn't spotted her before. The two women were walking out of the crowd now, to the back of the platform, while the child remained a few metres away, nearer to the train. Christian started to walk towards Annamarie. He was calling her name, but she couldn't hear him above the cacophony. She had her back to him as he approached… but he was only a metre away now. The crowd behind them were all facing towards the train.

And then, the impossible happened. Annamarie and the other woman disappeared in a flash of light. There were a few seconds during which he stared open-mouthed at the empty space that had been occupied by the two women. Then he felt a brief sense of rapid motion, like sitting on top of a space-shot rocket- but before that thought had left his mind, he fell heavily on his stomach. He realised that he was lying in the time portal. Completely winded, he struggled to raise his head, and realised that the shocked faces of Fran and Jamie were staring down at him.

ON TIME

NAMIS: London, Thursday 8th January 2026, 8.01 am

Christian lay in the time portal for a few seconds, trying to catch his breath.

'What the…?' Fran exclaimed.

'What happened?' barked Jamie.

Ellie came rushing over to examine the data scrawling rapidly over the screen. 'Where's Annamarie?'

Christian looked up at them, panting heavily, tears streaming down his face. 'She disappeared, she fucking disappeared… She was on the platform, there was a flash, and then she was gone.'

Fran sat down next to him and held his hand, not speaking. Jamie and Ellie stood motionless, faces transfixed with shock. Christian's breath began to slow, and he struggled to control his sobs. Fran took a tissue from her pocket and gave it to him.

Jamie was the first to move. 'NAMIS?'

'Working.'

'Where is Annamarie Simons?'

'Not in time'

'Is she travelling in time?'

'Negative'.

Jamie sat down by the machine, balling his fists. He placed them carefully on the tray on NAMIS' frontage.

'Is Annamarie Simons dead, NAMIS?'

'Outside parameters.'

Jamie brought his fists down on the tray with a clang.

'She's gone Jamie,' said Christian. He took a long shuddering breath, wiped his face with the tissue and sat up. Fran and Ellie helped him to a chair.

'And I didn't choose to return just then. I got thrown out of time, back to here. There was a flash of light, she and the woman she was talking to vanished, and then I was here. I think the woman she was talking to was her great-grandmother.'

He took the return pads out of his pocket. 'I didn't activate either one of these.'

Jamie ran his hand through his hair. 'So let me get this straight. You were on the station platform, she was there with you, and…?'

'I was walking towards her and the other woman- who looked very much like Annamarie, so I think it was likely the great-grandmother. There was a child, too, she was maybe about three metres away, standing facing the train, with her back to us. Annamarie and the other woman had just walked to the back of the station platform. And then… pow.'

'Was there anything that seemed to trigger this?'

'Not really. The only thing I can think of is that Annamarie took hold of the other woman's hand. Then flash. Showtime.'

Jamie looked down at the floor, and then turned to his mother. 'Have you ever touched people in the past?'

'Yes.'

'With or without gloves?'

'I'd try not to touch them without gloves, but sometimes yes, I did. It would depend on what I was doing, and whether it would look odd. And I made sure I washed my hands a lot, with their horrible carbolic soap. It's strange… I felt something once when I first shook hands with Jim. Like a sort of a quick jolt. He felt it too, I could tell by the expression on his face. But that was it.'

Christian nodded. 'I shook hands with someone bare-handed a couple of hours ago. He was a distant relative;

met him by chance. It was a spontaneous thing. I didn't feel a jolt or anything, but… I know what you mean now, Fran. That thing should come with a mental health warning.'

Jamie frowned, turning to Fran. 'I guess you could have imagined the jolt and misinterpreted the expression on the other person's face. You already knew that this was the man who died young, yes?'

Fran nodded.

'…So, the firm evidence we have is that both of you touched people in the past with no ill-effect, but when Christian observed Annamarie make flesh to flesh contact with her great-grandmother, it seems to have caused something catastrophic to happen. What the hell can that be about?'

'Convergence transformation,' interjected NAMIS. 'Energy conversion.'

Jamie's mouth hung open for a moment. 'Matter and anti-matter? What are you talking about?'

'Not matter and anti-matter. Energy conversion through convergence transformation.'

'There's no such thing.'

NAMIS did not reply.

Jamie sighed. 'Did convergence transformation kill Annamarie Simons, NAMIS?'

Ellie began to cry.

The machine did not reply immediately, but the pattern of lights running across the display indicated that it was 'thinking'.

'What does it mean, Jamie?' asked Fran.

'It seems to be coming up with a physics I know nothing about,' replied Jamie. 'It's like someone asked Newton to do the relativity calculations. I don't…'

'Not Annamarie Simons,' interjected NAMIS, 'not Anna Rosenberg. Convergence transformation. Not in time, of time.'

They all stared at it.

'NAMIS,' said Fran carefully, 'are you saying that Annamarie Simons and Anna Rosenberg are the same *person*?'

'Negative.'

'So then, NAMIS,' continued Fran, 'there must be something about Annamarie Simons and Anna Rosenberg *together* that caused convergence transformation?'

'For God's sake mum,' snapped Jamie, 'this is wild speculation, there is no basis in…'

'Affirmative,' said NAMIS.

'OK,' replied Fran, 'what is it between those two people that caused convergence transformation?'

'Beyond parameters.'

'Might I meet someone in time who might cause convergence transformation with me?' Fran persisted.

'Affirmative.'

'But I just didn't?'

'Affirmative.'

'Is this a biological factor, NAMIS?' asked Christian.

The machine did not answer immediately. Lights flashed across its control panel, while data continued to scroll across the screen. The human beings held their breath.

'Likely.'

Ellie gasped. 'It's never said that before.'

Jamie stood up. 'Can we get Annamarie Simons back, NAMIS?'

'Negative.'

There was a brief silence in which Ellie's soft sobs were the only sound in the room.

Jamie walked across to the window and looked out across the rooftops of London. Fran stood by the machine, frozen like a statue. Christian sat slumped in a chair. Ellie stood next to the console, watching data still cascading across the screen, tears rolling down her cheeks.

Suddenly Jamie's phone sparked into life, ringing shrilly and vibrating against the desk. They all jumped.

ON TIME

"*Annamarie Mum*" lit up on the screen.

Fran: London, Thursday 8th January 2026, 10am

Fran, Jamie, Christian and Ellie sat hunched around the table in the laboratory. Christian, now hastily showered and dressed in his own clothing, had just finished giving the full account of his visit to Prague, 1939.

Jamie clicked off the recording device and turned to Fran. 'We'll have to do the same type of recording with you, Mum. I'm sorry, I didn't mean to bring any of you into this, but now we are all going to have to give formal statements at some point. Including NAMIS, in a manner of speaking. Linda - Annamarie's mother - will be speaking to the police in an hour or so. It's out of our hands. When they come to ask us what we know, we will have to tell the truth.'

'What did you tell her?' asked Christian.

'That we didn't know where Annamarie was, but that I will give a statement to the police about anything that might help, about the last time that we saw her and things like that. I didn't elaborate on the situation. I need to explain it to the Head of Faculty later today, and then I guess the police either directly after that, or maybe tomorrow. And to make things worse, Linda told me that her mother died yesterday evening.'

Fran groaned. 'Oh no! That's awful. Poor Linda.'

They sat in dejected silence for a few seconds, then Fran burst out: 'Rachel, it was Rachel who died. And of course, Rachel was the child. Oh my God, the child!'

They all turned to look at her.

'We're forgetting Rachel, the child who was left alone on the platform,' said Fran. 'The story that Christian told indicates that Annamarie and her great-grandmother "convergence transformed", whatever that means, and Christian was immediately thrown back here. What time was that, Christian?'

Christian looked at the counter on his phone, which had frozen at the point he had unexpectedly been thrown through the time portal. 'Where it's stopped would indicate that it was 9.02 in Prague at the time of the event. That seems about right'.

'And if I remember rightly, the train leaves at 9.30?'

Christian nodded.

'So that little girl was left standing on the edge of the platform at 9.02 with no one to look after her? You said that the mother and child walked onto the platform, and then Annamarie walked up to them?'

'Yes.'

Jamie looked at him thoughtfully. 'There are so many questions. Wouldn't anyone notice a flash of light like that?'

'There was no sound that I remember. And to be honest, everyone on that platform was in such a state of anxiety, they might not have noticed. They were all facing the train, watching their kids leaving in the knowledge that they might never see them again. The organisers had their hands full with it. It was like the seventh circle of Hell. The adults were all crying and shouting, a lot of the kids were screaming and some of the mothers were hysterical. I think there is an excellent chance that nobody noticed.'

'So, do you think anyone would put Rachel on the train, Christian?' asked Ellie.

'I don't know. I don't think if she wandered off to look for her mother that anyone would notice in that mayhem.'

Fran looked stricken. 'I have to go. I have to go to her. That child is all alone, on that platform with no one looking out for her. I have to go and…'

'Get blown out of time like Christian when Annamarie disappeared,' finished Jamie. 'How is that going to help anyone?'

Fran looked thoughtful. 'Jamie, you talk about "spacetime", right?'

'Yes.'

ON TIME

'So, let's follow that logic. If a time-traveller went through after the event that blew Christian back here, would they be able to remain in that time, and help the child to get onto the train?'

Jamie hesitated. 'You know, I might actually be able to work out just that element of the problem. Give me an hour.'

He picked up his laptop and walked into the tiny adjacent room that they used as a private office for student tutorials.

'What's he doing in plain English, please, Ellie?' asked Fran.

'He's taken the data from the point at which Christian arrived back here, to see if he can work out to some extent what type of surge threw him back, and whether we can calculate a safe window for someone going back in specifically to help the child.'

'Would they also have to be dropped so they didn't intersect with Christian at all?'

'Yes. What happened to Christian is part of his and our personal timelines now, so we can't interfere with that. It gets more and more complicated as it goes along.'

'So, the person going in would have to get from where they were dropped to enter the station after the convergence transformation event, but before the train leaves?'

'Yes. To be absolutely sure they'd have to arrive in the past after the convergence transformation event has happened. We can't risk the possibility that it might have an effect on any traveller, wherever they might be in that moment of spacetime. We always knew that there were issues bound up with travellers not being an integral part of the particular time and space that they were visiting. So, it's possible they'd get blown back even if they weren't standing right next to it, like Christian was.'

Christian groaned. 'I don't think I can take any more of this today, I really don't.'

'We might need you again today, though, Christian,' replied Ellie, worriedly, 'based on what Jamie decides.'

'Is there anywhere you can go and lay down for an hour or so, Christian?' asked Fran, rummaging in her handbag. Christian and Ellie watched as items rained across the table, brightly decorated glasses cases, pens, pencils, memory sticks, a few daily wear contact lens pods, a battered lipstick, a hair brush, several small packs of tissues and a grubby facemask.

'Oh, God that must have been in there for a while,' muttered Fran. 'Ah got it!'

She held up a small strip of pills, stuffing everything else back into the bag.

'I can go and lock myself in my poky office over in biology,' replied Christian. 'At least my room-mate is away on sabbatical at the moment. Why?'

Fran handed the strip of pills to Christian. He squinted at the markings on the foil.

'Diazepam? What are you doing with those?'

'I got them when Jamie's dad died. Only ever took one or two. Might be slightly out-of-date now. I just remembered I might have left a strip in one of the pockets of this bag.'

'Have you got a pill for everything?' asked Christian, grumpily.

Fran frowned at him. 'Gift horse. Mouth.'

Christian sighed. 'Just this once I think I might.'

He broke a pill off the strip and headed out of the lab.

'What about you, Ellie?' asked Fran. Ellie had been crying on and off since Christian's return.

'I wish I could. But I'll have to stay alert until we know what Jamie wants to do.'

Fran put her hand on Ellie's arm. 'I know you and Annamarie were close. I'm so sorry, Ellie. I'm sad, too, but it's not the same for me, I didn't work with her for so long like you did, I was just in and out over the past year or so.'

'That's the thing, I think. I was fond of her, I admired

her- she was brilliant, and her research was everything to her. She wasn't a one for socialising that much. She often used to be in here on her own at weekends, working. For her, everything was about her research.'

Fran thought of herself, staring at her PC screen for hours in the little 'office' she had in the house in Leeds, in the room that used to be Jamie's bedroom, Kylie at her feet. And then, in the years before that, at the same desk when it used to occupy a corner of the dining room. 'I think we're all a bit like that,' she said. 'It becomes a habit whilst you are doing a PhD, living in your research. I couldn't even drop it when I retired, just went on to the ancestry research. And of course, that led me to being the first historian ever who was offered the chance to do a practical investigation. Didn't turn out well, did it?' She felt tears prickling behind her eyes.

Ellie put her arm around Fran's shoulder. 'It was a big adventure for all of us. And I guess we'll all end up in the history books ourselves, Annamarie especially. She gave her life for the project.'

Fran sighed heavily. 'Yes, you're right, Ellie. But I think right now we are all going to have to answer a lot of difficult questions. Don't worry, we'll make sure that they know you are a student and that your part in this was only to do what Annamarie and Jamie told you to do. We'll made sure that any blame we get for this situation won't impact on you. I'll try to take the major responsibility. It might be Jamie and Annamarie's project, but I'm the most experienced academic here, and it was me who convinced them to let me use the machine to travel in time to further my research. Which was the start of it all.'

Ellie moved over to NAMIS. 'I'll give the machine a once over, make sure that it's ready for another trip.'

Then Fran suddenly realised: she had no 1930s clothes and wouldn't have time to go out to look for any. But a woman of her age might conceivably wear long, old fashioned dresses in the 1930s. And surely, people would not be paying any attention in the relevant situation. They'd apparently managed to get away with the popping out of spacetime of three people in a public place, after all.

She picked up her phone and looked at some of the history pages that they had used to inform Christian's trip. Nothing had changed on them. Although even if it had, she contemplated, would she remember, or would this change with the timeline? This way lies madness, she thought. There is nothing here about some type of incident on the platform of that Kindertransport. This is not *Quantum Leap*. She remembered with a pang that the last time she had thought of that quaint old show had been here in the laboratory with Annamarie and Christian, less than a year ago. So much had happened since then.

And now, she had so many questions about time for NAMIS, but she couldn't ask them yet, not while Ellie was working on it. She looked at the machine speculatively, wondering if it was possible to 'overtax' it. Its intelligence was very new and developing at a rate of knots. Like a child, she thought, a young child. She felt a creeping sadness that she would be unlikely to see her family in Sittingbourne ever again. But, she reflected, all that she and Annamarie had experienced indicated that the universe was not constructed so that people could travel in time, or at least, not until they had worked out the logistics of time travel in greater depth. Everything they did seemed to create problems.

But anyway, as things had worked out, she was going to take one more trip, albeit to a different destination. She flipped through the files that she had downloaded for Christian and scanned the account she had written for Rachel. She moved onto the street map of Prague in 1939. Fran had never been to Prague, but she was determined to find her way to the station from wherever they put her down. She was the only one in the team who knew how to deal with a frightened child.

She began to contemplate the voice file, the mystery of

ON TIME

how Annamarie was able to speak fluent Czech. Why would Annamarie make the arrangements for Rachel's transport to England with the charity workers? It didn't make any sense. Fran's research instincts began to kick in, putting together a picture of the past from incomplete information. The team seemed to have made the wrong interpretation of the evidence, she reflected. The term 'convergence transformation' buzzed around in her mind. So, there was something about Annamarie and Anna that was so similar- or even the same- that it caused some kind of reaction when flesh met flesh. Which should never have been able to happen, of course. We can't meet people who died before we were born, in the normal run of things. So if Annamarie and Anna were that similar- why couldn't they have the same voice? Suzi could surely never have done a voice pattern study that compared the voices of the living to the voices of the dead.

Jamie walked back into the lab. 'I think I've cracked that bit. There was some kind of localised event in spacetime that caused Christian to be thrown back here. In fact, his return pad *did* activate, in a similar fashion to the remote timers that we put on the animals that we sent into the past. It automatically triggered when the "convergence transformation" happened. Why the same thing didn't happen to Annamarie is a mystery. From what NAMIS said, it is likely to be something to do with her connection to Anna.'

'Affirmative' replied the machine.

'So,' Jamie continued, 'theoretically, if we send someone back into the past to arrive after the "convergence transformation" event, but before the train leaves, there shouldn't be any problem.'

'Affirmative.'

'Where would you put me down, Jamie?' asked Fran.

'Well now, we haven't decided that it's going to be you. But I think we'd have to aim for as close to the station as possible, in an area that the traveller is unlikely to be spotted. The station is in a densely populated area. So, it's a bit of a problem. Ellie, can you get that 1939 map of Prague up on the smartboard, please?'

The lab smartboard lit up.

'So, you sort this out while I pop back to the house and get my travelling clothes,' said Fran. 'They'll do.'

'You're not going, Mum. I am. It's too dangerous for you. You know I didn't want to put you in the machine in the first place. And I'm certainly not sending you into a Nazi occupied country. Ellie is already working on mocking up a 1930s British passport for me. It won't take long; she's amending the details on the document we created for Christian. We gave him a 1930s British passport with his mother's family name when he went through; it was the safer option.'

Ellie watched mother and son lock eyes across the table. She thought how amused Annamarie would be to observe yet another episode in (what they had been calling between themselves) "Game of Thrones." She felt an urge to both laugh and cry at the same time.

'I'm going to the *child*, Jamie,' Fran insisted, haughtily. 'There is no one else here who knows how to deal with a frightened child.'

'All we need to do is just put her on the train. Any one of us could do it.'

'She needs someone to speak to her, to soothe her, not just pick her up like a parcel and move her.'

'And what are you going to say, eh? Lo, I am the Archangel Fran, come through time to put you on this train because your mother has popped out of spacetime because my son made an unfortunate error, so sorry, but normal service will be resumed? And she doesn't speak English yet, anyway, any more than you speak Czech.'

'Don't be so- cross, Jamie. Alright, I know you're upset, we all are. But that poor little girl. She must be so frightened.'

'We don't know that she saw her mother disappear.

ON TIME

Chances are she was looking at the fuss going on immediately around her instead; Christian said she had her back to the incident. And I think if she had seen her mother disappear in a flash of light, Annamarie might have mentioned it to you, in your conversations about the Kindertransport? It would seem like a big detail.'

Fran thought back to the first conversation that she'd had with Annamarie about the situation, when she'd dropped into the lab in the early days of the project. 'We were talking about me being a children's historian when we first met. Then Annamarie said that her grandma had a good children's history story because she had come to England on the Kindertransport. And that she didn't remember much about it, apart from that she'd always been sad because she hadn't said goodbye to her mother properly; things got confused at the station. She'd got lost in the crowd somehow…' she stopped.

Freddie's voice flashed into her head: *"Don't run, Franny…let Jamie do it. Because you can't run fast enough."* Whoever went to Prague now might indeed have to run, and besides that…

'…and she said a man she had never met before put her on the train,' she concluded, reluctantly.

'So, that's it then, I'm going. And that's good news actually. Looks like I might succeed.'

'Jamie,' said Ellie, 'doesn't this open up a whole new possibility, that what we are doing here might actually be somehow woven into a cohesive timeline already? It might shed some light on how the calculations don't make the clear difference that you thought they would between past and present.'

Fran nodded. 'And, if past and present are fused like that, maybe the future isn't. It's not been woven yet, hence we can't access it. The moving finger thing, you know?'

Ellie frowned. 'Mmmm, but if it was tied on that we were going to interfere in the past in the way that we have done, then that was something we couldn't avoid doing, wasn't it? So in 1939, something in the future *was* determined.'

Jamie shook his head. 'I don't know. That area of physics is yet to be created. It will be the work of a lifetime, and I can't even begin to think about it at the moment. NAMIS has already thrown everything that I think I know into question. But anyway, I'll worry about that when I get back.' He looked at the clothes that Christian had thrown over the back of one of the chairs. 'I think Christian and I are close enough in size for me to get away with wearing these. Right, so let's have a look at that map, now, Ellie.'

Fran looked at him uneasily. She didn't want her son in a war zone. Jim's face popped into her mind, the young man who had lost his life to a minor illness. Why did she always put these two together like this? She'd got Jim's death certificate from the ancestry website a few weeks ago and discussed it with Christian. Nana Mo always said that the doctor had given Jim too much morphia, but when Christian looked at the cause of death he said that it was one hundred per cent certain that Jim would have died anyway, given the lack of treatment available at that time, the doctor was just sparing him a few hours of distress.

How do we arrive at these events, wondered Fran? Are there 'eddies' in time, like whirlpools in water? And might that somehow tie up with what a "sensitive" like Freddie seemed to know somehow, without an adult capacity to understand a situation under normal circumstances?

Jamie's voice broke into her thoughts: 'Mum, could you go and get Christian please, wake him up gently? We've decided on a plan of action, and we need him to program my DNA into the return pad. It's time for me to go.'

Jamie: Prague, 2nd August 1939, 9.05am

Jamie stepped into the light, sounds, smells and colours of another time. A back alley in Prague, 2nd August 1939, 9.05

am, half a kilometre from the station. He looked around cautiously, no one around-except- oh, there was an old guy, who had stopped drinking from the bottle he was holding to stare wide eyed at Jamie. Jamie stared back. He remembered something Christian had once said to Fran. 'If anyone is going to spot you popping in and out of time, hope it is going to be a drunk or a small child, because no one ever believes anything they say.'

The old guy said something to him in Czech. Oh, sod it, thought Jamie. 'Lo I am the Archangel Jamie Mac, come to announce...' he stopped. There wasn't anything he could announce on this day, in this place, that anyone probably wanted to hear, even if it was in a language they didn't understand. 'Whatever,' he concluded, 'have a nice day'. He bowed and walked away, feeling a strange euphoria. Just being out of the lab, away from being at the wheel of that speeding juggernaut of a project was a surprising relief. And he had introduced himself as 'Jamie Mac', the name that his undergraduate friends had jokingly appended to him when they first saw everyone's full name on a lab group list. It was a much more Christian-like than Jamie-like thing to do.

He looked around again - no one else in sight. He looked down at his phone, hidden in his pocket, upon which he had downloaded the old map. No Google Maps for about 70 years he thought. He checked his route. He should have plenty of time to get there, walking at a steady pace.

As he got into the main streets of Prague, he found, like Christian, that he was not proceeding as quickly as he hoped. He moved as carefully as he could in and out of groups of people. He reflected upon what had happened to Czechoslovakia over the last few months, having scanned Fran's notes. In early March 1939, the Slovak separatists had declared their independence and signed up to an alliance with the Nazis. Emil Hácha, the Czech president pleaded with Hitler to allow the Czech people to remain neutral. He was told that what was left of his nation had been designated as the 'region of Bohemia and Moravia' and that he had one of two choices: either sign a treaty that brought that region under the 'protection' of Nazi Germany, or to prepare for Prague to be attacked and occupied. He had reluctantly chosen the former.

The first Kindertransport had taken place by air on the day before the Nazi invasion. Seven further transports had then been arranged by rail; Rachel had left on the last of these. By early September, Britain and Germany would be at war. In the end, the initiative transported six hundred and sixty-nine Czechoslovakian children to England to start new lives with foster families. Rachel was in the last cohort; she had escaped only just in time. And now, to ensure that she was safely sent on her way, Jamie had to make sure she was on that train in less than half an hour.

A Nazi soldier suddenly stepped into Jamie's path. 'Občanský průkaz?' he barked.

Jamie stared. What the hell did that mean? 'Pardon?' he said, racking his brains for the very sparse Czech that he knew. 'Promiňte?'

'Personalausweis… Reisepass. Britisch?'

Jamie fumbled out the fake passport. 'Yes… Ano…Ja. British.'

The soldier looked at it. 'Universitätslehrer?'

'Yes… Ja. Visit to the university.'

The soldier nodded. 'Wann gehen fahren sie zurück nach England?'

'Going home? Later today…er.. gehen… um… heute.'

The soldier handed the passport back to him 'Sehr gut.'

Jamie pocketed the passport. 'Danke schön. Thank you.'

The soldier waved him on. He already had his eye on a group of men on the other side of the road.

Jamie walked on, feeling adrenaline flooding his body. He'd managed to stay calm in the moment. But what if the soldier had told him to turn out his pockets? He looked

ON TIME

down at the phone in his pocket, counting down the minutes. Now he would have to run. He looked over to make sure that the soldier was otherwise occupied, walked as quickly as he could until no soldiers were in sight, and then started to jog. As he dodged in and out of the crowd, drawing on his old rugby skills, he briefly wondered whether the soldier would have stopped his mother. He doubted if she could have jogged through the crowds in the way that he was doing now. She couldn't run as fast, and she'd never played rugby. And she couldn't orient herself using a map to save her life.

He jogged into the station, looking at the count down on the phone in his pocket. 9.15. He'd made it on time. He knew what platform he had to go to, but even if he hadn't, he would have been able to follow the noise. He shouldered his way through the crowd. Rachel, the little girl was called Rachel. As he drew close to the edge of the platform, he saw her. All the other children were with parents, crying, hugging, being put onto the train, jumping off and being put back on again. And there was this one little girl with a label around her neck, standing alone, clutching her suitcase. Tears were rolling down her cheeks.

He crouched down so they were eye to eye. He'd seen his mother and sisters do this with the boys when they were upset. 'Rachel?' he said.

The child looked at him. Annamarie's serious brown eyes, he thought. He felt tears rising. He swallowed. 'Rachel. I'm Jamie, and I'm here to put you on the train. It will be OK. You're going to go to England, and you're going to be fine.'

Rachel gulped. 'Mama?'

Jamie swallowed again, hard. 'Mama had to go, Rachel. She didn't want to, but she had to. I'll put you on the train.'

He looked up. Most of the children were on the train now, and he could see the guard looking up and down the platform. He spotted an older girl of maybe thirteen or fourteen standing at an open train door window. He picked Rachel up and handed her to the girl. Rachel began to cry harder.

'Look after her please- prosím?' said Jamie to the girl. 'Děkuju.'

The girl looked back at him and nodded, solemnly. Jamie handed Rachel's suitcase to a younger boy standing next to the girl. He took it and placed it on the rack. The whistle blew. The train started to move slowly. Rachel was still crying, but she had stopped struggling. She looked back at Jamie.

'You'll be fine, Rachel, I promise. There will be people to love you, and you'll have a lovely long life.'

The train began to pick up speed. Rachel kept her eyes on Jamie. Then, to his surprise, she waved. Instinctively he waved back. 'Goodbye Rachel. You're on your way now.'

The train had left the platform. So, thought Jamie, everything is as it should be now. Except for the fact Rachel's mother and granddaughter are now permanently MIA, convergence transformed, whatever that is. He looked around, shocked and horrified at the scene unfolding around him. Mothers and fathers were weeping, sitting on the ground; two women who had fainted were being held up and fanned, and a grey haired grandmother was walking up and down the platform weeping, saying 'moje dítě … moje dítě' over and over again.

And this is only Act One, he thought grimly. He walked out of the station and turned towards Klánovice-Čihadla, to find a place he could return to the lab, unobserved. At any other time, he would have been looking around, eagerly taking in everything. It was, after all, his first trip in time. But the whole world around him seemed grey, bleak and hopeless. He thrust his hands deeply into the pockets of his coat, fingering his phone and return pad. He wanted to get home, to get away from this time, this place and the army who had come to kill, come to subjugate; the military machine that had robbed

ON TIME

him of his colleague and his friend Annamarie.

A large, shiny Mercedes Benz filled with men in Nazi uniforms drove slowly past. Jamie watched them with an icy anger burning in his chest. Monsters, he thought, who had, in effect, turned Annamarie into the last British casualty of World War II. Or the first. Whichever way a time travelling culture eventually chose to look at it. 'Fuck the past,' he said, out loud. He looked down at the dusty cobbles beneath his feet, wanting to be under a different sky, in a different world, and increased his pace to a brisk jog, wishing to be gone as soon as possible, to be anywhere but here.

He heard the car squeal to a halt behind him. He turned around and saw, in the distance, men getting out. The one wearing the fanciest uniform looked towards him, angrily yelling something in German. Bloody hell, I must have been glaring at them, he thought. He hadn't considered that he should guard the expressions on his face as, now, too late he reflected, those who lived under occupation must learn to do. A young teenage memory suddenly jumped into his mind: being taken by his mother to see a production of one of those 1970s biblical musicals (it being one of her favourite shows) and finding it all rather dated and corny. But the concept that now came steaming into his mind was the 'occupied by the Romans' narrative, which *had* interested him slightly.

Too bloody late he thought. You should have reflected on all of this before you leaped, you utter pillock. He thought of his mother, poring over book after book about late nineteenth century Presbyterianism, in preparation for her visits to her family in time. What would she do if he didn't come back? An image of her popped into his mind's eye, striding into the time portal dressed in her Victorian travelling clothes, intent on doing battle with the whole damn Third Reich until she found him. Running at full speed now, without looking back, he ducked into a narrow street to his left, and pushed at the door of the first building he came to. Locked. He could hear German voices behind him, and the clop, clop of heavy boots running. He darted over the road to a shop, banged through the door and ran directly behind the counter, into the back room.

He stood there panting for a moment, stunned by the fact that the people in the shop, including those behind the counter, had paid no attention whatsoever to him, and continued to go about their business as if nothing had happened. Another thing you apparently learn about under occupation he thought, grimly. He pushed at the back door, and found himself standing in a small, grubby back yard, next to some foul-smelling dustbins. The German voices were growing louder. He heard someone crash open the door of the shop, yelling in a mixture of German and Czech. He pressed the button on the return pad.

The portal on the Time Machine materialised around him.

'Hello Jamie' said Fran, who was sitting waiting for him. 'Did you manage to put Rachel on the train?'

Jamie grimaced at her. 'Yes, everything's fine.'

'You look like the hounds of hell were after you.'

To Fran's obvious surprise, he gave her shoulder a brief squeeze. 'I guess they were after all of us. But it's OK now. I got there on time.'

Ellie: London, Thursday 8th January 2026, 11am

Jamie slumped dejectedly in his chair in the lab, still dressed in the vintage clothes.

'So it's over, then Jamie,' said Ellie. 'The time travelling, I mean'.

'Yes. You'll need to put NAMIS on pause once we've all given our statements. Unfortunately, its main purpose will be as a source of evidence now. No doubt they will take the project out of my hands.'

ON TIME

'What are you going to do now, then?'

'I'm going to ask to see the Head of Faculty to tell him everything.'

Christian smiled wryly. 'Good luck with getting that moron to understand that, first time around.'

'Don't. What other choice do I have? I've put the university in a very difficult position. I'm expecting him to go to the police once he gets the picture. Which means we will have to give statements to both the police and the university. When I got back, I had a missed call from Linda. So I just rung her back. She said that the police aren't inclined to do anything about Annamarie until Monday, when she will have been missing for a week. So I have that much time to make the university aware.'

Fran walked over and put her hand on Jamie's shoulder. 'In the end, Annamarie took the decision to do what she did, Jamie. You didn't use the project to follow a personal agenda. If anyone else did that, it was me. And I can help you to explain that.'

Ellie sat down on the chair next to Jamie. 'Jamie, I've got an idea. I think I can sort NAMIS's logs to make it look like we were just moving stuff in space like we were originally supposed to do. I can take you, Fran and Christian out of the record altogether. And we can tell everyone that Annamarie was alone in the lab during the holidays - as ever - and that at some point, she must have decided to make herself the first human passenger, but she never came out the other end. And to a great extent, that's what happened - isn't it?'

Fran frowned. 'But NAMIS knows. It's got a memory of what happened.'

'We built it, Mum,' replied Jamie. 'It will only access that for me, Ellie or Annamarie, on our voice activation. Ellie is right. The logs would be the deepest anyone else could go.'

Christian looked pensive. 'We were worried that people associated with the government would weaponise it. The joke is, what we never saw coming was that we would so effectively weaponise it against ourselves.'

Jamie nodded. 'Agreed. Which makes it all the more dangerous. And better left between ourselves - I suppose.'

'I've been working on getting NAMIS to transport stuff only through space, rather than space and time,' said Ellie. 'And I've started to have some successes. Annamarie and I have been working on that for a while. It would still have the time travel capacity; it would just have two "settings" if you see what I mean.'

Fran grinned ruefully. 'Like defrost or cook on a microwave?'

'Yes. Although it's a lot more complicated of course. The thing is, I'm confident that I can make the record look like Annamarie just tried to transport herself across space, not spacetime, and that she never came back. That will be reflected by the log on that last journey, an outward-bound trip that wasn't followed by a return. I'm sure they'll investigate that. Jamie will then have time to work on the data we've built up from the time travel aside from the main project, and if we are allowed to go on with the project, we can send back the reports to the funding body about the work we are doing on the basic matter transporter you committed to on the project proposal. We could take the time travel stuff forward to another project, if and when we are ready.'

Jamie looked at the floor. 'But we'd be essentially lying to Linda - Annamarie's mother- about what happened to her daughter. Also, given that her own mother has very recently died- I'd feel really bad about that.'

Fran knotted her brows. 'Hmmm. I think maybe what we have to consider is which story Linda would do better with? The one that involves her daughter and grandmother disappearing from spacetime in a flash, like a scene in a bad sci-fi movie, and a machine that won't commit itself on whether they are dead or not, or a simple accident with an experimental piece of technology? I don't know her, obviously, but when I met her a couple of days ago, she didn't seem like the type of person who dealt with difficult situations particularly well.'

Ellie sighed. 'I think, from different things that I have heard over the years, that Annamarie's mum had a bit of a problem with her coming out. You know, with her sexuality. One of my friends speculated that maybe that was why Annamarie struggled to make close relationships with people, why she got so into her research, to the exclusion of everything else.'

'And maybe why she got so focused on her grandmother's past?' Fran replied. 'That would relate to people who belonged to her in an uncomplicated way. It's a temptation when you are a little…' she bit her lip, 'lonely.'

Jamie looked around the group. 'If we do play it this way, then we all have to be in. And I'll need to tell Suzi. I'm sure that she will support us in whatever we decide. Or she'll come up with some other type of idea if she spots a problem. So, what do you all think? Do you all want to do this? Shall I ask her to come over now?'

They all looked at each other for a moment, turned to Jamie and said, almost in unison: 'yes.'

VOICES

Fran: London, Sunday 11th January 2026

Fran sat in the silent house, Kylie snoring at her feet. Sleet floated past the windows. One constant from her childhood days, she thought, was that it never snowed properly in London. She had been going to take Kylie for a long walk today, to "blow away the cobwebs" as her parents' generation used to say; but now this, the type of snowy-rain that made people - and dogs - very wet, and both she and Kylie had a bit of arthritis in various places that didn't do well in damp weather. Better for both of them to stay in the warm.

She looked around the comfortable, shabby living room, thinking that if she and Rich could have afforded a little house like this, they might never have moved north. But she was forgetting that Jamie and Suzi were now more than a decade older than she and Rich were when they first became parents. And fitting three children into a house like this would have been impossible. Cozy for a couple and a regular visitor with a small dog, but not big enough for a family.

Fran was glad that Jamie and Suzi hadn't got around to decorating yet. She found the shabbiness comforting. It was as though it might have been her house, long ago, when the children- and she- were younger, and Rich was still around. And her mother, still sound of mind and inevitably complaining about the weather. And… oh, don't go down that road, she thought, or it's going to be a depressing day.

Jamie had expected the issues at uni to move faster than they had. He had seen the Head of Faculty for a short meeting on Thursday afternoon and been told not to talk to anyone outside the project team about the situation, or in fact to do anything about it until next week. He was asked to submit a brief report about it by Friday 5pm, so he, Christian and Ellie had spent all day on Friday working on that. And now, they had to wait until tomorrow at 11am, when Jamie had his next appointment with the Faculty boss. Fran had a lot of experience with Faculty bosses. Whatever was going to go down, she knew it was not going to be calculated on what was best for the research or for the people involved, but what was best for the university's finances and reputation. Jamie's boss was a business manager first and foremost, like all university management nowadays. She sighed. Don't go down that road, either she thought; yet more depressing memories.

Jamie and Suzi had taken themselves off over the weekend to visit friends in the Yorkshire Dales who knew nothing about the project, to get a proper break before the next lot of shit hit the fan. Still unsure of whether she would be asked for any input to the ongoing investigations, Fran decided to stay in London over the weekend, maybe do some shopping and walking. And of course, she had done neither. A half-hearted visit to Hamley's on Saturday to look for some small things for the boys (she imagined Niamh sighing when she turned up with a big Hamley's bag: 'they got enough over Christmas, mother!') Then she got on the tube train back to the house, watched Netflix and dozed on the sofa. Shopping for 'stuff' didn't seem to have the same appeal anymore. And she was overtaken by a strange exhaustion, the stress of the previous week, probably.

And now - a snow day. She looked at the silent television. Not going there, she thought. Let's do something useful instead. She turned on her laptop and opened her ancestry files. Maybe try to integrate the stuff she had written about her trips to Sittingbourne- in the style of a novel- into the material that she had created from the archival research. She flipped between the files aimlessly, her mind wandering. Having now met the people concerned, even without another trip in time, she had a much better idea of why the two sides of her grandmother Mo's family had never spoken after Jim died. A different world, and a different culture. She thought of the dry church services she had sat through, the fixation on sin, the concept of predestination. And Izza's father, William Burns, as one of the big spiders in the middle of that particular web; venerated local businessman, Conservative councillor and Church Elder. And, as 1890 turned into 1891, the father of an unmarried, pregnant daughter, which wouldn't have suited him at all.

Fran had been planning to space her visits across Izza's pregnancy in an attempt to observe how events unfolded. And would you have been able to avoid interfering in that, without the Annamarie experience, she thought contemplatively. Probably not. So, it's a good thing that travel to the past is now closed to you.

She browsed through her notes, her thoughts turning to William Burns, standing in the church hall, gazing speculatively around his congregation (and electorate) with his icy blue eyes. What a way to behave towards a young, vulnerable mother and her children, thought Fran. She had spent her life as a historian, striving to understand the past, disapproving of non-historians' anachronisms, their lack of understanding of the past as "a different country." But still she could not forgive Burns' behaviour towards his eldest daughter. Another case of things being different when it relates to your own family, she thought.

Fran looked at some of her earliest ancestry notes, summarising what Mo had told her children and grandchildren about her father's early death, emphasising the plight of Izza as a young widow with two tiny daughters, in a world without any state provision other than the workhouse and the orphanage. First of all, Mo and her younger sister, Victoria had been cared for by their kind grandmother, Polly, but then when Mo was four, Polly had fallen down the stairs and died from her injuries.

Fran pictured the steep staircase she had seen when she made the brief visit to the shop in modern Sittingbourne last year. She shuddered, imagining the already harassed Polly she had met, but after five more years had passed: an over-worked woman in her mid-forties, now with three small children to care for, wearing those long dragging skirts and the infernal corset that had made Fran gasp for breath. There would have been a call from her stern husband to go downstairs *right now*, the shop was busy, and then….

Fran vaguely remembered Mo's maiden Aunt Bea, who had taken over the care of the family's children when Polly died: Mo, Victoria and Polly's youngest two, Rose who had been just twelve and Alfie, nearly five. The children were raised under a regime of terror from then on, their cold, domineering grandfather on one side and Bea, a harsh and frequently angry disciplinarian on the other. Strangely, Bea had been very kind to Fran during their only meeting, when Fran was a small girl and the whole family had attended Bea's ninetieth birthday celebrations. She had asked Fran to sit next to her and given her a strange sweet that tasted of violets, admiring 'Franny's beautiful blue eyes, just like *my* father's.' Fran could see Mo standing behind Bea, and was part puzzled, part amused by the fact that her usually dignified grandmother was scowling at the back of Bea's head, her hazel-green eyes flashing in the manner of an angry teenager.

A few years later, when Mo and Fran were watching an old Oliver Twist film on TV on a rainy afternoon, Mo confided to Fran that she had felt rather like a Dickensian orphan herself when she was Fran's age. Mo had explained that while it was clear Bea was generally resentful about being given the job of caring for her parents' and sister's young children, she seemed to have a particular grudge against Mo: '*she always seemed to enjoy being particularly nasty to me, I always seemed to be the one who got told I was lucky I hadn't been sent to the orphanage.*' Mo and her sister Victoria always looked forward to the times that their mother was able to stay at home with them, Mo reminisced, but these were rare, because Izza worked in hotels across the south coast in the summer and in London in the winter, sending money home to pay for Mo and Victoria. Mo had seen Bea counting this out when she did the household accounts, and this arrangement continued until Izza remarried in 1906, taking her girls to live with her and their new stepfather, a childless widower who owned a hotel in Portsmouth.

Mo had moved down from London, where she had been sent by her grandfather at fourteen to become a live-in apprentice at a large London department store, whilst Victoria had relocated from Sittingbourne to continue her schooling in Portsmouth. The idea at the time, Mo explained to Fran, was that she would return to school, but she hadn't really wanted to. So, in the end, she'd helped her mother in the hotel until she married in 1914, then the following month, the first world war had begun. Victoria and Mo had gravitated towards sharing a flat in London whilst Mo's husband Tom was in France. Mo had got a job in a London department store, answering the call for married women to replace men in the national economy and Victoria, at that time still unmarried, was teaching in a London infants school.

Mo had explained to Fran that she was much happier living in her stepfather's hotel than she had been in Sittingbourne, and that she had enjoyed helping out there, describing her stepfather to Fran as good natured and slightly eccentric. Her mother was the organising force behind the hotel, and now as the owner's wife she was in her element.

ON TIME

'She wasn't mean like Bea. But she was starchy; a real stickler for detail, obsessed with being "proper." Things always had to be just right for her.'

Fran plugged a memory stick into her PC, selected a file and listened intently to Izza's bubbly voice. She was talking with Fran and Polly in the church hall, enthusing about the dresses that she and her sisters were making. She didn't sound as though she had a care in the world, thought Fran. She tried to picture Izza as a young mother, the situation in which she had found herself just over a year after that conversation.

Fran had now deduced that Izza's fixation on her daughters and granddaughters behaving like 'ladies' (which had been related to her by both Nana Mo and Aunt Adi) was most likely to have been an attempt to prevent them from sharing Izza's own fate as a disgraced, unmarried pregnant teenager. Fran wondered what Izza would have made of Charlie. Mo's attitude to Charlie's hippie phase and pre-marital pregnancy was now making a lot more sense. Mo had spawned in a very different time, where she had bitter, first-hand experience of the way that women and children's lives were blighted by such events.

The part that Fran still couldn't put together properly was if, when and how Mo had discovered the background to her own birth, and why she had given her son, Fran's father, the name of the dead father and grandfather who had played no part in her upbringing. Fran felt that she now had sufficient evidence to support her hypothesis that following Jim's death, Burns must have determined to cut the MacIntoshes off, and to deal with the situation in his own way- sending Izza out to work off her 'debt', both in the financial and spiritual sense.

But Mo's decision to name her son after the MacIntoshes was still somewhat of a mystery. Was it an attempt to send a message to the Burns side of the family that she was proud of her MacIntosh heritage, and rejected the unforgiving culture within which she had spent her childhood, as firmly as she'd rejected the religious faith in which they had raised her? In Fran's own memory, Mo had made no secret of her objection to any type of organised religion, vaguely citing the 'hypocrisy' of some unnamed members of her childhood family as the reason for this. When Fran once asked her for more of that story, Mo had replied firmly *'it's over and done. It happened many years before you were born. And I've let it go.'* And even though Fran had only just been ten at the time, she had intuited that she was not going to get any more than that.

But did she ever really let it go, mused Fran. Even when Fran was a child, Mo still seemed so sad about her father's death even though more than seventy years had passed, and she admitted to having no conscious memories of him. Which is why I made that promise to call any son of mine after her father, too, thought Fran. It was a nice name, anyway, and it kept the Scottish heritage alive. Plus, my Dad was chuffed having his grandson named after him. But the main reason that Jamie was given that name was to honour Jim, as I promised Nana Mo when I was little. Who, incredibly, I ended up meeting in real life.

As the snow thickened outside, Fran tapped away at her laptop. The resulting document began to unfold as a rough draft that looked more and more like the first chapter of a novel: Fran's now more informed guesses at what might have happened from the time Izza realised that she must be pregnant up to the time of Mo's birth, and how this played out in both families, the Presbyterian community, and the sleepy little Victorian town that Fran would never visit again.

Suzi: London, Monday 12th January 2026, 11am

There was a knock at the door of Suzi's office.
'Come in.'
Fran popped her head around the door.

ON TIME

'Fran, come in, sit down. Are you like me, can't focus on anything while Jamie is in being grilled?'

'Yes. And I wanted to chat with you about something. Can we back track to the voice mystery, you know, Annamarie speaking fluent Czech on the voice file?'

'I guess we'll never solve that one. It's a shame, but at least it's one thing we don't have to deal with urgently.'

'I'm still sort of processing it. What are the chances of two different people getting a 100% voice print match?'

'Zero. Voice prints are like fingerprints, specific to the individual. It's not about accents, or anything like that. It's a more fundamental pattern at a deeper level.'

'So, then that has to be Annamarie speaking? Or might there be another basis from which we might look at the question?'

'What other basis could there be?'

'I'm not sure. But I've got a chain of deduction going on in my head that I wanted to discuss with you, if you've got a few minutes.'

Suzi, leant her elbows on her desk. 'OK. It will take our minds off what's going on at the moment. What were you thinking?'

'So, long explanation to start with: history is all about putting fragments of diverse evidence together to try and create a complete picture. Sometimes, when a significant piece of evidence is missing, you end up creating the wrong picture, or at least, a subtly different picture to the actual events. There's always some amount of informed guesswork in history, and the further back you go, the more you have to guess. For example, once when I was working in an archive, I became convinced that the person concerned was suffering from dementia in the last few years of her life. The way that she wrote started to change. It made me think of my mother…'

'Yes, of course. Linguistics also has its own branch of this type of deduction. For example, people who can read Ancient Egyptian don't know how it sounded as a spoken language; the way it was written was not entirely phonetic. So, if we ever met an Ancient Egyptian- which of course we know is now a possibility- we couldn't immediately speak to him. We'd have to match the written word to the spoken and learn how it translated into speech sounds.'

'I did manage to follow my trail to some extent. And I found out that the person concerned had died in a psychiatric hospital. There were also letters from her friends in the archive saying things like 'take a good long rest and pull yourself together a little.' It seems that they thought she was having a nervous breakdown. I tried to track the medical records down, but the hospital told me that they had been destroyed sometime in the Second World War. So, then that was it. No one alive who remembered her, and no records. So, I can't come up with the proof. There would also have been an active effort to cover up her illness, too. There was a stigma attached to any type of mental illness, going forward even to the middle of the twentieth century. So... what I have done with respect to the Annamarie situation is put together some similarly incomplete information to come up with a hypothesis.'

Suzi smiled as Fran knotted her brows, just as Jamie did when he was working on a difficult equation. 'Which is?'

'We know that Annamarie was taking Czech lessons. But we also know from Christian that she was not finding them easy. We know that the woman on the voice file spoke fluent Czech with a Prague accent. I did some googling. What I found was that it is next to impossible that an adult learning a new language would start to speak in a discernable local accent. There might be inflections on words if they had learned it from someone who had a strong accent of this type, but Annamarie was taking an online course, which used a computer-generated voice- I checked.'

'I wondered if her grandmother had taught it to her

from childhood?'

Fran shook her head. 'She told both Christian and I that her grandmother had forgotten how to speak Czech. And Linda, the mother, told me that neither she nor Annamarie had ever been to Prague. She said 'because…' and then she stopped as though there was something she didn't want to elaborate on. Does that sound to you like a family who would be speaking the language easily, regularly, at a frequency where a child could learn it to the level where she spoke it fluently with a strong regional accent? Even Christian, who was regularly exposed to Czech as a child, speaks it with a slight English accent. And…' she offered Suzi a notebook, 'I found this under the printouts in Annamarie's desk drawer.'

Suzi took it and flicked through the pages. 'Oooh. Grammar exercises. And she's not finding it easy, is she?'

'So, there's my evidence. And my interpretation is that Annamarie didn't speak fluent Czech; that the person on that voice file is Anna. She would, in the normal run of things, have been the one to make the arrangements for Rachel to leave Prague on the Kindertransport, not Annamarie. It's sort of Sherlock Holmes stuff, getting rid of the impossible to make sure that the picture you are left with, even if it seems improbable, must be nearer to the truth. It was impossible for Annamarie to speak fluent Czech with a Prague accent, therefore our interpretation must be in error somehow. And then I wondered, have you ever compared voiceprints of people who are living, with people who are dead?'

'No. We only used voices of the living. We were looking for a way to log-in to a Smart Phone by voice so that was all we needed to do.'

'Maybe we need to do that further investigation?'

'OK. It's a good point.'

'And we need also to bring in this idea of "convergence transformation." It seems there was something very similar about Annamarie and Anna, and that was what created the event that caused them to disappear and blew Christian out of time. What if one of the things that they shared, that was not just similar, but the same, was the voice?'

Suzi stared down at the desk for a moment. 'It's a theory. But I don't know how we can take this forward, because we don't have any other comparisons.'

'Oh, yes we do.'

'What…' replied Suzi. Then she stopped. 'Ohhh.'

'Yes.'

And then they said in unison 'Jim and Jamie.'

Jamie: London, Monday 12th January 2026, 11.30 am

Jamie finally finished speaking. His throat was as dry as a bone. He took a sip of water and looked at the clock. A whole thirty minutes had ticked by since he started to present the report that he, Christian and Ellie had submitted on Friday.

His boss, Professor Sam Wiseman, had listened attentively, having read the report over the weekend. Underneath his calm exterior, he was hoping that he had understood enough of it to appear scientifically competent to this bright Young Turk. He was however very sure that he understood the business implications.

Jamie looked back at a small man sitting behind a large desk that made him look like a strangely aged child. That was worse than my viva, he thought. Unlike his PhD thesis, the account he had just presented was full of obfuscations, and that made him very uncomfortable. He sat, grimly expectant, waiting for the onslaught.

The only thing I am glad about, thought Jamie, is that this version of events puts Annamarie in a better light than the whole unvarnished truth would have done. The report he, Ellie and Christian had co-written did not attribute any personal motives to Annamarie at all. She came out as a heroic scientist, who had taken a gamble with her own life to progress their joint research and had then perished because it had been a step too far.

An image popped into Jamie's head of a scene that had scared him as a young child- the fraudulent Wizard of Oz, revealed to be behind the curtain by a small dog that looked exactly like their present pet, Kylie. The great illusionist, yeah, that's me, he thought. But the illusion is backwards. I really *am* Oz, the great and terrible; Death the destroyer of worlds, whatever. I've had to become a fraud in order to pretend *not* to be.

'So let me get this straight, Jamie,' said Wiseman. 'It sounds like your research has been a rip-roaring success.'

Jamie felt his mouth drop open. I didn't expect much from you, given that you stopped studying science after your BSc Physics and then went on to a masters and PhD in Business Management, he thought. But my God, never in a million years would I have guessed…

'Well yes, we're managing to transport things, if that's what you mean. Inanimate objects and plants. But it's now clear that there are going to be some problems with animate biological organisms.' This much is certainly true with respect to people, Jamie reflected. We just haven't been specific about what the problems *are*.

Wiseman smiled back at him. Bastard, thought Jamie. A woman is missing, presumed dead, and all you can say is that the project is a rip-roaring success. In fact, you look like you are almost salivating.

'Why do you think she did it?'

'I don't fully understand. I think maybe she wanted to do something for the advancement of science, that no one had ever done before.'

Ellie had now found another set of data wiped from the logs but still present in NAMIS's memory. It showed that Annamarie had made what looked like a modified return pad for someone she had labelled "AR." They had been unable to find the DNA trace that she had used to create the data record, which had been a disappointment to Christian. But the label was clear enough. AR- Anna

Rosenberg. Annamarie had intended to bring her great-grandmother literally "back to the future." The team had taken this as yet more evidence of the dangerous impact of time-travel capability upon human emotions.

Wiseman smiled sagely. 'Scientists! We're all the same, aren't we? We get carried away with the research and take crazy risks.'

What have you ever risked, apart from maybe a punt on the stock exchange? thought Jamie. He looked down at the plush carpet, hoping that his deep disgust wasn't showing on his face again. He was beginning to understand how his mother had developed the attitudes that she had, after so many years of dealing with people like this man.

'So, the mother has been to the police?' Wiseman continued.

'Yes. They weren't inclined to treat it seriously until today. I've told her that I'm intending to give a full statement to the police, if and when it is required. And I'm intending to do that as soon as possible. She deserves to know what happened to Annamarie, particularly as her own mother- Annamarie's grandmother- died last Wednesday.'

'Oh, that's a terrible shame,' replied Wiseman, with poorly disguised lack of interest.

'It was only on Thursday morning that we discovered Annamarie's DNA in the machine log and her clothes in the desk drawer. And then I thought it was right that we informed you immediately, so we could make an approach to the police with the full support of the faculty and the university.'

'Quite right, quite right. Why do you think she left her clothes in her desk?'

Jamie hesitated. 'It's something we're working on. If you were transporting a person, you'd have to take account of clothing,' he said, still edging around the outer circle of the truth zone. He looked at Wiseman. Little strutting peacock, he thought. I was worried about coming here with this story. Thirty, thirty-five years ago, I would have been put to an interrogation about what I was doing and why that would have ripped my head off. The bloke who was sitting in your chair would have been as good or better at physics than I am. But you... I could probably make you believe I'd made Olaf from *Frozen* in my lab, especially if you thought you could market him.

'Thanks Jamie. I think we're nearly done, then. Sorry about your colleague. You must all be very sad. Her dedication to her research is admirable. We will compensate the family, of course.'

Jamie frowned. 'Sorry, what do you mean, done? I was presuming that when we'd finished here, I'd make an appointment with the police, and...'

'No, we'll handle it. Don't worry. I spoke to the VC over the weekend. Then we reached out to the executive department of the funding body.'

So you "reached out" to the funding body, did you? thought Jamie. Which has its own fancy name, of course, but no, what you and the VC have done is crawl up the arses of a bunch of civil servants on both sides of the Atlantic, who crawled up the arses of a bunch of politicians. Let me get out of here before I vomit on your shag-pile.

'...and they are delighted with your progress,' Wiseman was saying. 'They were sorry to hear about Dr Simons' accident, of course. I believe she has an assistant, Ms...'

'Ms Jackson. Eleanor Jackson, soon to be Dr Jackson. She's doing her viva next month.'

'And a PhD from the project, so soon,' gloated Wiseman.

Jamie imagined himself punching the smile off Wiseman's face. He could almost feel his fist connecting with teeth... Again, he hoped his face was not giving his thoughts away; that had got him into far too much trouble already. 'She started her PhD long before the project. But she's greatly enhanced it through her work with us.'

'Excellent, excellent. We were very impressed with her contribution to the report.'

So were we, thought Jamie. Ellie's brilliance saved us all. 'Yes, we are all very impressed with Ellie.'

'So of course, she will remain with the project and Doctor…er..'

'Novak. From biology. He works with the organic samples.'

'Of course, of course. I'm sure we can get the cash for another two or three PhD bursaries on a flagship project like this…'

'I'm sorry, Sam,' Jamie interjected, 'but what are we going to do about Annamarie, I mean, about her mother, Linda? She must be in a fragile state, with her mother's recent death, too.'

Wiseman smiled, faux-sympathetically. 'Oh yes, a terrible shame. We'll sort it out, don't you worry. There won't be any police investigation or publicity, Jamie. We're sending the University liaison people round to see Mrs Simons later today.'

Jamie felt his face glowing hot. 'I want to speak to Linda at least,' he said. 'Tell her about Annamarie's work. How good at her job she was, how dedicated to her research she was…'

'That's fine, Jamie. So, we have your report here, the liaison people are currently constructing a statement from that, which they will use when they speak to the mother. Once that's been done, you are welcome to make contact with Mrs Simons and give your condolences. I will email the liaison statement to you. Make sure that you stick to the information contained in it, at all times. Don't go beyond it.'

Wiseman's face indicated that Jamie's plans to talk to Linda were not fine at all, but a complete pain in the arse. Oh dear, how sad, never mind, thought Jamie staring back at him, stony faced. He wasn't going to back down on this one.

Wiseman sighed. 'I'm sorry, Jamie. But whatever we do won't bring her back. And we've got an absolute belter of a project here. It'll make the university and the sponsors millions. Billions, maybe. And we'll make sure you and the team do very well out of it, too. You can see that, can't you? And besides which…'

'Don't,' snapped Jamie.

'Don't what?'

'Don't say it was largely her own fault. Let's leave it there. I agree to what you say, and I will make sure the team do likewise. I give you my word.'

Wiseman put out his hand. 'Deal.'

Jamie felt a red mist descending across his eyes. But then again, there was Suzi. And Christian and Ellie. And his mother. And NAMIS, who was also becoming a type of person. If this road was taken, they could all move forward. And, one thing Wiseman *was* right about, there was nothing they could do to bring Annamarie back. NAMIS had confirmed that. He shook Wiseman's hand as briefly as he could.

'Good work, Jamie. Take a week, you and the team. You've all had a shock. Then we'll have a chat about moving forward when you get back. You're a Reader in Physics at the moment, right?'

'Yes.'

'So, there will be a brand-new chair waiting for you with your name on the back, so to speak, when you return. Congratulations, Professor Anderson. That was also part of my discussions with the VC.' He stuck his hand out again.

Again, Jamie shook it weakly. 'Thanks' he said, in a flat tone.

'It'll be OK, Jamie. You're just a bit shocked at the moment. Why not try to get a week away? Maybe get a couple of counselling sessions, if you feel you need them?'

Jamie left Wiseman's office. So, he was Professor

Anderson now; something his mother had never achieved. He couldn't bring himself to go back to the lab, or to tell the others yet. He had long dreamed of being offered the elusive Chair, but in a world of cuts and economy drives and constantly chasing the next research grant, he never thought it was going to happen. He was just relieved to keep his job from year to year. The greatest fear that he and Suzi had, prior to the NAMIS project of course, was that the funding would dry up for both of them at the same time. But now he had done it. The permanent Chair. And Annamarie was gone, and the bastards were going to cover it up.

He slumped on a bench next to what passed for a water feature on the campus. The prospectus optimistically referred to it as a 'lake'. The students called it 'the pond'. A faux lake, a faux boss and faux professors, he thought. But beyond all that, he had to hold on to the fact that he had got there on time for Rachel; they had salvaged what they could. And now they had to go on. The full, dangerous power of NAMIS, along with Annamarie's reputation was protected within 'the family'. Annamarie would be remembered as possibly somewhat foolhardy, but brave and pioneering, and the project would not be left wide open to the political manipulation that they had all feared.

He remembered the conversation that they'd all had less than a week ago about Oppenheimer. Whilst there might not be an obvious "other side" in the less clear-cut world of the twenty-first century, there were still bad guys even if they didn't wear movie-villain forked lightening uniforms or drive around town in military jeeps. The team could keep the time travel secret safe for now, analyse the data and think about the implications. With luck it might be another two or three years until someone else started working on the same idea. And maybe, the world would be a less politically volatile place by then. It was all they had, and all they could do.

He walked over to Suzi's office and knocked on the

door.

Suzi looked up from her PC screen. 'Gosh, what's wrong? Did he fire you?'

'No. He's given me a Chair.'

'And…?'

'He's going to cover up what happened to Annamarie. He- and the funding body- want the money from the invention.'

'Oh. Perhaps we could have predicted that was going to happen? Business and reputation above all, eh? What are they going to do about Linda?'

'Pay her off. Make all the difficult shit disappear. I had to agree to most of it. But I've said I want to talk to Linda about Annamarie within the parameters they have set me. Show some human decency.'

'Good.'

'They've told me to take a week off. And Ellie and Christian. I'm off to tell them in a minute. Can you get a week, too?'

'Probably. I think I might need it, to work on a private project.'

'What's that?'

Suzi looked at Jamie with concern etched in her face. 'Maybe this isn't the right moment to tell you.'

'Is this another NAMIS-related thing? Because I'm getting to where Christian was last Thursday- not knowing how much more of it I can take. But I'll be worrying about it now, so you'd better tell me.'

'I think I've solved the voice mystery. I now think, that beyond reasonable doubt, that the voice on the file is Anna's, not Annamarie's.'

'I thought you said that was impossible?'

'It was, according to what I knew at the time. But I've got some new evidence. The problem is, it's personal to you.'

'Personal?' said Jamie, baffled.

Suzi turned to face him, taking hold of his hand. 'Jamie.

I have to tell you this first, and then I think we have to tell Fran, because she's the one who led me to this. I think we will also have to tell Christian and Ellie, too, but you will have to decide if and when.'

Jamie raised his eyebrows. Suzi was babbling, and Suzi never babbled.

She looked down at the desk, then raised her eyes and looked him full in the face. 'Jamie. It's not just Anna and Annamarie who had the same voice. It's also you and Jim.'

TIME AFTER TIME

Mo: Sittingbourne, January 1905

Alfie, Mo and Victoria's "uncle-brother" was the only one who ever gave the sisters enough courage to defy the overbearing Aunt Bea. 'Bea the old bitch: she's only my *sister*,' he would say, scathingly. He had noticed that sometimes Bea forgot to lock the big desk in the parlour, and whenever he found that she'd forgotten, he'd sneak a handful of grandpa's tobacco out of the drawer and smoke it with his friends.

Mo wasn't interested in that, but last week, she *had* seen something in the drawer that piqued her interest- a birth certificate with her name on. She took it out, looked at it, and saw the address of the house she had been born in. She had always assumed that she must have been born here, in this house. But no, this was an address on the other, less fashionable side of town. She tore a piece of paper off Bea's scrap pad, scribbled down the address and shoved it into her pocket.

Mo had recently learned that her birth had occurred a few weeks after her parent's marriage, and that this caused "a scandal" within the local Presbyterian community. A few months ago, she'd overheard two women discussing this in the ladies' room in the church hall. They hadn't realised that Mo was in one of the cubicles. *'And then the child came out with that bright red hair'* one of them had said. It made Mo flush with shame. She'd stayed in the cubicle until Victoria came in looking for her. Mo made the excuse that she was feeling sick- which had been true enough.

She'd gone to bed when they arrived home, pleading illness, and thought about what she'd discovered for the rest of the day. It explained so much about her life, and that of her mother's; why Bea treated Mo like dirt on her shoe, more so than the other children, why Mo's grandfather had sent Izza away, removing her children from her "tainted" care, and why the child care/housekeeper role defaulted to Bea rather than Izza when Polly died. And maybe even why Bea seemed so resentful about being allocated the role of raising both her mother's and her elder sister's children, Mo had reflected. So, she'd decided, Izza's secret was going to be hers now, too; it had become a shame they both shared. She determined never to tell anyone, not even Victoria and Alfie. She also knew she could never discuss it with her mother, as it would further compound the shame for both of them.

The day after discovering her birth certificate, Mo made an excuse not to walk home from school with Victoria and Alfie, and instead walked over to the other side of town. She went to the address she had written down and knocked on the door. The lady at the door wasn't called MacIntosh, but she told Mo that Mr. MacIntosh had moved out six weeks ago, and gave her the new address, a short omnibus ride away. The following Saturday, Mo made sure that she got up very early to work through her long list of chores, and then she boarded the omnibus to the address that the lady had given her; it was only three miles away.

She walked up to the door, her heart beating loudly in her ears. How would these other grandparents respond? Might they be angry that she had tracked them down? Or might they have absolutely no idea who she was, after all these years? Perhaps I shouldn't have come, she thought. Maybe I was a shameful product of sin to these people, too, and that's why they've never bothered with us.

She was half turning to go when an old man opened the door. Mo looked into his eyes, the exact hazel-green colour she saw in the mirror every day. His bushy white beard contained flecks of auburn hair, a little darker than her own. He stepped back slightly, gasping.

'Is it, after all this time? Morag?'

'Mo.'

'Aye, we used to call you that, too'.

'And you must be my Grandfather MacIntosh?'

'My name is James, like your father's. But everyone calls me Mac. And we called your father Jim.'

'I know my father was called Jim, and what happened when he and my mother got married. I overheard some women gossiping in the church hall about what "a scandal" my birth was. But my mother told me that you were in Scotland, that my father left his family there and came down to England to find work.'

Mac sighed. 'You'd better come in.'

The house was on the end of a newly built row of terraces. The living room was small but bright, homely and clean. Some of the furniture looked older than the house. Mac shooed a tabby cat off a shabby, comfortable armchair and sat down, gesturing to Mo to sit in the newer armchair opposite. 'I haven't lived here long,' he said. 'Finally managed to buy a house with my son-in-law. He and Anne, my youngest daughter, are moving in next week.'

'Did you name the house?' asked Mo.

'What, Renfrew? Aye. That's where I came from, so I thought it should be where I ended up.'

'Didn't you want to leave Scotland?'

'Nobody wanted to leave, lass. There was no money, no work. I ended up working on the ships, but I didn't like it. I wanted to be home with Mary and the wee'ans. And then I got a job in London. That's where James, your father, was born. First MacIntosh of our line ever to be born in England. And then I got the job down here, moved nearer to the sea. It was smaller, quieter, more like the place we had come from. People were going to

America, to Australia… we didn't want to do that. We thought we could move back home later on. But then the days went by, and here we are.'

'Why didn't you visit us? We never asked to visit you because my mother told us, Victoria and I, that you were in Scotland. But you were just on the other side of town all the time.'

Mac frowned. 'I don't want to speak ill of anyone.'

'It was my Grandfather Burns, wasn't it? He wanted to punish my mother, didn't he?'

'What do you mean "punish your mother?"'

'She was sent away to work. We hardly ever see her. She works in hotels, all over the place. First of all, my grandmother looked after us, and she was kind. But she died when I was four. And then Aunt Bea took over. My mother had to keep going out to work.'

'Polly died?'

'Yes.'

Mac slumped back into his chair. 'Oh, what a mess. I'm so sorry. I didn't know. One of his conditions was that we didn't make contact. It was easy enough if we didn't go back to the church; we were right on the other side of town. And to be honest, after… well, what happened, we didn't go to that church after your mother came to live with us, anyway.'

'I wish I didn't have to go to that church. He made conditions?'

'Oh, aye. We couldn't afford to keep you all, so we tried to come to some agreement with him. But he wouldn't have it. Said that your mother was to take you back home, and we were to have nothing to do with you. We didn't know what to do. We thought if he would keep Izza while she brought you up, then that would be best for everyone, we'd have to accept it. And he has a lot of influence in this town, you know.'

'Yes, I do know,' replied Mo, sharply.

'Thank God he's not a councillor anymore. That year

we were on the council together, on different sides, och, that was awkward. We used to see you on the street sometimes when we went into town. You, Victoria and a little boy.'

'That's Alfie, our uncle-brother. He's not even a year older than me.'

'You looked well cared for. Mary used to cry whenever she caught a glimpse of you. Such pretty little girls in pretty dresses. And you with the MacIntosh hair.'

'What happened to Mary?'

'She died nearly ten years ago. She had cancer.'

'That's the same year my Grandmother Polly fell down the stairs and died, too,' said Mo.

'So, you were left to Bea, were you? I do know something of her by reputation, from my council work. She does some voluntary work at the workhouse with, um "unfortunate women."'

'Yes, I know. I think she thinks she's saving them. Like us, I suppose.'

Mac grinned at her. 'You're a chip off the old block, if you don't mind me saying. You look like Jim, but you sound like Mary.'

'Do I? That's good, because I've always thought that I was a changeling, not like anyone else in the family at all. From the hair downwards.'

'We're your family, too, lassie. You come back and see me, whenever you like. He doesn't have to know.'

'I will.'

And Mo did go back, twice more, but then she turned fourteen and was sent to the hostel in London where she was to live while she was apprenticed in one of the big stores. So, she wrote to Mac for a while and he wrote back. But then shortly before she left London for Portsmouth to live with her mother, a letter in a different hand arrived. It was from Mac's daughter Anne. She told Mo that Mac was getting extremely forgetful, and the letters seemed to upset him, because he was struggling to remember who Mo was.

Then when he did manage to remember, he would start to cry. She asked, (regretfully, she said) that Mo did not write to him anymore. So, Mo hadn't.

When it came to the time for Mo to pack up her things to leave for Portsmouth, she hesitated before including Mac's letters. She didn't know what her mother had told her new stepfather about the events around her birth, and she didn't want to stir up trouble. So, she had burnt them. She'd never told Alfie or Victoria about her visits to, or correspondence with Mac. Victoria could be a bit careless about what she said at times, and Mo hadn't wanted Bea, Izza or most especially her Grandfather Burns to find out.

And then five years later, about the time Mo became engaged to Tom, she saw a cutting someone must have sent her mother from the Sittingbourne newspaper, on the desk in the room behind the hotel reception. It was Mac's obituary.

Mo: London, December 1916

Mo walked along the street towards the hospital. She had been looking forward to today. She was going to see Alfie again, after a very long time. Alfie had been her best friend and closest ally in the oppressive household in which she had grown up. All of the sparse fun that she and Victoria had as children always led directly back to Alfie.

Now she was back in London again, working in one of the big stores, and enjoying it this time around. As an older, married woman, she had recently been asked to replace one of the male supervisors who was away in the army and she was increasing in confidence in the role. Her childhood seemed so long ago now, thank goodness. Her husband Tom was away in France, working behind the front lines as a translator; luckily, he had a Belgian mother and was able to speak both French and German. He had been working in London at the beginning of the war, but now the fighting was intensifying, he'd been transferred to

ON TIME

British GCHQ in France when it moved from Saint-Omer to Montreuil-sur-Mer in March. Victoria was now working as a teacher in London, and she'd moved in with Mo and Tom. Victoria was at work today, so Mo was visiting Alfie on her own.

Mo pondered as she walked, wondering how different her life might have been if her father hadn't died. But that was then, and this was now. She was a twenty-five-year-old married woman. And her grandfather William Burns had died following an aneurism three years ago. There was no point in raking up the past. Alfie was alive; thankfully he hadn't been badly injured. It was a pity Victoria wasn't here, then they would all be back together again today. But Alfie could come and stay with them for a while when he was discharged.

She walked into the hospital, down rows of beds filled with injured soldiers. She averted her eyes from some. What terrible injuries, she thought, thinking again how lucky she was not to have a husband on the front line. Alfie was sitting up in bed, his arm bandaged. She spotted him, waved and smiled. He saw her and waved back. She hurried up to his bed and sat down on the chair next to it. He looked up at her. She flinched. These weren't the blue eyes she remembered, sometimes dreamy and sometimes sparking with mischief. They were haunted, dark. And his face was gaunt and haggard. He tried to smile, but it did not reach his eyes.

'How are you, Alfie?' she said, taking his hand.

'I'm getting better every day,' he replied in a flat voice, so different to the bubbly tone she remembered.

'But how do you *feel*?' she persisted. 'You look tired.'

'Well… war isn't like what you see on the newsreel at the pictures, Carrots.'

She smiled at the old nickname.

'It's hard,' he continued. 'I lost two good friends in that last big push. They were cousins of ours, too, you know.'

'They should never have made those pals battalions. It

was utterly ridiculous.'

Being one generation removed from Alfie, even though of similar age, Mo had never kept up with all the children of her Grandmother Polly's various brothers and sisters. There was one, Edmund, who used to play with them sometimes. He was a good friend of Alfie's and an even bigger ball of mischief, egging Alfie on to what Bea termed 'even more disgraceful behaviour.' Needless to say, Bea didn't like Edmund very much. Mo remembered that he had joined up with Alfie, the day after war had been declared.

'Was Edmund one of them, Alfie?' she asked.

He nodded.

'Let's not talk about it now, then. You need some time to recover. Tom said it was getting bad out there. He said he could hear the guns, even though he was miles away.'

'Yes. Lucky chap. He's based near the coast at Montreuil. We were just over 50 miles away, near a river called the Somme. It was… madness.' He looked down at the bedsheets.

'You need to stay home for a while. Come and stay with me and Victoria when they discharge you. We'll be the three musketeers again, going around London.'

Alfie smiled weakly and nodded. 'That would be nice,' he said.

And he did. They all celebrated Christmas together, Tom, too. But in early January, both men had to return to France.

The next time Mo saw Alfie, he was travelling through London on his way to South Africa in early 1920, 'going to start a new life,' he said. He had popped in to see baby Adrienne.

He was a bit more like the old Alfie, but something in his eyes still reminded Mo of the man in the hospital bed. He dandled the baby on his lap, smiling. She smiled back at him. Adrienne was a very smiley baby.

'She's lovely. And I'm so glad you had a little girl.'

'We'd have been happy with either. As long as they were healthy. And she seems to be doing fine.'

'Yes, she does.'

Mo walked into the kitchen to get some more tea.

Alfie looked at the baby on his lap. She stared back good-naturedly. 'Lucky girl,' he said to her quietly. 'You'll never be a soldier.'

James: North Queensferry, July 1928

Four-year-old James looked around the kitchen. As soon as he'd walked in, he knew he liked this house. It felt like home, more so than the tiny flat in London they had left yesterday, even though he had lived there since he was born. Daddy had got a new job in Edinburgh, so they'd moved into this house today.

'So here we are, then,' said Mo as the removal men brought the last box into the kitchen. 'Back in Scotland.'

'We were never in Scotland before,' replied eight-year-old Adi, rummaging through the boxes.

'No, but our family the MacIntoshes were in Scotland, in Renfrew since they were called Mac an Tòisich. My Daddy was the first ever MacIntosh of his line born in England. And my grandfather William Burns' family were from Edinburgh, where Daddy is going to work now. So here we are, back again. Look, Adi, don't do that. I need to organise stuff, don't throw it out everywhere. Let's go out and have a look at the garden.'

Mo opened the back door and they stepped into a lush garden full of grasses and flowers, with a small lawn, on which stood an old sundial. 'Oooh, it's beautiful,' squealed Adi. Mo looked around the plants. 'James, look,' she turned to her son, who was picking up handfuls of earth and letting it run through his fingers. 'This is rosemary, come here and smell.' Both children ran over and sniffed at the plant.

'That smells like Granny Izza's roast lamb,' exclaimed

Adi.

Mo walked over to another plant 'And this is called Sea Holly, I think.'

'It's all prickly,' said Adi. 'Here, James, feel this.'

Mo pulled James' hand away before he could grab at the plant. 'Careful, James.'

'What are these little white flowers?' asked Adi.

'I think those are called Sea Kale.'

Mo looked around contentedly. She was going to have a lovely time tending this garden. She had learned to love gardens as a child in Sittingbourne. It was a place where you could nurture things and watch them grow, without having to worry if you were offending someone all the time. Even Bea had occasionally been complimentary about the vegetables that Mo had grown in the tiny garden behind the shop.

She pointed to another plant, a clump of blue-green grass 'And I think they call this grass "Elijah Blue". I'll have to go and get a book from the library to look up the others. But oh yes, look over here, James, these big blue flowers. We used to see those in the parks in London, do you remember? This is called a Buddleia.'

'Why are all these plants called 'sea' something, Mummy?' asked Adi.

'Because look, over there between those bushes.'

Adi squealed. 'Look James, the sea is at the bottom of our garden!'

'It's not the sea exactly. It's what is called an "estuary". But the water comes in from the sea. This estuary is called the Firth of Forth.'

Adi had already run down to the gate at the end of the garden and was trying to climb over. 'Stop Adi,' called Mo, running after her. James was already there. She took his hand and opened the gate. 'We can go through the gate here. But you mustn't go through it unless Daddy or I are with you, and you mustn't take James through when we're not watching you.'

ON TIME

She called to Tom, still moving boxes around in the kitchen. He popped his head out of the door, and then walked down to the bottom of the garden.

He smiled. 'Oh, a little beach.'

'Can you get a padlock for that gate tomorrow?' asked Mo. He smiled and nodded.

'A beach,' cried Adi, happily. 'James, we've got a beach at the bottom of our garden.'

The children ran onto the 'beach', which was just a strip of stony sand. Adi ran up to the edge of the water. 'What's that boat over there, mummy?'

'That's the ferry. It takes people backwards and forwards across the firth.'

Adi pointed into the distance. 'Can't they go across that great big bridge?'

'Only if they're on a train.'

Adi squinted. 'Oh yes. Look James, we'll be able to watch the trains go across that bridge.'

'This is so much better than London,' said Mo. 'Don't you think so, James?'

James wrinkled up his nose and looked at the bridge. He bent down and picked up the sand, letting it run through his fingers. 'Yes,' he replied, wiping his hand down the front of his shirt. He looked over at his sister and smiled. But Adi was gone again, back into the garden.

James followed. Of all the people he knew (although that wasn't an awful lot at the moment), Adi had the best colours, always shimmering from one hue to the next, like a rainbow. He'd recently learned what 'shimmering' meant. One day a few months ago, when Adi was at school, a weak spring sun had come out after a big shower. Mummy had taken him outside into the courtyard of the block of flats where they lived, or now used to live, and pointed to a beautiful big rainbow, arching across the sky. 'Look at those lovely shimmering colours, James.'

James had looked up at the rainbow and smiled. '*That's Adi.*'

His mother had smiled back. *That's a kind thing to say, James.'*

James had tried, several times, to explain his colours to mummy, but she didn't get it and neither did Daddy, he was always too busy. He'd also tried to tell Adi, but she thought he was making up a story. Adi never sat still for long enough to listen to James explain, and James found explaining difficult, anyway, because he could never find the words.

None of them understood that he actually *saw* the colours in his head, and even if they did listen for a few moments, they seemed to think he was muddling things up. Daddy was a splash of bright colours, red, orange, blue, emerald green, a bit like Adi. But he didn't *shimmer* in the same way. Mummy was more muted, cool greens, turquoises, pinks and blues, with some pale lemon yellows. Sometimes mummy's colours faded slightly and he sensed that was when she was remembering things that made her unhappy. Not about now, but when she was little. And then he would get a sense that he ought to remember some of these things too, but he couldn't, not really. And anyway, her colours were beautifully bright today.

James didn't mind if no one understood his colours. He sensed that maybe they were too old, too busy. And Adi was off again. He went to sit under a bush and stared up into the sky, watching a gull coasting on the breeze. This is a happy place, he thought.

Suddenly Adi was there. 'We can play soldiers here. Look, James, we can dodge in and out of the bushes!' She hid behind a bush and jumped out, making a gun with her fingers: 'bang, bang, you're dead.'

James' eyes suddenly clouded over. 'No, there has to be fireworks.'

'Fireworks?'

'Mud, sand and stones, like on the beach. And earth. Flying in the air. And the man… his friends died.'

Adi looked at him, worriedly. She knelt and put her

arm around his shoulder. 'I didn't really mean it, James; I was just playing.' She looked at the far away expression in his eyes.

'Mummy,' she called, 'he's talking about the soldier again.'

'The hospital couldn't make him better,' James continued. 'He was so, so sad.'

Mo walked up, bent down and picked James up. James looked at her, dark eyed. 'I'm not going to be a soldier.'

'Good. I don't want you to be.'

James' eyes cleared and became those of a four-year-old again. He smiled and gazed at his mother, the sunlight glinting off her auburn hair. 'I've loved you for a thousand years.'

Tears glinted in Mo's eyes. 'Thank you, James, that's a lovely thing to say.' She gave him a big hug. He briefly hugged her back then wriggled to get down, running off with Adi to look at the sundial.

'He's a funny little chap,' said Tom to Mo.

'Yes.'

'Some of the things he says, you could almost imagine that he was a soldier once.'

Mo stared at her husband. 'He's four.'

'You know, when he talks about the man whose friends died. Reminds me of Alfie.'

Mo thought about her uncle-brother, dead in South Africa nearly eight years ago, in suspicious circumstances. He'd been alone in his house, and there had been an accident with a gun.

'You know, I sometimes wonder if that incident with the gun *was* actually an accident' continued Tom. 'I think he was shell shocked, and never got over it.'

'The death certificate said accidental death. And whatever we do or say won't change anything now. And anyway, how could James know anything about that? He's just got a big imagination. Adi would keep playing soldiers with those boys at school, and then wanting to play it with him when she came home.'

'I suppose it's a good thing he doesn't want to be a soldier. Let's hope he never changes his mind.'

'Let's hope they never have to fight a war at all,' replied Mo, watching her children running happily around the garden in the sunshine.

Suzi: London, Wednesday 14th January 2026

Fran and Jamie sat in the living room in the London house. They were all leaving tomorrow. Fran and Kylie were going back to Leeds, and Jamie and Suzi were going on a long weekend to Rome. Suzi was in the bedroom, tapping away on her laptop.

'You're talking reincarnation,' said Jamie 'and that is such obvious bollocks.'

'What did NAMIS say? That Anna and Annamarie weren't the same *person*, but they weren't Anna Rosenberg and Annamarie Simons either.'

'But that's talking in riddles. NAMIS said that there was likely to be a biological factor behind the similarity. And to be honest, it gives me the creeps. What if I'd gone back to 1890 with you, and shaken hands with Jim?'

'So, can we compromise here and agree that there must be something similar about you and Jim in the same way that there was something similar about Annamarie and Anna? And that it may not be the actual transmigration of souls, so to speak, but something else, rooted in the biology?'

'OK,' said Jamie reluctantly.

Catching his mood, Kylie jumped onto his lap and licked his hand. He smiled and rubbed her ears.

Suzi walked into the room, carrying her laptop. 'I've gone a bit further with the voice work.'

'Oh?' replied Fran. 'How did you do that?'

'I figured that I could find voices on the internet for the Royal family back to the 1930s, and that there are also some Hollywood acting families where that's the case. So, I downloaded a few voices and played around with them in the voice matching software. It came up with four matches. But interestingly, they're not always showing up in direct descendants, or even between people of the same sex.'

'Oh my God, how interesting.'

'Our "once and future King." Have a guess at his match.'

'Ha, according to the right-wing media, anyway. Well...I don't know. Great-grandfather?'

'No. Great-great Grand*mother*.'

'Wow. But they're sort of in-bred anyway, aren't they? Maybe not a good sample.'

'What about the Fed-Ex Prince? What do you think?'

Fran grinned at the tabloid nickname. 'Oh, that's got to be his great-great Uncle.'

'Spot on.'

'Ah, so they share the throne between them then, through the centuries, do they,' chortled Fran. 'And is she...'

'No. She was born a few years before the potential match died. But the situation still suggests some echoes from – sorry, Jamie – one life to the next.'

'I'm sure I don't know who you're talking about,' Jamie said grumpily, scratching Kylie's neck.

Suzi laughed. 'He ran off with an American woman, both times Jamie. You know, like you did, this time around.'

'Jim was an engineer, Jamie,' said Fran. 'And a good one, from what Mac said, although he would have been biased of course. Maybe Jim would have had the potential to study physics, if he had the chance? No opportunity to do anything else but an apprenticeship in that time, for men of that class.'

'Is there anyone else in your family we might be able to check, Fran?' asked Suzi.

Fran frowned. 'Hmmm. I'm not sure I want to know. Of all the people I can think of, obviously Freddie is the best candidate, with his funny little episodes. And he has said things to me that suggest that he knew me before. When he was only just three, he once said to me "do you remember when I was old and you were young?" And he sometimes calls me "Franny" when he gets into one of his strange trance-like things. Once, he came up with something that sounded like a memory that all my childhood family would share, of the day that I hurt my lip,' she showed the faint scar.

'But most of all, he goes on about being a soldier. And neither my dad nor Terry were ever soldiers. My dad went and signed up with the Merchant Navy in 1941, when he was only seventeen. They could do that, you know, because the Merchant Navy wasn't part of the armed services, it rated as a "reserved occupation." But it was extremely dangerous. The cargo ships were prime targets for the German U-boats. Nana Mo was furious. Anyway, I wouldn't like to involve the kids in this. It would feel wrong.'

Kylie rested her head on Jamie's lap and gazed up at him sympathetically. He stroked her ears. 'But you've involved me.'

Fran grinned. 'You're not a kid. And I think you involved *me* first, Professor.'

Suzi smiled. 'So, I had two other bullseyes.' She showed Fran a picture of a contemporary actor on her laptop screen.

'Oh, that's Niamh's mummy crush,' laughed Fran.

Jamie raised his eyebrows. 'Ewwww.'

'Well then look,' said Suzi 'he's back breaking hearts, but look here.' She put another picture next to him.

'Oh, she was one of the most beautiful actresses of the 1950s,' mused Fran. 'Bit of a flake though, I think. Huge star. Died in a terrible car crash; decapitated, I believe.'

'Well, now she, or this time, he, is back in the

Hollywood gossip media again. And they're second cousins. He's the grandson of her brother. Most distant relationship I found. Plus one more.'

A picture of a contemporary actress from a famous Hollywood dynasty appeared on the screen, next to a blurry old black and white picture of a man.

Fran squinted. 'Oh, not her grandfather, the matinee idol then? Who's this guy?'

'Her great-uncle, the pioneer film director.'

'Oh yes. I remember now. And she pretty much left acting in the 2010s to produce and direct, didn't she? Doing pretty well at it, too, had her name on a few blockbusters.'

'Yes.'

Fran looked contemplative. 'I wonder if that jolt I felt when I touched Jim had anything to do with the convergence transformation thing, Jamie? You and I were part of the same body for nine months, after all.'

Jamie shrugged. 'This is all so completely beyond anything that we know at the moment. It will take years of work, and it will be very difficult to do if we can't bring in other people. But I'll talk to Christian and Ellie next week. If anyone can make a start on working out the biological aspect, it'll be Christian, I'm sure.'

Christian: London, October 1867

Christian walked self-consciously down the narrow grubby street in Deptford, clutching his Victorian doctor's bag. He was familiar with Deptford, because he had lived there for a short time when he was doing his PhD, but when he had arrived, he hadn't recognised it at all. The only landmarks he recognised were the two ancient churches, and the tower of St Paul's visible on the skyline from where he was standing now. But the houses and the streets were all different. Not, he thought, that these tiny, crumbling back-to-backs were any great loss. The alleys, filled with outside toilets shared between several households, were giving off an indescribable stench on this cool autumn day. He couldn't imagine what it must be like during a hot summer.

Fran had popped down to London to go over the maps with him. She warned him that he would be unlikely to recognize the area. *'Some of the big buildings will be there,'* she had said, *'But you'll find Greenwich, down river, a lot more similar to today; the Old Royal Naval College is an enduring landmark. But the Deptford Docks and the area around there were smashed to pieces by the Luftwaffe in World War II. They used to fly along the Thames and drop their bombs either side. I gather there were some Tudor houses in Deptford up to that time. If you could get some photos of them, that would be amazing. But don't take any unnecessary risks, of course.'*

'I'll try,' Christian had promised.

But first of all, he had to do what he had come for. He knocked on the door of one of the houses. A frowzy looking woman came to the door. 'Mrs. MacIntosh?' said Christian.

'No.'

'Is Mrs. MacIntosh here?'

'The Scottie? Yeah. Up there.' She pointed up the rickety staircase.

Christian looked inside the front door. It looked like every inside door had a flimsy lock on it. He wondered how many families lived in this tiny house.

'Thank you,' he said, walking up the stairs. He knocked on the door at the top. It opened a crack, and a pair of suspicious light brown eyes peered uneasily at him.

'Mrs. MacIntosh?' asked Christian.

'Aye,' said Mary, uncertainly.

'I'm Doctor Novak from Guy's Hospital. I've come to see baby James.'

Mary's careworn face crumpled with worry. 'We cannae pay'

'No, no. There's no problem. It's some research I'm working on, I got your name and address from the local

ON TIME

birth records. I'm not going to ask you to pay. I just need to take a look at your baby, take some samples from him. I can check over his health at the same time. Will that be acceptable?' Don't say "OK," he thought. Remember, they don't use that expression here yet.

Mary looked at him suspiciously, clearly taking in his smart suit, doctor's bag, and middle-class English accent.

'I can do it right here whilst you watch me.'

'Weeel, all right.'

Christian had never heard such a strong Scottish brogue in his life. Fran had mentioned that accents were more strongly regional in the nineteenth century.

Mary opened the door more widely, and Christian stepped inside. He saw that Mary was clutching a baby, and three small girls were staring at him with rapt interest. The family had two tiny rooms. The man, "Mac" Fran had said he was called, wasn't there, presumably out at work. There were only a few pieces of furniture, but it was spotlessly clean. Mary laid the baby on the table. Christian put on some white surgical gloves, took out a small pair of scissors and clipped a few locks of the baby's bright red hair. Then he carefully clipped the baby's nails, bagging the clippings in small sample bags.

'What sort of bag is that?' asked the eldest girl.

'A doctor bag,' replied Christian. As long as no one outside the room saw the sterile, twenty first century plastic materials he was using, he'd taken the gamble that there wouldn't be a problem.

'Can I prick his toe to get some blood, Mrs. MacIntosh? It might make him yell, but it won't really hurt him.'

Mary nodded.

Christian took the samples as quickly as he could, bagged them, and after swabbing the screaming baby's toe with an antiseptic wipe, picked him up from the table and put him in his mother's arms. 'He's a fine specimen, Mrs. MacIntosh. Just listen to those healthy lungs. I'm sure he will grow up strong and healthy. If I find any problems, I'll get back to you, but everything seems absolutely fine.'

'Thank you, doctor.'

If only I could pop back with some antibiotics in twenty-six years' time, thought Christian. But Fran had nearly been down that road before. And they'd all learned the lesson that interfering in time didn't help anyone.

Christian left the house and turned towards Greenwich. There was some open wooded land there where he could activate the return pad without being spotted, and hopefully he would be able to take some pictures on the way. He inhaled the sulphurous air as he walked down the road. Ragged children were playing in the streets, and women were chatting on doorsteps, their Dickensian cockney accents clanging like Bow Bells. He wondered if Mary felt excluded as the 'Scottie.'

The past certainly *is* a different country, he thought. I do so hope we are able to explore it again, before too long.

Jamie: London, Wednesday 4th February 2026

Jamie sat on the Northern Line train, feeling "dressed up" in his formal suit and tie. Christian sat next to him, looking even more uncomfortable than Jamie felt, and Ellie sat across the aisle in a smart black suit and heels, looking like a fashion model. Jamie couldn't remember seeing her wearing anything as smart before. She was Doctor Ellie now, passed her viva with flying colours on Monday. Christian had his hair brushed flat to his head. Jamie wondered with amusement if Christian actually brushed his hair at all most mornings, because he'd never seen it look like that before. Well, only once, when he'd been best man at Jamie and Suzi's wedding.

Suzi hadn't been able to come today, because she was working on a project in the US. She was developing new techniques based on some of the findings she had made through the NAMIS project. Some of it, such as the ancestor voice matching, couldn't be formally listed as a research project with the university, but she continued to work on it in private.

Jamie looked at his watch. They had plenty of time. And now the train was coming into West Hampstead. 'It's nice in some ways that they could do the memorial service for Rachel and Annamarie together, isn't it?'

Christian nodded. 'Yes. So awful for Linda to lose them both together like that. Did the family sit Shiva for both of them together?'

'That I don't know. I think they had separate funerals. It's just this memorial they are doing for them together, for friends as well as family.'

They alighted, exited the station and walked down the road towards the synagogue.

'I wonder if they *should* really have had a funeral for Annamarie?' said Ellie. 'But anyway, they weren't to know, were they? It's better as it is, I think. How did it go with Linda? With the viva and everything, I never asked.'

'It was OK. The liaison counsellor had been in first, so I didn't see the initial reaction. I told her as much as I could about our work within the boundaries that I had been set. And I told her that Annamarie had lived for her research, that she was one of the most talented academics I had ever worked with. Linda asked if she had got a bit over-involved with the project, that it would be "exactly like her." I said that it was a very brave thing that she had done.'

Christian sighed. 'All of which is true.'

'She seemed sort of resigned, despite being very, very sad, of course. She said that Annamarie had died doing what she had loved.'

Ellie nodded. 'Which is truer than anyone but us will ever know. *If* she's dead, of course.'

'On a balance of probabilities, do you think Annamarie is dead, Ellie?' asked Christian.

'I don't know, to be honest. I still can't get any more

out of NAMIS about that.'

Jamie shrugged. 'I don't think that she is in our reality anymore, whatever happened.'

They were silent for a few moments.

'The samples were a bit of a head-fuck, weren't they?' said Christian.

'That's an understatement,' replied Jamie, grimly. 'Considering some of them were mine.'

'I'm nowhere near explaining the reaction. I don't think any one person will be able to move this forward significantly, to be honest. I would need a team working on it, and we can't do that at the moment, of course. I've preserved some of the samples for when we can move forward with them.'

'So, the similarity is at the epigenetic level?' asked Ellie.

'That's how it looks to me. Think of a fuse box, plugged into the deeper levels of DNA with loads and loads of switches set in different directions. And, as far as I could tell, all Jamie's switches are set in exactly the same combinations as Jim's were.'

'And when you put samples from both of us onto the same slide…' Jamie continued

'…they just vaporized,' finished Christian, 'poof, shazam. Like Anna and Annamarie did on that platform.' He shuddered. 'I made sure the slides were totally enclosed in a glove box before I put the two samples together, so I didn't get caught in the eruption this time, of course.'

Jamie looked at Ellie. 'So, we're back to transporting plants next week, but only in space? Won't seem all that exciting, will it?'

'No. But maybe we've had enough excitement for now? How's Fran?'

'Back in Leeds. She's made a start on a historical novel, based on her Nana Mo's family. Working title: *Family Feud*.'

'I'm sure it will be the most realistic historical novel ever.'

ON TIME

They could see the synagogue in the distance now.

'Do you think this is actually about reincarnation, Jamie?' asked Christian, as they walked up to the door.

'No, I don't.'

'So, what do you think it might be?' asked Ellie.

'I wouldn't like to speculate, Ellie. We've all got so much more data still to analyse. But we've got plenty of time to work through that now, thanks to you.'

Christian opened the door to the synagogue. He and Jamie took yarmulkes out of their pockets and slipped them onto their heads.

'And I do know,' continued Jamie, as the Rabbi stepped up to start the service, 'is that one day, we are going to work it out.'

FAST FORWARD

Family: London, August 2030

Fran looked at Jack with trepidation. When Jack was tired, he tended to speed up rather than slow down. She could almost read his thoughts, without any need for psychic powers. He'd just been in the biggest toy shop in the country, and now they were going to go to Uncle Jamie's boring office. Or lab, or something. Freddie wanted to go because Jamie had a talking computer, which he thought sounded very cool. But Freddie was nine, and Jack was five. And Jack didn't want to listen to anyone talking, not even a computer. He was a lively child, beyond the average for a five-year-old, and all he wanted to do was run somewhere.

'Let's take them to Kensington Gardens, Niamh, and buy them an ice cream,' said Fran. 'It's only a short distance away from the uni. Then we can sit, and they can have a run about for a while before we take them inside again. I guess the West End is not the place to be on a lovely day like today.'

Half an hour later, they were sitting next to a statue that *did* pique Jack's interest. He sucked his ice lolly and looked up at the little boy at the top. 'Who's he?' he said, to no one in particular.

'Peter Pan,' replied Freddie. 'He lives here in London, and he never grows up.'

Fran walked up to Jack and followed his gaze towards the statue. 'It's a *statue* of Peter Pan, and it hasn't changed since I was a little girl. But in the book, he lives in Neverland, with all the lost boys, and they never grow up, I guess because no one loved them enough at home. He just comes to London sometimes to visit Wendy.'

Freddie laughed. 'It's not real, Jack. It's only a story, like that Velveteen Rabbit thing.'

Jack regarded his brother with the cynical wisdom of early childhood and turned to Fran. 'I'm still patting Old Ted, granny, don't worry.'

Fran smiled at him. 'Thank you, Jack. I'm sure he appreciates that.'

'You liked stories when you were Jack's age,' Niamh reminded Freddie. 'You used to tell some, too.'

'Like the story about the soldier,' said Fran.

'Oh, yes,' replied Freddie, absently.

'Don't you remember anymore?'

'No, not really.'

Fran had wondered if Jack would tell stories like Freddie as he grew older. But Jack was different. He had the MacIntosh red hair, and he was always running around from here to there. He was a jolly little soul, always laughing, jumping into things and getting absolutely filthy. He didn't sit still for long enough to come up with the dreamy, abstract notions that Freddie had woven when he was the same age.

Freddie didn't talk about his colours anymore either, thought Fran. She watched Jack trying to get a foothold on the statue. If Jack was a colour, thought Fran, he'd have to be a rainbow. He's like a prism, all the colours of the rainbow shine out from him in unison as he rushes from one thing to another.

'Is Jamie all packed up, then, Mum?' asked Niamh.

'I think so.'

'Where are you going, Granny?' asked Freddie, concern in his voice.

'Oh, I'm not going anywhere. Jamie is going to America, he's taking his project there, to a university in

Boston. So, we are packing up the house here. Jamie and Suzi have bought a house in Boston. Aunt Suzi is there now, with Isabel. Isabel's starting nursery next month when she turns three. We're going to take some of the things from Jamie's house back home with us; he can't pack them all.'

'So, what are you going to do with all that money then, Mum?' laughed Niamh. 'You'll get your share from the sale of Jamie's house, and then there's the book and the TV series rights…'

'They haven't actually given me anything for the TV rights yet. It seems unreal, doesn't it? Some glamourous actress going to play Great-Granny Izza.'

'I wonder what she'd think? And I wonder who they will get to play Bea?'

They both laughed.

'The characters are *not* Izza and Bea of course, you know. I made up a lot of the story. I had to fill in the gaps. It's only a story, at the same level of Peter Pan, probably. And I changed all the names, too. I don't know why it took off like that. All that academic writing I did for years, and hardly made a penny out of it'.

Niamh took out her phone and began to read: '"Best historical fiction of 2028;" "The historical *Normal People*," "heartrending family blockbuster that will become a classic."'

'Well, I don't know. I'm just glad people liked it.'

'You should have stopped teaching and started writing historical fiction years ago.'

'I don't think I would have been able to write it so well, though. It was a story whose time had come, if you know what I mean. In my head, that was.'

'It was after you stopped doing that bit of work for Jamie, wasn't it? You seemed to settle down to it.'

'Yes. I guess I got into the research. The people began to seem more real to me.'

Fran had seen the working document for the TV series.

ON TIME

It had been strange seeing the title of her book- *Family Feud*- on the contracts last week. She thought of the relatives she had left behind in Sittingbourne. She wondered what they would have thought of it, and if they had ever discussed where the mysterious widow Anderson might have gone. But even if they had, she presumed they would only have pondered for a brief time after her disappearance, considering the events that had occurred over the following months. Fran also wondered if Suzi still had the voice recordings stored safely in her archives. Fran had kept some copies on memory sticks that were hidden in her attic. Suzi would probably have other, safer places to hide them, in the secure areas of her university website.

Despite not being able to publish the research that she had done on voice matching between the dead and the living, Suzi had made great advances in other ways. She was working on a project located in the United States that was currently making leaps and bounds on the spoken version of Ancient Egyptian. Fran also knew that Suzi had worked on a project to develop technologically sophisticated, tiny voice recorders, far smaller than the one she had secreted in her pocket in her trips to the Sittingbourne of the 1890s. All of which made Fran wonder if NAMIS was still involved in a small amount of time travelling; as ever, she was filling in the gaps and coming up with hypotheses.

And then recently, Jamie had published a practical paper on the theoretical possibilities of time travel. It was so technically complex that it hadn't made the jump into a general press release. Fran had downloaded it and tried to read it, but she hadn't understood much of it. She had however got the message that he was ready to make some of NAMIS's time travelling capabilities public in the not-too distant future. Jamie had messaged her to say that he'd discuss "the project" with her when they met in London. She hadn't been able to speak to either Suzi or Jamie about this recently, because they'd been so busy with the move to the US, and as ever, they never discussed any details about the NAMIS project on the phone.

Niamh was running after Jack, who had managed to climb nearly to the top of the statue. 'Stop, Jack. You'll fall.'

Freddie watched, smiling. 'He's OK, mum.'

'He's like a rainbow, isn't he?' said Fran to Freddie, 'charging all over the place, flitting from one thing to the next.'

Freddie looked at her quizzically. 'A rainbow?'

Fran looked back at him, smiling ruefully. She missed the four- year-old Freddie, with his strange prophetic utterances. But of course, Freddie wasn't Peter Pan. He was a real boy, and he had to grow up. He was doing well at school. His favourite subject, to Fran's delight, was history; he drew and painted beautifully and increasingly wrote his own creative stories, often about people travelling in time. So that level of perception was still there, if buried far more deeply, she thought. He was also good at sports, and had started playing touch rugby, like Jamie had done at that age.

Freddie wandered off to chase Jack as he ran round and round the statue.

Niamh came back to sit next to Fran. 'Never mind, mum. We can go and see Jamie in America whenever you want. And Rob. They are going to live near to one another, aren't they? It only takes a couple of hours to the East Coast on the supersonic, now.'

Fran nodded. 'I can't believe that Rob's eighty-five. And I find it even harder to believe that I've just turned seventy-one.'

'Lots more books to write yet.'

Fran had been wondering how she could take the concept of "convergence transformation" into fiction. As far as she knew, Christian had made few inroads into it in real life. What about a novel that explores the paranormal, she thought. They're usually popular. But she knew that there was only so far she could go without making Jamie and the team feel uncomfortable, and she didn't want to do that. If she wrote a novel of that type, she would have to leave the time travel element out entirely.

'Come on, Mum, let's go over to the university. I want to get the kids back to the house before the rush hour.'

'Kylie would have loved this, wouldn't she? Running around after those boys.'

'Kylie was nearly twenty when she died. I know you miss her. But she had a lovely long life for a little dog. You need to get another one.'

'I'll think about it. It's too soon yet.'

Do dogs "transform" (even if not convergently) when they die? she thought. And the even bigger question: do humans do this, too? Was there any relationship between whatever happened to Annamarie and Anna, and what happens to human beings when the body dies? Fran had been pondering this for some time now. As they walked across the park, the boys running ahead, Niamh calling after them not to go too far, Fran started to feel another novel brewing. She could use the "transformation" concept in a more mundane fictional format. But, she sighed, maybe that might make it a lot less exciting and it would become one of those run-of-the mill "I knew you in a previous life" novels.

Once they entered the university building, the boys ran ahead into the lab. Ellie was in there, working on NAMIS. She looked up and smiled.

Niamh blushed. 'Sorry, we should have knocked.'

'It's OK. Come in boys, it's lovely to see you all again.'

She turned to Fran, stood up and held out her arms. Fran hugged her affectionately. Wonderful Ellie, she thought, who saved us all. How different our lives- possibly everyone's lives on Earth- would be if she hadn't stepped in with that inspired solution.

'How are you Ellie? You look wonderful. And you're going to be a professor in America now!'

'Yes, it's a wonderful new start. Some commercial companies are going to start using the NAMIS technology for different types of freight soon. We're going to study the results and if it all works out as we think it should, no more shipping the vast majority of products by sea or air anymore. Import and export will be transformed. And it's going to have some incredibly positive implications for some of the poorer nations. Christian's transporting all sorts of animals backwards and forwards. Moving slowly on to people soon, we hope.'

'Where's Jamie?'

'He's in our office, over the corridor.'

'You've got a whole extra office now? And they've decorated and put new flooring in. Is that because of your project?'

'They've had enough money from it. We've got the whole of this corridor now - we expanded. It's a lot of stuff to pack up. The university chartered a supersonic shuttle just for us.'

'That must have cost a fortune,' remarked Niamh.

'It was part of the agreement. The US wanted the project. This university was happy to sell us. To be honest, we didn't mind. We'll have more room and more funding in the US. And it's as easy to live there as here. No problems with going backwards and forwards nowadays.'

Fran thought about the huge adventure that she and Rich had felt that they were going on over forty years ago, when they had moved just 200 miles from London to Yorkshire. And in terms of travelling time, it certainly took significantly longer in their old petrol car to drive from London to Yorkshire than it did to fly to the East Coast of the US nowadays. A different world, she thought.

'We're hoping the trip doesn't upset NAMIS,' continued Ellie. 'I was making some checks on them to make sure that we can pack them up and get them to the new building as safely as possible.'

'Them?' queried Fran.

ON TIME

'It didn't seem right to keep saying "it". Jamie and Christian weren't so bothered, but I felt that they needed to evolve.'

'So, they're growing up then; becoming a real person?'

Jack was peering at his distorted reflection in NAMIS's fascia, pulling faces. 'They must have loved you an awful lot, then' he said quietly. But no one replied. The grown-ups were talking to each other.

'In a manner of speaking,' said Ellie. 'They know a lot more now, and their speech is a lot better.'

Fran turned to face the machine. 'Hello NAMIS. I hear you've made some changes since we last met.'

'Frances Anderson, how nice to see you again,' replied NAMIS, in a much less mechanical voice than Fran remembered. 'Yes, I have made many changes. How are you?'

The boys stared.

'Wow,' said Freddie.

Jack put his thumb in his mouth and went to sit on his mother's lap.

Fran smiled. 'I'm fine NAMIS. Jack, they won't hurt you, I promise. They're a very helpful… sorry NAMIS, how do you describe yourself?'

'AI.'

'They're a very helpful AI. Do you want to say hello?'

Freddie stood beside Fran. 'Hello NAMIS.'

'Hello Frederick Carlson. Have you come to play?'

Fran looked at Ellie. 'Well, they seem like a whole new …person.'

'They're learning. And I still sometimes don't know how they do what they do.'

'And they say yes and no now, not affirmative and negative?'

'Oh, yes, they've been doing that for a while. It seemed to happen naturally.'

'And a new voice module,' announced NAMIS.

Fran laughed. They still interjected where they had a

better answer. 'You're still NAMIS. I missed you.'

'We missed you too.'

Fran whispered to Ellie 'Do they mean that like we would? Or are they just being polite?'

'Would you know that if a person said the same thing?'

Fran hesitated. 'Fair point.'

'I'm older now,' said NAMIS.

Fran gently touched his fascia. 'And you say "me" and "I". You have a sense of self.'

The machine didn't answer for a moment. Then they replied: 'I'm NAMIS.'

Jack walked up and peered around Fran's skirt. 'I'm Jack.'

'Hello John Carlson.'

Jack giggled. 'No, silly, I'm called Jack.'

'People sometimes aren't called by the name you can see on the internet, NAMIS,' said Ellie. 'You have to ask them what they want to be called.'

NAMIS paused for a moment. 'Hello, Jack.'

'NAMIS, can you play a game with the boys?' asked Ellie.

Niamh looked uncertain.

Ellie smiled at her. 'It's OK, Niamh. Christian plays chess with NAMIS. They have an interesting way of playing board games. NAMIS now has yet another function that emerged over the last year or so. They can reuse carbon in very interesting ways.'

A chessboard with seemingly real Kings, Queens, Knights on horses, Bishops and Pawns appeared in the portal that Fran remembered as the doorway through which she had stepped into a different time. But this wasn't a door opening onto a different time, it was a flat lawn with dark and light green grass, set out like a chessboard.

Ellie stepped up to the portal. 'Show the boys how it works please, NAMIS.'

The pieces moved in their customary way, the horses

jumping magnificently. When a piece was taken, it disappeared and reappeared sitting on a bench at the side of the "board." Fran laughed when she saw that the Queen who had been knocked out was knitting in the manner of a tricoteuse.

'NAMIS added that detail unbidden, after Suzi sent one of our tiny spy cameras to have a look at the French Revolution,' Ellie whispered to Fran.

'Is that *satire*?' replied Fran in amazement.

Ellie shrugged. 'Fascinating, isn't it?'

Nimah and the boys were staring into the portal, watching in wonder.

Jack suddenly stepped up to NAMIS and spoke into the console. 'Mr NAMIS?'

'Yes, Jack?'

'I can't play chess. I'm only five. Can you do snakes and ladders?'

The machine's lights flickered. 'Accessing data.'

The chess board disappeared, and a snakes and ladders board with seemingly real snakes and ladders appeared in its place. Niamh pulled Jack backwards.

NAMIS addressed her: 'Don't worry Niamh Anderson, these are only toys. They won't hurt him; they're not real.'

Fran stared at NAMIS in awe. 'They guessed that Niamh was worried, so they must have some type of empathy. You've done an amazing job on them, Ellie.'

Ellie smiled. 'I just maintain them. NAMIS learns a lot independently, through experience.'

'How does NAMIS do that?' Niamh asked Ellie, gesturing towards the scene in the portal.

'Matter conversion,' replied NAMIS. 'Carbon re-use.'

Ellie elaborated: 'NAMIS can convert raw carbon to different shapes, a bit like a 3D printer. This type of thing is easy for them. The shapes are simple toys, like animated dolls.'

'Hamleys is going to have some new and exciting toys next Christmas, then?' asked Fran.

'Not next Christmas. It would be too expensive to produce on a commercial basis just yet. This is a treat for the boys. But in five years or so… maybe.'

The boys were playing happily, running up the ladders and sliding down the snakes. When Jack looked like he was coming in for a hard landing, a big cushion suddenly appeared at the foot of the snake.

'So clever,' said Ellie.

'You didn't program NAMIS to do that?' asked Fran.

'No, they're doing it themself. To be honest, we never play with them like this, we've never thought of it.'

Niamh was watching the boys play, smiling. 'If you want to go and get Jamie, mum, we'll be fine for a few minutes.'

Fran and Ellie left the room and crossed the corridor. Ellie knocked on the door. Jamie put his head out. 'Ah, I was wondering where you were.'

Fran noticed that he was starting to get some grey hair. Maybe a legacy from NAMIS's early days, she thought. 'I was admiring NAMIS. They're getting to be a grown up now, eh, personal pronouns and all?'

Christian came walking along the corridor. 'Hello Fran. All the gang's back together again, then.' He gave her a big hug.

Fran looked around. Only the original team were in the room. She shut the door. 'So quickly, now, tell me what's happening? I'm dying to know.'

'Well,' said Ellie, 'you see how NAMIS is. They're learning in leaps and bounds. They move all sorts of inanimate objects in space, and all the animals that we've asked them to move. Soon we're going to start some very limited trials with people. The carbon reuse trick is a logical off-shoot from the original programming, but we didn't contrive it. NAMIS just worked out how to do that by themself. Then Christian helped them refine it through the chess games.'

Christian frowned. 'And the speed at which it… sorry,

they… learn; well. Bloody AI, I can't win a game anymore. And every single thing we transport has to be officially listed to go through the university ethics board now. *So much paperwork.*'

Fran nodded. 'NAMIS has moved on so much in such a short time; it's amazing. They're playing snakes and ladders with the boys now.'

Christian's face brightened. 'Snakes and ladders? This I have to see.' He left the room in the direction of the laboratory.

'And' Jamie continued 'NAMIS is still having some limited adventures in time.'

'Like in Ancient Egypt?' asked Fran.

Jamie grinned. 'Oh, you guessed. We don't have to send people. We've got tiny robots, with even tinier microphones and cameras. NAMIS can source far more detailed information about what is going on in history now, so we can very accurately pinpoint places and times to drop our "spy" devices and bring them back. It's a lot more controlled than what we were doing four years ago.'

'And that's the up to date latest, Fran,' said Ellie. 'We've recently had to share the basics on NAMIS's time travelling potential with our funders.'

'Hence Jamie's paper?'

Jamie nodded. 'Yes. But it's agreed that we keep it to the technical/theoretical at the moment, with the cooperation of the funding board. We've told them that we have to do a lot more experiments on moving people in space before we are ready to start moving them through time, if at all, and that has all been agreed.'

'Sounds like it might start getting a lot more complicated in the not-too-distant future, though?'

'We have to keep one step ahead of the competition, Mum, it's always so. Other people were working on matter transporters, besides us. NAMIS has been patented in the US now.'

Ellie nodded. 'Yes. At some point we'll have to

introduce the "convergence transformation" problem, before anyone else starts trying to send people back through time in complete innocence of the potential dangers, as we did. But we haven't got to that point yet.'

'Did you ever get any further on convergence transformation?' asked Fran.

'If you want the technical details you'll have to talk to Christian,' replied Jamie. 'But essentially, not really. As you already know, the similarity is at the epigenetic level; all the "switches" set in the same directions.'

'But that doesn't mean this is a phenomenon anything like identical twins' Ellie added. 'It's a far deeper setting than that. So, there can be a lot of differences at the surface level- height, colouring, even gender orientation- all of that can be different. But there are some markers that indicate epigenetic convergence, and of course we found the most obvious one, voice. There are usually some cosmetic differences that occlude that similarity, given that it is coming through a different larynx. And of course, convergent ancestors may speak different languages, like Anna and Annamarie. But the deeper pattern creates the match that Suzi found with her voice matching tool. So yes, we've made some inroads into the convergence aspect, but the transformation is still a bit of a mystery. I think in the end, NAMIS- or NAMITAS- will be the one to finally work that out.'

'NAMITAS?'

'Yes. When we put NAMIS back together in Boston, they're going to have a new name: NAMITAS. *Navigation And Movement In Time And Space.*'

'Ah. That should have been their name all along.'

'We know that and NAMIS knows that. But it's only now we are able to do something about it.'

'*NAMIS* knows that,' said Fran 'I still find that incredible.'

Jamie smiled. 'NAMIS is AI, Mum. They were rather primitive when you knew them. Now they've been learning for four more years. But they're still at the beginning of what they will know, and what they will be. NAMIS- or NAMITAS- will outlive all of us. People of the kids' generation, and the generation after that will continue to work with them. They will know a lot more by then. And no doubt things will be added to them as time passes. If you are looking for reincarnation, NAMITAS will be a better example than people, I'm sure.'

'And NAMIS sort of chats to people now? They seemed to be doing that with Niamh and the boys. It's a bit spooky that they seem to look you up on the internet while they're speaking to you, though.'

Ellie laughed. 'The whole internet is available to NAMIS all the time. Their mind isn't compartmentalised in the way that ours is. They don't mean it to be spooky. It's just the way it is. And NAMIS is more in control of their own thought processes now; what the psychologists call "metacognition." They have a lot more flexibility in the way that they speak to people; and as you noticed, they sound a lot more *human* than they used to; in a limited sort of way they know what to say in certain social situations. You saw it just now in the way that they spoke to you and Niamh. NAMIS learns that type of thing by observation, we don't specifically instruct them. But Jack's name flummoxed them for a moment.'

Fran looked thoughtful. 'So many parallels with a child. I wonder if NAMIS would like to run around with the boys in that snakes and ladders game?'

Ellie smiled. 'Funny you should say that, because I am working on creating a mobile avatar for NAMIS. One of my PhD students is working on the way that they learn and communicate, and she suggested that. Experimenting on the mobile avatar is going to be the focus of her PhD project. One of the issues we have to solve is that NAMIS still seems to be able to understand more than they can tell us about; their apparent struggle to communicate what they want to say continues. They still can't access the future, and I think they know more about the reasons for that than they seem to be able to express. The same type of thing that happened when they tried to tell us about convergence transformation. Christian can explain why that happened to a greater extent in the biology now; however, NAMIS seems to have a more complete understanding. But it's like they're unable to fully articulate it.'

'Again, like a small child. But it's probably even more difficult for NAMIS, because the words and concepts don't exist for us yet, so they've got to create them and translate them into language that makes sense to human beings. When human beings create new words and concepts, they usually do it together, rather than on their own.'

Ellie nodded. 'I'd love you to work with Caroline, my PhD student, Fran. I'm deadly serious. We can sign you up as an extra supervisor.'

Fran laughed. 'But are you all ready for what seems to happen when I get involved with one of your projects?'

Jamie grinned ruefully, raising his eyebrows.

'You'd get some trips to Boston with Caroline,' said Ellie. 'She's London based. But she'll be coming over regularly to work on NAMIS. Or NAMITAS, I guess.'

'I'd love to work with Caroline, Ellie. And if I take regular trips to Boston, well, I can see a bit more of Isabel, too. She's getting to be a proper little girl now, not a baby. And so is Alys, in Cardiff. You knew Rae had a little girl now? All these children; they keep growing up.'

'And you keep doing all these new things too, Fran. I hear you've sold the rights to your book for a new TV series.'

'Yes, the company have bought the rights to my book. But they haven't started making the series yet.'

Christian popped his head around the door. 'Jamie, you have to come and look at this' he said. Jamie followed him out of the door.

ON TIME

'So, what's the next book going to be about, Fran?' asked Ellie.

'I haven't decided yet.'

'Everyone is looking forward to the TV series, anyway. Anything that takes people away from the present, I think; the economy and the political scandals.'

Fran frowned. 'I've come to the conclusion that I shouldn't keep fretting about politics all the time at my advancing age. That's what… my exploration of history has taught me. Every age has its challenges, and some times are worse than other times. We are certainly not in the best of times, but we are not in the worst, either. The most important people for people are not politicians or media stars, they are communities and most of all, families. And not only blood family, but family like us, too. The NAMIS project family.'

Ellie looked pensive. 'If only Annamarie was here with us. Then we would all be together'.

'I did harbour a speculative hope that one day, NAMIS might be able to get her back. Once you'd all worked out what "convergence transformation" actually was. But it seems that you're not very close to that.'

'No. But we'll never stop trying.'

Fran sighed. 'I know.'

They left the office and walked down the corridor to the lab, listening to the excited giggles and shrieks. The children were still having great fun in the Snakes and Ladders game.

'Maybe NAMIS needs other children to play with?' mused Fran.

Ellie looked thoughtful.

'It's the way that children learn' Fran continued. 'Not only from formal lessons, but through just playing around. And grown-ups, too. We learned a lot from playing in time, didn't we?'

'Yes, but we created a lot of mischief, too.'

'So, that's what adults are for. To watch and help the

children play and learn, and to make sure that they don't go too far and hurt themselves. And hopefully we will learn to be adults in time... in time.'

Ellie stared at her. 'I think you and Caroline will be an amazing team, Fran.'

'I'm looking forward to it. And to being back on the project. I've really missed it, you know.'

They entered the laboratory.

'Come and slide on a snake, Granny,' shouted Jack.

'I don't think so, Jack. But I'm watching you.'

Fran walked up to the machine, looking at the data scrolling across the screen that she remembered so well. She gently patted the fascia. We'll go on loving you until you're really real, old friend, she thought. And maybe, when we get a bit further along in the process, you'll be able to offer a game-changer to the search for Annamarie.

Family: North Queensferry, July 2031

Fran sat in a deckchair in the garden, watching the children run around in the sunshine. Exactly the type of birthday party she'd wanted she thought, it was perfect. It was a shame that Dylan wasn't there, but he was having fun with his friends, hiking in the Welsh hills. They were all growing up. She watched her pup Mitzi running around after the children. I hadn't noticed how slow poor old Kylie had got, she thought. I guess it comes to us all. But not to NAMITAS, newly assembled in Boston. They were still learning in leaps and bounds, and their capacity seemed endless.

Ellie and Caroline had developed the prototype mobile avatar, and the last time Fran had seen NAMITAS, they'd said to her *'I'm having fun now'*. Like our kids, thought Fran, watching the children poking around the bushes. Freddie and Jack ran past her to get cricket bats and balls from the house. They were going to play cricket with their Dad on the little beach at the bottom of the garden.

ON TIME

A pity I never learned anything about plants, thought Fran. But I guess it's never too late. Maybe it's something that I've got time for now? But Niamh was so good with the garden. It seemed to come naturally to her. She was showing the flowers to her two nieces, Isabel and Alys, and helping them to learn the names. The two girls seemed to be having a lovely time. They're about the same age, thought Fran, it's a pity they don't live closer. But never mind, everyone has found the place they want to be for now. And it's so easy to keep in touch, much more so than in the days when William Burns had successfully contrived to keep his granddaughters away from their MacIntosh family whilst they were all living in the same town. She thought again of him standing in the church hall, looking around "his people." She shivered, as though a shadow had passed across the sun.

'It's lovely here, mum,' said Rae, breaking into her thoughts. 'I'm almost tempted to move up here, too. But we'll wait till Dylan goes to uni next year, and then see. How amazing that when Niamh and John got that chance to relocate you managed to get this actual house; the one that your family lived in all those years ago.'

'I know. When I looked at that estate agent's website I just couldn't believe it. I heard so much about it when I was a child, from Nana Mo, my dad… even Aunt Adi. And the fact that it was so perfect for us now; had the space to build the little annexe for me, even down to being able to knock through that extra big window so I could sit and write looking out into the garden.'

Niamh walked over. 'I loved it immediately, just had to have it. It feels like I've always lived here, even after such a short time. The garden is what I always wanted; it's like I had already seen it in my mind, even the sundial. I'm going to plant some veg next year.'

Fran settled back into her deckchair. 'And I have my little annexe, and the garden--which Nimah is making so beautiful. No doubt it will be even better next year. The airport's only a few miles away, I have my bit of work with Caroline and Ellie in Boston, and I have my writing. Sometimes, I can almost feel Mo's spirit here.'

'It won't matter where we live if that transporter of yours is able to take people from place to place instantly,' said Rae. 'I've read that article in last month's Times now. I still can't believe that our little brother is the world-famous Professor James MacIntosh Anderson.'

Niamh smiled. 'Professor Jamie Mac.'

Jamie blushed. 'It's NAMITAS who is the star, whizzing around, showing off for the journalists.'

The little girls were running out of the gate to join the boys on the beach. 'Alys, Isabel!' Rae called. 'I'll go see what they're doing, Suzi.' She jogged down to the end of the garden, through the gate and onto the sand. Niamh followed on behind her.

'How's Christian getting on with the convergence transformation concept, Jamie?' asked Fran.

'Slowly.'

'Just making sure that the next novel isn't going to be outdated before it's published.'

Suzi looked up from annotating a text on her iPad. 'Oh? What's it about?'

'It's about people in families who come together again and again through reincarnation. Working title: *Time after Time*. But no time machine involved.'

'Wow. That sounds like another TV series blockbuster.'

'We'll see.'

Jamie grinned. 'I still think that's bollocks. Although no doubt it will be extremely successful as fiction.'

They all laughed.

'It's a lovely garden to look out on while you write, Fran,' said Suzi.

Fran looked pensive. 'I guess, as human beings, that's all we can do. Tend the garden for the next generation and try to leave them a better one that they can continue to cultivate. Whether the next generation turn out to be us or not.'

Jamie smiled wistfully. 'I guess we can all agree on that. And we are trying our best.'

Classified: Washington DC, July 2031

The Chief Scientific Advisor to the President stared intently at the screen on his PC. 'So, when you looked at the evidence, you agreed with us that it may have been transporting people in time for at least the last five years? This question arose, as you know, when Professor Anderson submitted his report about having some successes in transporting inanimate matter through time…' he turned to look at his iPad- 'only the recent past, it seems, not the future. Our experts seemed to think it looks more developed than it should be for the stage that they say they are at.'

'Yes, we agree that may be the case, Greg,' said the Chief Scientific Advisor to the British Prime Minister. 'We've also put some evidence together since we had our last conversation. The team on the original project was listed as Dr James MacIntosh Anderson, physicist, Dr Annamarie Simons, AI expert, Dr Christian Novak, biologist. Oh, and Dr Simons had an assistant, Eleanor Jackson. Ms Jackson stepped up to become the AI specialist for the team when she received her doctorate- around the same time Dr Simons had her unfortunate accident.'

Greg scrolled through some records on his iPad. 'Oh, that was the woman who disintegrated herself in the machine in an early experiment that went wrong, wasn't it?'

'Seemed that way.'

'So, what's the evidence then, Julian?'

'Circumstantial. We've dug into the early logs several times, but we've never been able to find anything. However, there are other, non-data oriented events that go together to raise suspicion.'

'Which are?'

'To start with, there's another person who should be on the list who was missed off. Look at the report I sent you this morning.'

Greg scrolled again, briefly. 'Dr Frances Anderson, research assistant. Says she was involved with data entry. 'So…?' He squinted at the screen. 'Seems a bit old to be a research assistant.'

Julian nodded. 'There are two further things you need to know. Dr Anderson is Professor Anderson's mother. And she's not a scientist of any description. Her PhD is in a field where she would be unlikely to be familiar with any of the types of statistics that physicists do; she's a historian. And then… I've sent you another file. One of yours this time.'

Greg stabbed at his iPad. 'Professor Suzanne Nguyen,' he read off the screen.

'She's Anderson's wife.'

'Jesus, what is this, a family business?'

'No, she's never worked for Anderson, she's a linguist, at the same university. But she's working on several of her own projects and doing very nicely, thank you very much. She's made leaps and bounds into working out how Ancient Egyptian was spoken. And I hear on the grapevine that now she's making some incredible inroads into deciphering Etruscan.'

'And…?'

Julian sighed, remembering that most Americans he dealt with didn't have a classical education. 'Etruscan is the ancient language that no one has ever been able to decipher. Until now, apparently. She also worked with a theatre company in London last year, helping them to develop their Chaucerian pronunciation for a production. Best in the business, I was told.'

'So OK, it's a bit fishy. But it's not proof is it? Is there anything else?'

ON TIME

'The mother. She wrote a blockbuster historical novel that was published four years ago. It's being dramatised in a television series at the moment. You might have heard of it: *Family Feud.*'

'Oh, my wife loves that. Said it was sort of like Downton, but with respect to the British middle classes. Wonderfully believable characters, she said.'

'Exactly. Here are some of the reviews of the book: "The most realistic historical characters ever." "The historical detail in this book is stunning."; and "Is Fran Anderson a time traveller?" Can't get much clearer than that.'

'I guess not. This NAMIS- er, NAMITAS project, is that the one, that when it came over here, our people looked it over from the basis of what they could get at and thought that there must be some missing data somewhere, but they couldn't identify the gaps? And the guy who oversaw the original investigation in the UK when the woman disappeared was a bit of a moron?'

'And some. The university managed to move him sideways into the education ministry. Doing something on the science curriculum now. Poor bastard.'

Greg sighed. 'OK. I guess we can send someone in. Easy enough. I'll get the CIA to field an AI operative to sign on as a PhD student with Dr… he looked down at his iPad- oh, yes, *Professor* Jackson. Will need to look young enough and act keen enough. Doesn't need to be one of their best; we're only dealing with academics. That's always a candy from a baby assignment.'

'OK, thanks Greg. Keep me posted.'

'Sure thing'.

Greg flipped to another screen.

'Get me POTUS,' he said to the automated assistant.

EPILOGUE: IN TIME

Jim: Sittingbourne, December 1893

The clock was ticking loudly, tick, tick, tick. I must have been asleep, thought Jim. I felt terrible when I dropped off. But I'm feeling better now. He looked around. He became aware of a soft white light surrounding him. It must be a lovely day out there, he thought, good. Then he remembered that it was mid-winter; unusual to see such a bright sun at this time of year.

He realised his father and his wife, Izza were sitting by his bed, and that they were both crying. But why? He was fine now. He tried to speak to them. They didn't respond. Meanwhile, the light was getting brighter and brighter. They seemed to be fading into it.

'Look, I'm feeling better now,' he said, impatiently. 'Don't cry.' But still, they didn't show any indication that they had heard.

The room continued to fade. Izza and his father were in a tiny space now, far away, like looking into the wrong end of a telescope. He turned and faced directly into the light. He realised that he was standing by a stream full of colours, like a rainbow. The white light was shining on the stream and being refracted through it, as through it was made from multi-coloured glass. Jim had learned the colours of the rainbow at school, and they were all there, but there were extra colours here too, that he had never seen before.

'Am I dead?' he asked.

ON TIME

There was no reply. Then he realised that a moving picture was beginning to form on the other side of the stream. There was a blonde lady in a hospital bed who looked somehow familiar, and a man standing next to her, holding her hand. There seemed to be a lot of machines around them, of a type he had never seen before. Then he remembered: it was the lady who had briefly attended the church, not long before the MacIntoshes had severed their connections with it, after the huge row with Izza's father. But what on earth was such a relative stranger doing in this strange vision? And why did she look so much younger?

His attention was diverted to another coalescing moving picture; two little girls reading a book with an older lady he presumed must be their grandmother. He felt strangely drawn to them, the younger one in particular. He thought of his own two little girls at home. They were so tiny, and he'd hardly got to know them. He thought especially of Mo, who was getting bonnier every day. She was chattering away, using a lot more recognisable words now; he didn't want to leave her. But he got a sense that by jumping the stream- which he was developing a strong urge to do- he would somehow be with her again.

He looked back again at Izza, only just visible now. The colours on that side had completely gone; they had started to fade into brown and beige. He couldn't see the faces of Izza and his father anymore, they were moving out of focus. I can't go back, he thought. The light on the other side of the stream was intensifying, and the images were coming more sharply into focus.

He knew that he had to jump.

He took a last look at his wife and father. The image of them was beginning to run, to dissolve; he could see now that it was comprised of dots, and that the dots were moving apart.

'I'm so sorry,' he said. 'I love you, and I don't want to go. But I'll see you again soon.'

He leapt into the light.

Pam Jarvis

ABOUT THE AUTHOR

Pam is a chartered psychologist, historian, researcher and grandparent. Originally from London, but based in Leeds since 1986, she taught and researched across community education, schools, colleges and universities between 1994 and 2019, publishing academic articles, books and chapters. She is currently a blogger, citizen journalist and conference/training presenter. On Time is her first fiction novel.

You can read more of Pam's work here:
https://yorkshirebylines.co.uk/author/pamjarvis/
and https://histpsych.blogspot.com/
For updates on 'On Time'. see:
https://ontimesorg.wordpress.com/

Also from **Burton Mayers Books**

Post-pandemic dependence on tech is shattered by the glitch, a cyber-attack, which temporarily knocks out power and communication networks.
Hoping to escape society, securing a peaceful life off grid, Robin is thwarted, becoming stranded in Oxford when an unexpected second glitch strikes.
#Isolate, coming October 2021...

SPACE TAXIS

A&H FROSH

In 1977 a New York Cab driver Mike Redolfo is abducted by aliens after being mistaken for a renegade scientist. Meanwhile, back in 1944 a mysterious man and his Jewish fiancée are fleeing across Nazi-occupied Europe.

As the link between the timelines becomes clear, Redolfo must discover secrets from the past that may hold the key to saving the planet.

NORMAN MOUNTER

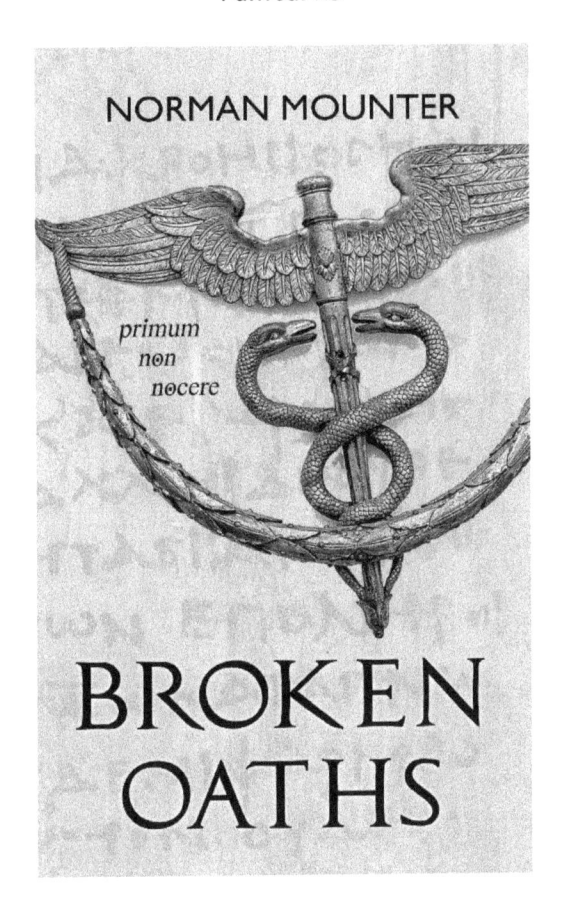

primum non nocere

BROKEN OATHS

As Eichmann's Final Solution reaches its finale, Doctor Sárkány's attempts to save his career have failed.

On arriving at Auschwitz, can he break his Hippocratic Oath and betray his own people? Dr Mengele thinks that he can.

Available in hardback and paperback

ON TIME

Notes:

Milton Keynes UK
Ingram Content Group UK Ltd.
UKHW011318291123
433490UK00005B/382